Boneyard Beach

Other Folly Beach Mysteries by Bill Noel

Folly

The Pier

Washout

The Edge

The Marsh

Ghosts

Missing

Final Cut

First Light

Boneyard Beach

A Folly Beach Mystery

Bill Noel

Hydra
Publications

Printed in the United States of America

ISBN-13: 978-1-942212-29-4

Cover photo by Bill Noel
Author photo by Susan Noel

Hydra Publications
Goshen, KY 40026

www.hydrapublications.com

Prologue

"Beauty is in the eyes of the beer holder!" rang out one more time on the boat crammed with eleven of my fellow college students. I clasped my hands against my ears. How many more times would I have to hear it before my brain exploded? How had I let Cleveland talk me into going on the euphemistically-named "moonlight marsh educational activity" when everyone knew that it was an excuse to get away from the pressures of tests, studying, and boring professors? More importantly, it was an excuse to get smashed.

If I had any doubt about the intent, it was clarified when the guys lugged three large maroon and white coolers down the pier and hefted them onto the twenty-five foot long Carolina Skiff with letters on the hull announcing to all but observers with severe cataracts that it was *MAD MEL'S MAGICAL MARSH MACHINE*. This was my last chance to let reason prevail and scamper off the pier and hitch a ride back to the college library to study for Dr. Hansel's test. I'd turned to go when Cleveland came up behind me, put his arms around my shoulders and said, "Drew, ready to party?"

He didn't wait for my answer as he led, nearly shoved, me toward the boat, stepped around an old bald-headed guy, dressed in camo gear, who I would have guessed from a mile away was Mad Mel, and then deserted me to grab a beer. I didn't drink, but didn't dare ask if they thought to bring anything non-alcoholic on the "educational activity."

Thirty minutes, or about twenty renditions later of the obnoxious 'beauty is…" chant, on a boat now cluttered with two-dozen empty beer cans, the captain slammed the bow of the skiff onto the beach.

"Holy crap!" a classmate yelled. "We've landed on the moon."

He was 239,000 miles off—see, I do pay attention in class—but I understood what he'd meant. The sand was dotted with large, white, windswept trees, straggly vegetation, and other than the nonsensical sounds and laughter from the boat, dead silence. The sun was on its descent behind the trees and their eerie shadows reached out to the boat like a witch's talons drawing us in.

We had reached our destination and half the group bounded over the side to the wet sand. One of the coeds landed in water that lapped over her feet. "Shit!" she yelled and high stepped it out of the surf. The student behind her laughed, not the sympathetic response the tennis-shoe-soaked coed had hoped for.

Six guys lugged the coolers over the side and staggered, more from beverages consumed on the journey than from the weight of the coolers, up the small incline to where the sand met native vegetation. The rest of us—yes, even I—followed the coolers like ants following the lead ant dragging a cake crumb.

"Halt!" Mad Mel bellowed. "Before you go farting around and doing whatever worthless college students do, this craft is departing at twenty-two hundred. Be here! If you don't have a moon beam, stay with someone who does. It'll be dark in ninety minutes."

Charming, I thought, and wondered how he'd managed to book any tours. Two guys were mumbling something about when twenty-two hundred was and two gals were giggling about finding the nearest porta pottie. And, Timothy, standing beside me, asked what a moon beam was.

I said, "A flashlight."

"Why didn't Rambo say so?"

I didn't have an answer and it didn't matter because Timothy had already beelined it to the cooler. Once again, I wondered why I had come.

I'm not naïve to the ways of my fellow College of Charleston students; after all, I'm a junior and live in a dorm, but I'm also a loner by nature, have never been one to get caught up in the partying that is as normal in colleges as student loans and all-nighters. I stepped away from the crowd and realized that I only knew four of the eleven students and would consider none of them friends. I knew the names of four guys because I'd met them while attending Gay-Straight Alliance meetings. Yes, I'm gay. It's no big deal and I don't flaunt it. I don't march in gay pride parades; I don't have any interest in crusading for gay rights or protesting intolerance. Most people who know me casually don't know anything about my sexual persuasion. For that matter, they don't know my religion, my political affiliation, or whether I prefer hamburgers to hot dogs. I'm a loner who happens to be gay.

I'm also an observer and would rather listen to a conversation than participate in it. That's why I'd chosen to move to the edge of the vegetation, sit on one of the horizontal branches of a sun and sand whitewashed oak and observe: observe my fellow students attack the beer cooler, observe the historic Morris Island lighthouse off shore as only the top third benefitted from the setting sun, and observe the seagulls as they circled the exposed sandbar in front of the lighthouse.

I also observed two guys as they walked away from the others, stepped over two of the downed trees, and disappeared down a path toward the marsh. They were backlit by the sun, but I could tell that they had been strolling hand-in-hand.

A little later, I was in the same spot, a hundred yards from the coolers, and the sky had gone from bright orange, to a muted blue-orange with darkness soon to follow. There were three people gathered around the coolers like they were afraid that a band of marauding pirates would sneak ashore and steal the beer. The boat hadn't moved and I saw Mad Mel's silhouette as he leaned against his Magical Marsh Machine. I couldn't see anyone else, but the sounds of laughter and an occasional whoop in the distance let me know that there wouldn't be beer left for pirates to commandeer.

I had finally stopped rehearsing my answers for tomorrow's

test and had begun relaxing. Participating in this educational activity wouldn't have been on my to-do list, but it wasn't as bad as it could have been. That was until I heard a rustling sound behind me. I turned in time to see a three-foot long, thick piece of a whitewashed oak branch coming at me. I felt nothing as it slammed my head.

Drew Casey never heard the laughter as his fellow students climbed onboard *Mad Mel's Magical Marsh Machine*. He never heard the captain shout, "Everybody here?" Nor did he hear the slurred voices of a few of the students say, "Yes." And he missed hearing their drunken voices chant seven times on the return trip to the dock, "Beauty is in the eyes of the beer holder."

Chapter One

The pulsating roar of an engine from a retro-styled Chevrolet Camaro, unencumbered by a traditional, sound-deflecting muffler, reached me seconds before someone pounded on my door. My keen perception told me that my peaceful morning enjoying a cup of freshly-brewed coffee while I regaled in not having to be anywhere was about to end.

I had retired to South Carolina eight years ago. Since then, someone in a pick-up truck and another person in a car had tried to run me down; someone else tried to shorten my life with the sharp end of a pair of shears; I've had a gun pointed in my face more than once; another person had tried to drown me, and a malcontent with a torch attempted to turn me into a crispy critter.

While pondering retirement for several years before I took the plunge, I had devoured nearly every book and magazine article about how, when, and where to retire, and regaled in stories of happy retirees living out their dreams as they rode off into the sunset on a golf cart. As shocking as it may seem, not a single publication had mentioned how many different ways a retiree could be murdered. I should consider writing that book, and I would if I enjoyed reading and writing. I don't.

If I'd spent my life working in law enforcement, what I had experienced may not have been unusual, but give me a break. I was in my mid-sixties, lived on a small barrier island, and owned Landrum Gallery, a tiny photo gallery named after yours truly in an egocentric moment. How dangerous should that be? The closest

I'd ever come to a law enforcement career was during a brief stint as a school crossing guard when I was in the sixth grade.

Now what? I thought as I exhaled and headed to the door to welcome one of my more outlandish friends, and owner of the Camaro.

"Hey Chris, got a question," Mel Evans shoved past me as I opened the door. He rushed to the kitchen and Mr. Coffee.

The new arrival grabbed a mug, poured a cup, and looked around the kitchen like he was looking for Frisch's breakfast bar. My kitchen was the most underused room in my small cottage and he should have been thrilled that I had coffee.

"What's there to eat?" asked the six-foot-one, sixty-year old with a salt-and-pepper, Brillo-pad haircut. He wore woodland camo field pants sheared off at the knee and a leather bomber jacket with the sleeves cut off at the shoulder and a frown that appeared surgically implanted.

"Is that the question you barged in and disturbed my peaceful morning for?" I asked and refreshed my coffee.

Mel's unlikely friend Jim "Dude" Sloan, an aging hippie and owner of the island's largest surf shop, had introduced us. Mel ran a marsh tour business that catered to young adults who wanted to get away from the judgmental crowd and party on the small islands or low-tide sandbars that surrounded my home on Folly Beach, or its better known big brother, Charleston, a stone's throw away.

"No, smartass, that's not it, but I can't get to it until I've had something to eat."

"Then you knocked on the wrong door unless you want corn flakes sans milk, or M&Ms, or Cheetos."

Mel returned to the living room and I followed. "Considering your culinary options, I long for the good old days back in seventy-three when I joined the Marines. They dropped us from a chopper in the swamp on a five-day training mission and we had to catch and eat bugs, cute critters, and snakes that didn't taste like chicken no matter what they say."

I pointed toward the kitchen and said, "There's been a mouse sneaking in. Have at it."

"Damned rodent'll starve to death in there. Where're the Cheetos?"

Instead of casing the kitchen for Mickey, five minutes later Mel had finished a half bag of Cheetos, gulped down a can of Budweiser Light that he managed to find tucked-in behind a box-wine in the refrigerator, plopped down in one of the kitchen chairs, and belched.

Mel looked at the empty beer can and then around the room like he expected someone to be hiding in the corner, or maybe he's looking for the mouse for dessert. I sat and waited.

"Now the question," he said.

"About time."

He waved my comment away. "Let's say hypothetically someone took a dozen kids for a moonlight ride and docked at Boneyard Beach."

Mel hesitated. Boneyard Beach was a desolate area at the north end of Folly Beach that overlooked the historic Morris Island lighthouse.

"Okay," I said and waited.

"The next day," Mel shook his head, "the guy who hypothetically booked the trip calls and says that only eleven of them made it back." He held out both hands and his frown deepened.

I suspected that Mr. Hypothetical had been feasting on my Cheetos and beer. "Did the hypothetical someone stay with the boat or was he on the beach with the group?"

Mel shook his head and then nodded, an incongruous visual message if there ever was one.

"Sort of both," he said.

I again waited, anticipating an interesting explanation.

"He left them on shore and stayed with the craft, except when he hypothetically had to piss. He didn't think that needed to be a group activity, so he went the opposite direction from the sorry-ass students."

I didn't believe that needed a response so I nodded. "Did the hypothetical captain take a head count before he headed back?"

Mel's brow furled and he stared at me. "Umm, he sort of

yelled, 'Everybody here?'"

"And?" I prompted after Mel's long hesitation.

"Heard some slurred yeses," he said, not more than a whisper. "Then shoved off."

"Anybody say no or act concerned about someone missing when they got to the dock?"

"Not a hypothetical peep."

"Anyone sober?"

"Only the hypothetical captain," Mel came close to grinning, but couldn't get his facial muscles to cooperate. "He didn't want to be a bad influence on today's spoiled, sniveling, rudderless brats."

I hesitated, shook my head, and wanted to ask what kind of influence a marsh boat operator who hypothetically specialized in ferrying groups of *spoiled, sniveling, rudderless brats* to isolated beach parties would have by staying sober.

I resisted and asked, "What did the caller want?"

This time Mel did grin. "Wanted to know if the hypothetical captain found any leftover bodies on the boat this morning."

"No, I assume."

"Affirmative."

"Affirmative to finding a body, or to no?"

"Affirmative to no."

"So," I said, still confused, "What's your question?"

"Think the hypothetical captain might be in trouble?"

"Affirmative."

After my no-brainer answer to Mel's long-coming question, he stared in his coffee mug, and then at his empty beer bottle. "Got any whiskey?"

"Coffee, white wine, beer," I said.

He shook his head. "This sure as hell ain't a well-stocked advice center."

"There's no shortage of advice, but you'll have to go somewhere else if you want a wider drink selection."

"I'll stick with coffee." He walked over to Mr. Coffee and refilled his mug. "I've got to stop the hypothetical crap. It's too big a word for this old, broken-down jarhead to throw around. It all happened to me."

I made a half-hearted attempt to act surprised. I had met Mel a few years back when a body had turned up in the marsh and a friend of mine had been accused of putting it there. Mel took a couple of us to the site where the body had been found and later helped us catch the killer. The former Marine was gruff, more profane than I preferred, but I was fascinated with his near-twenty year friendship with Dude Sloan, the sentence-challenged hippie. Dude was as opposite from Mel as two people could be. Mel had mustered out of the Marine Corp after twenty years of serving "your damned country and you'd better not forget it," as he was prone to say. He had moved to Charleston and hitchhiked to Folly on weekends to surf and fell in love with the area.

"You think I could be in trouble?"

"What did the kid say after you said that you didn't find a body?"

Mel stood and walked to the window. His white Adidas tennis shoes looked as out of place with the rest of his attire as LeBron James at a KKK rally. "The twerp mumbled something about hell to pay, cops, lawyers, lawsuits, and maybe firing squad. By that point, my ears were burning and my focus screwed."

He returned to the chair and put both elbows on the table. "So what do you think?"

By now I had no idea what to think, but did have more questions.

"When did you take the group out?"

He glanced down at his black, stainless-steel Fossil watch with more dials and buttons than a Boeing 747, and then back at me.

"Eighteen-hundred, two hours before sunset."

"And returned?"

He looked back down at his watch like the answers were engraved on the bezel.

"Twenty-two-hundred. Was black as a witch's … umm, witch's hat."

"What kind of group was it?"

"College students."

The phrase *pulling teeth* came to mind as I tried to drag information out of my friend.

"Why do you think that?"

"They were that age and acted stupid like college students."

"Stupid how?"

"Half were plastered before we left the dock. The whole way to Boneyard Beach they kept chanting, 'Beauty is in the eyes of the beer holder.' They did it over and over, and over and over." Mel gritted his teeth. "I was about ready to say, beauty in my eyes is throwing you twerps overboard."

Mel's career path after leaving the military had taken a rather strange direction for someone who had been accustomed, "brainwashed" according to Dude, to the rigors and inflexibility of the life of a Marine. He went from working for a septic tank cleaning company to buying a struggling marsh tour business from an old-timer who had actually cared about the ecology. Mel piloted the business into a lucrative niche market where none of the customers cared a whit about anything other than having a good time. I smiled when I thought of Mel and college students in the same sentence.

I needed to hear more about the group before offering advice.

"Were they couples?" I asked.

"Good question. Let me think, umm, don't think so. Didn't notice hugging, smooching, or pawing each other. But, I wasn't surveilling them closely and could be wrong. Remember, I wasn't with them on the beach."

"Did you get their names?"

"No need. Only got the name of the guy who booked the trip and paid with a credit card. He was the one who called today. Damned kid's name's Cleveland F. Whitstone." Mel scowled at his coffee mug. "Have you ever heard a snootier name? *F*'s probably for Farnsworth."

I agreed.

"If you're not going to feed me any better and aren't offering better liquoring, think you could get around to dispensing advice?"

Mel wasn't the type to ask for help, and I wasn't sure what he wanted, but it was time to give it my best shot.

"If I were in your Adidas, I'd go to the police and tell them the whole thing. It'd be best if they heard it from you instead of hearing it from someone else. You don't know what happened, but from what you said, there's a good possibility something did. Something bad."

"You're probably right."

"I'll go with you to tell Chief LaMond."

Chief Cindy LaMond was the head of Folly Beach's Department of Public Safety which included the island's police and fire department. She was also a close friend.

Mel leaned back in the chair. "I can damned well take care of it myself." He folded his arms like, *and that's final!*

I was surprised by his reaction, but shouldn't have been. Mel was self-sufficient, stubborn, and goal-directed.

"Tell you what you can do," he said after a pause. "I want to go back and see if there's anything to be found."

Like a body, I thought.

"Want to go?"

Why not? Mel had never asked for anything and I'd always enjoyed rides through the marsh and its ever-changing look and personality. Besides, he had me curious.

I gave him my best morning smile. "Sure, when?"

"Now."

He stood and looked around the kitchen. "Any grub to go?"

"Not after you inhaled the Cheetos."

"Then grab your gear and let's haul ass."

Chapter Two

Fifteen minutes after I had grabbed my camera and canvas Tilley hat we pulled up to the hand-painted, wooden sign nailed to a sawed-off telephone pole stanchion, announcing *Folly View Marina, Private Property*. The marina was less than a mile off-island and just past the Mariner's Cay condo complex and marina. Folly View had been dubbed the working-man's marina with its weather-worn dock and two dozen deep-water boat slips. Mel undid the rusty chain that blocked the entrance and pulled the growling V8 into the small, tire-rutted parking lot, slammed on the brakes, and skidded to a halt on the crushed shell, gravel, dirt, and weed-covered pavement. We would've made it sooner, but before leaving the island, Mel stopped at the Circle K combination gas station, convenience store, and Subway for three packs of Hostess Twinkies, two packs of Monster Size Slim Jims, and a six-pack of Budweiser.

"Breakfast, the most important meal of the day," Mel mumbled as he used his teeth to rip open the Slim Jims package as we crossed the lot and stepped on the floating dock. The smell of decaying fish thwarted my appetite.

Nine-inch high, black letters reading *MAD MEL'S MAGICAL MARSH MACHINE* on the side of a Carolina Skiff left no doubt about which craft was Mel's. Subtle was not a word I'd heard used to describe him. The boat was docked next to an older, smaller version of his skiff.

Mel nodded to a man working on the neighboring boat's

engine. "Morning, Nemo."

"Back to you, Double M," replied the thirty-something, chubby gentlemen about my height at five-foot ten, with a black, Charleston RiverDogs ball cap pulled down touching his ears. He turned from looking at us to the sky. "Don't get wet out there."

A wall of black clouds had gathered in the west. Mel followed the other man's gaze. "They're heading inland. Ain't coming our way."

Minutes later, Mel was navigating the narrow five-mile-long waterway that snaked its way through the marsh behind Folly Beach and opened onto Lighthouse Inlet, the body of water that separated Folly from Morris Island to the north. Mel took a right at the inlet; the iconic, and unfortunately deteriorating, Morris Island Lighthouse was surrounded by water on our left and the Boneyard Beach to the right.

I leaned closer to Mel and yelled over the roar of the engine. "Who was that at the dock?"

Mel turned his head in my direction and yelled, "What?"

I repeated the question.

"Goes by Captain Nemo," Mel yelled. "Real name's Nathan something. He's a competitor. Runs a tiny-assed marsh tour and fishing business. All he does is work on his boat. It's broken down more than it works. Nemo's okay but doesn't say much. Hang on!" Mel yelled over the roar of the boat's huge Evinrude.

Before I could grip the rail, Mel plowed the craft onto the beach. The bow jerked up as it skidded on shore. My Nikon was strapped around my neck which was the only thing that saved it from leaving the boat ahead of me. Instead, it clanked against the seat and my elbow hit the bulkhead.

Mel heard the camera hit, looked back at me, and smiled. "Told you to hang on."

I looked at my camera; there wasn't any apparent damage, and then glared at Mel. "How about more notice next time?"

Two pelicans had been perched on a log half-in the water and watched our abrupt entrance to their serene environment. One looked at the other one and they lumbered off to find a less human-infested resting spot.

Mel ignored my question. "These are the coordinates where we hit land last night." He pointed to his left. "Or it was a little more that way."

I didn't see evidence that anything had been here within the past twenty-four hours. Mel said that it had been low tide so overnight's incoming tide would have obliterated footprints. The beach was thirty yards wide and then patches of sea oats and various marsh weeds began taking over. There was a handful of dead oak trees rising from the sand that reminded me of a horror movie where zombie arms or some Hollywood monster rose out of the earth and grabbed the ankle of an unsuspecting teen. There were more of the twisted, bare, sun, wind, and salt-air bleached oaks closer to the vegetation line. Life had been suffocated out of the trees when the inlet had begun migrating inland over the last 150 years. Life-sustaining freshwater which fed the large trees' roots was replaced by saltwater as the beachfront eroded. From appearances, we could have been on a deserted island. It took little imagination to see how the area had acquired its nickname.

"You going to follow me or stare at those damned trees?" Mel screamed.

He had walked about forty yards from where he had nearly hurled me out of the Magical Marsh Machine and reached down to pick up two empty beer cans.

"I tried to get the twerps to police the area but it was as dark as the witch's hat I told you about earlier," Mel said as I mushed through the sand to where he was standing. "Let's see if there's more trash." He turned and walked away from the water, hesitated, and turned toward me. "Holler if you find a dead body."

I said that he could count on it and I walked away from him but still toward the thickening vegetation. A rumble of thunder broke the silence and I glanced up. Ominous black clouds were rolling toward us and the short, windswept-shaped trees began to sway with the increasing wind. The distinct smell of rain filled the air.

"Should we head back?" I yelled.

Mel was twenty yards to my left and looking over the lip of

a concrete foundation that was one of the remaining remnants of the Folly Beach Coast Guard LORAN station that inhabited the island's north end until 1980. Graffiti artists had adopted the military adage that if it moves, salute it; if it doesn't move, paint it. The military would have gone apoplectic at what was painted on their deserted foundations, but couldn't argue that it'd lacked creativity. Mel didn't find litter from last night's escapade or a body within the foundation's walls and walked to a narrow path that led to the edge of the marsh. He ignored my question; a talent that he had come close to perfecting.

I kept glancing at the darkening sky and at Mel as he walked deeper into the area nearest the marsh. He was focused on something out of my line of sight. I was more focused on the increasing movement of the charcoal-black clouds and thunder that sounded like it was just on the other side of the dune; the clouds that Mel had proclaimed were going inland.

"Damn!" Mel screamed.

During my first week on Folly, I was within two hundred yards of where I now stood. I had been minding my own business and photographing the sunrise behind the lighthouse when I heard a gunshot and moments later stumbled on the body of a seriously-dead Charleston developer. My dreams of a peaceful retirement were shattered and the next few weeks my life was turned upside down, not to mention that I was almost killed in the process.

Thoughts of that morning washed over me as I rushed to Mel, a few yards away. Instead of a corpse, I found Mel hopping on one foot and swatting at an army of ants climbing up his leg, chewing flesh as they went. He had trampled on their colony.

I swallowed a smile as he continued to curse and swat the small but painful insects. I also watched where I stepped.

Mel had hopped back to the beach when the storm clouds unleashed a torrent of rain on Boneyard Beach, Mel, the Magical Marsh Machine, and the person who had asked Mel if we should head back.

It took a couple of minutes to dislodge the boat from the rain-drenched sand and back into water deep enough for Mel to start the engine. He spewed a multitude of profanities that he had acquired from twenty years in the military as he navigated through the curvy stream on the return trip to the Folly View Marina. He had pulled his camouflaged fatigue cap down as far as he could on his head to help block the windswept, pelting rain from his eyes. I sat behind him and was glad that my Tilley provided much more protection from the elements. I couldn't help but smile as he continued to elevate his left leg and smack real and imaginary ants.

Other than profanely telling me not to drip on his precious seats, Mel said little on our return ride from the marina to my house. I asked if he had learned anything from the soaking trip to Boneyard Beach.

"Two things," he said as we crossed the new bridge to Folly twenty miles per hour over the posted limit. "Learned that we didn't do a good job policing the area last night, and that the damned rain clouds didn't go where they were supposed to."

I didn't think missing two empty beer can was a poor policing job, but did think Captain Nemo's weather forecast was more accurate than Mel's. I chose not to mention it to my chauffeur. What I did do was remind him to tell Chief LaMond about the call he had received and what he had remembered about the possibly ill-fated excursion.

"I heard you the first time," he barked.

Chapter Three

I had spent the majority of my working life in the human resources department of a large health care company in Kentucky. Many of the issues I dealt with were contentious, repetitive, and occasionally rewarding; but overall, the corporate environment with multiple layers of bureaucracy was, to put it kindly, tedious. Excitement, adventure, close friendships, and an overwhelming desire to get out of bed and go to the office each day were in short supply. On the other hand, it paid well, had regular hours, and if one didn't mind a rigid, rules-driven environment, it was a pleasant place to work.

And then along came retirement, Folly Beach, and Charles Fowler. Charles was two years my junior, twenty-five pounds lighter, two inches shorter, and had thirty years seniority over me on the quirky island and in retirement. He had moved to Folly from Detroit at the ripe young age of thirty-four and hadn't held a steady job since.

In addition to stumbling on a dead body my first week on Folly, I had met Charles, the man whom I would have bet my life savings on that I would never, yes, never, have become friends with. Thankfully, no one had offered me that bet. For reasons known only to the deities who rule the universe, Charles had become the closest thing I ever had to a brother, confident, and close friend. Over the years, I had taught him photography; he had taught me how to goof off. I had taught him ... well, I can't think of anything else I had taught him; but he had given me countless lessons on not taking things seriously, how to see the good in everyone, regardless of their station in life or degree of obnoxiousness, and how to overcome my lifetime of rigidity.

Charles and I had lived through encounters with murderers, threats and attempts on our lives, and be it through skill or pure luck, we had helped the police put a few evil folks behind bars and in one instance, helped send a murderer to hell.

"So it's final," Charles said.

I nodded.

We were sitting in two rickety chairs in the small storeroom, break room, and all-purpose gathering area, behind the showroom at Landrum Gallery.

"September first?" Charles said as he ran his hand through his thinning hair.

"Yes."

"Three and a half months?" he said.

One more nod.

Charles leaned back in the chair and I stared at the large, blue, *UTD* on his long-sleeve T-shirt. He looked down at the shirt.

"Like it?" he asked. "University of Texas at Dallas. They're the comets; mascot's called Temoc, that's comet spelled backwards."

Charles owned as many T-shirts—most college and university logoed, and all long sleeved—as he did books and he had as many books as the Library of Congress. I had quit asking him about the shirts years ago, but that had never stopped him from offering tidbits about them.

I lied. "Interesting."

"Positive?"

I figured he wasn't making sure that I thought his shirt was interesting and was verifying that the gallery would be closing in September. Charles was good at many things; at awkward transitions, he was exceptional.

"Yes," I said. "We've been over this many times and you know I can't continue to lose money. It's time."

"And we're only going to open Saturday and Sunday until then?"

We had also had this discussion more than once. Charles figured that if he said it enough times, I'd change my mind. When I opened the gallery seven years ago, he assumed the position of sales manager. I say assumed, because I had never asked him to work here nor had I paid him a dime for the work he'd done. He'd said he preferred it that way so he wouldn't have to deal with the "Feds" which meant the Internal Revenue Service. A while back he promoted himself to executive sales manager. From what I was paying him, I was in no position to object.

"Yes," I said to the Saturday and Sunday question.

He closed his eyes and lowered his head. "Okay," he whispered.

I felt like a heel.

My cell phone rang and yanked me out of my misery.

"Morning, Cindy," I said, after seeing *Cindy LaMond* on the screen.

"Don't think I agree," Chief LaMond said. "I'm sitting in my car at the end of the road on the old Coast Guard property. Sweat's running down my face, the danged sun's in my eyes, my polished shoes are all mucked up with wet sand and my socks are speckled with sandspurs." She took a deep breath. "And, oh yeah, I just finished ogling a stinky corpse. And you want to be cheery?"

This was not the way I wanted to be distracted from Charles's distress over the gallery's closing. I knew precisely where Cindy was. A locked gate at the end of East Ashley Avenue stopped public vehicles from accessing the former Coast Guard property, but police and fire officials could unlock it and proceed to the end of the paved road and the beach. She was also no more than three hundred yards from where Mel and I had stepped ashore yesterday.

"A drowning?" I asked as calmly as I could muster.

Charles looked up from the table and stared at the phone.

"Let me think," Cindy said. "Body's fifty yards back from the high-tide line; it's up a path from the beach to the marsh; in the middle of some straggly old trees. It's half covered with a bunch of palmetto leaves; and, oh yeah, his head's smashed in. Drowning, don't think so, but hey, I'm only the lowly police chief. COD will come from folks with a higher pay grade and medical-school learnin'."

"You said *his head*, so it's a guy," I said.

Charles leaned close to the phone and struggled to hear Cindy's side of the conversation.

"Can't slip anything by you," she said.

I tapped *Speaker* on the phone so Charles wouldn't fall out of the chair listening.

"How long's he been there?" I asked. "Know who he is?"

"The ME's here now and thinks not more than a couple of days, but will have a better idea later. Don't know who he is, no ID on the body."

"Age?" I asked and gave a silent prayer that he was an old man.

"Early 20s. Listen, Chris, I've got to go. I knew you'd want to know since you're such a nosy Nellie."

"Quick question," I said. "Has Mel Evans contacted you?"

"No, why?"

"Just wondering," I said, knowing she wouldn't believe me.

I heard the muffled sounds of someone talking to Cindy. "On my way," she said to the other voice.

"Don't forget the party tonight, Chris," she said and was gone.

I won't, I thought, but it wasn't the party I was thinking about.

Chapter Four

Reasons—excuses—to have parties on Folly Beach have been footloose and plentiful. St. Patrick's Day, Fourth of July, local events like the Sea and Sand Festival, Folly Gras, or special events like "I saw a dolphin, let's celebrate," or "Clint's got a case of beer, party's on," can gather a crowd. So I wasn't surprised when Cindy's shorter-half, Larry, had called to invite me to a *zero party*, I didn't ask what it meant, I'd asked when and where.

Three days before the event I had run into Cindy at Mr. John's Beach Store and she told me that the *zero party* was to celebrate two memorable birthdays that ended in zero and which fell within two weeks of each other: Cindy's 50th and Larry's 60th. They had decided to host the party since they figured no one else would appreciate the calendar-unique event as much as they would. I told her that it wasn't true, but we both knew that she was right, and besides, she had the nicest yard for parties of anyone I knew.

The evening was cool for May so I walked six blocks to the LaMonds's home on East Indian Avenue. Cindy and Larry moved into the attractive, elevated, house five years ago when they got married. Behind it was their private, narrow wooden walkway that traversed a section of the marsh and ended at the Folly River. The house would have cost much more than the local hardware store owner and a public servant could afford but Larry had inherited the property from Randolph Hall, who had owned Pewter Hardware until he sold it to Larry fourteen years ago. If Hall had lived anywhere other than on Folly, he would have been considered eccentric. In addition to owning the hardware store, Hall had inherited a fortune, had no living relatives and left the store and house to Larry and the balance of his estate to area animal shelters. Larry had tried to turn down the more-than-generous inheritance, but Hall had crafted his will so Larry couldn't disclaim the store, nor could he sell it for ten years. Larry had hidden it well, but he was embarrassed by the windfall and felt that he hadn't deserved it.

I heard voices coming from behind the house and walked around to the backyard instead of going to the front door. Several people were gathered on the large, crushed-shell patio. White smoke poured out of a high-end, stainless-steel gas grill at the far corner of the yard. Larry waved smoke out of his face and was swinging around tongs that were as long as his arm. He wore an apron with *Hell if I know if it's done!* in red script on the front. Larry was five-foot-one in elevator sneakers and had often been asked if he'd been a jockey. He hated horses and had learned over the years to smile and say no, rather than spew insults. The apron ended at his white socks. He looked flustered but by holding the tongs showed that he knew more about cooking than I did. I wasn't inclined to offer assistance.

Cindy leaned against the wooden rail on the pier and was talking to Brandon, Larry's only full-time employee, and to a tall, trim couple I didn't know. Cindy saw me at the corner of the house and waved me over. I shook Brandon's hand and Cindy introduced me to her next-door-neighbors, the Muensterman's. I suspected that they had passed the zero milestones that the party was celebrating.

"I see Larry has things under control," I said with a grin.

Cindy laughed. "I gave him one rule before he started the grill. It had to be at least twenty feet from the house. I didn't want my fire department showing up."

"New grill?"

She looked at the smoke billowing from the appliance. "Its debut, special order. He got a humongous discount because he buys a bunch of cheaper models from the company. In my government world, it's called a bribe. In addition to bellowing boss smoke signals, that one's supposed to do everything including getting cable TV and all thirty-seven ESPN channels." She shook her head.

"Hope it can cook burgers," I said.

Cindy continued to watch the smoke. "It's no accident that I have Woody's Pizza on speed dial."

Brandon excused himself and left to help Larry, and the Muensterman's drifted toward the bar.

"Where's Karen?" Cindy asked.

Karen Lawson was a detective in the Charleston County Sheriff's office and the woman I'd been dating for four years. She was also the daughter of Folly's former police chief and current mayor, Brian Newman, a fact that occasionally made my life interesting.

"She left this morning for a two-week training session in Charlotte. Something about making her a better detective."

"I doubt that's possible. She's already the best the sheriff has."

Cindy's Folly Beach Department of Public Safety provided police services for the town but the county sheriff's office investigated the more serious crimes on the island. Karen had handled all the major crimes on Folly until about two years ago, when politics and petty disputes raised their ugly heads and in his infinite stupidity, the sheriff decided she shouldn't work cases where her father was chief and now mayor.

"Speaking of detectives," I said, "know more about the body?"

"Not . . ." she looked over my shoulder toward the corner of the house and interrupted herself. "Holy crapola, he came."

I turned, followed her gaze, and echoed, "Holy crapola!"

"Come with me," Cindy said as she pushed herself away from the wooden railing.

"What's he doing here?"

"In a moment of monumental foolhardiness, I invited him," Cindy said and smiled in the direction of her newest arrival, Brad Burton, and his wife, Hazel.

Brad had retired from the sheriff's office six months ago

and moved to Folly. In what must have had the irony-gods giggling, the Burtons became my next door neighbor. I had had one brief conversation with him since they moved, but had never spoken to Hazel. She had spent most of her time preparing their house in Charleston to be sold. During Burton's last few years as a detective, our paths had crossed several times, none positive. He had been Detective Lawson's partner and investigated the murder that I had stumbled across eight years ago. He pegged me as the murderer and had never forgotten that he was wrong. I had stuck my nose in his business on a few occasions since and he had treated me with distain. From my perspective, he had been a terrible detective; he was lazy, rude, and all-around incompetent. To reach the rank that he had achieved, he had to be better than I'd speculated, but it seemed that the closer he'd come to retirement, the closer he had come to worthless.

Cindy reached to shake his hand. "Welcome Detect … Brad."

"Thanks for the invitation, Chief," he said as he shook her hand. "Meet my wife, Hazel."

"Nice to meet you, Hazel. Please call me Cindy."

I stood a few feet behind Cindy and watched her exude more charm, smiles, and slobber than I had ever seen from her. I got a sugar high from watching.

Brad noticed me standing behind Cindy and offered a weak smile. Hazel walked over. "Hi, Chris, I'm Hazel. I've seen you in the yard but haven't had a chance to talk. Brad's told me a lot about you."

I followed Cindy's lead and smiled. "I bet he has."

We spent a few seconds talking about the weather before Cindy pointed the Burton's toward the bar and told them to help themselves.

Cindy took my elbow. "Let's check on Chef Emeril LaLarry. Looks like a forest fire over there." She led me toward the grill. "Honest, I only invited Burton because he was new here and had been a cop."

A cop who had no use for the Folly Beach force, I thought.

"Who would've thought he would come?" Cindy continued

before we reached the grill and Larry who waved smoke out of his face and coughed.

"How can you tell when these little buggers are done?" Larry asked as Cindy joined him in waving the smoke away.

I hadn't realized how prophetic his apron was.

Cindy took the mitt from the alleged chef and lifted the top of the oversized grill. More smoke bellowed out and twenty-five former beef patties appeared through the smoke. They were about thirty seconds from cremation. I'd seen juicier charcoal briquettes.

"Dear," Cindy said, and gritted her teeth, "I believe these were done five months ago." She turned the grill off and turned to me. "What'd I tell you about Woody's?"

Larry shook his head. "The freakin' sales rep didn't tell me that this thing'd get hot enough to start a nuclear reaction."

Larry and Cindy conferred and she called Woody's to order half-dozen pizzas and then announced that the smoke-signal exhibition was over and that everyone should grab another drink and that food would arrive shortly.

I left the hosts discussing how the grilling had gone astray and walked over to Cal Ballew, a former country music "star" who owned one of Folly's more popular bars, officially titled Cal's Country Bar and Burgers. He had an uncanny resemblance to Hank Williams Sr., wore a sweat-stained Stetson that had travelled thousands of miles with the six-foot three inch crooner, during his forty-plus years touring bars, nightclubs, and anywhere else that would allow him to perform. His lone hit record was on the charts in 1962. In the spirit of Folly-fashion, Cal's Stetson was complimented by a faded-black golf shirt, shamrock-green short shorts, and cowboy boots. I counted Cal as a good friend.

"Where's your guitar?" I asked as he dangled his arm over my shoulder.

Cal was known to start singing country classics wherever two or more people were gathered.

"Arthritis in my strummin' fingers. Old age is travelling by jet; used to come by train. Way too fast, way too fast. I moseyed past another big *zero* birthday last year."

"Seven?"

He nodded and bowed.

Cal leaned closer and asked if the latest arrival was Detective Burton. I told him yes and that it was now Brad Burton. Cal said thank God and looked toward the river. "What do you know about the body they found?"

I cringed and told him not much.

That would change for the worse.

Charles, usually the first to arrive at an event and thirty minutes before the announced time, appeared next. He looked around and spotted me and was at my side before I could wave him over.

"What'd you learn about the murder?" he asked.

Words like *hello* and *hi* were nearly extinct on the barrier island and I had begun to feel disoriented whenever I heard a conversation starting with one of them. It had been weeks since I had experienced that feeling.

"Nothing you don't know."

He waved a homemade, wooden cane around the yard; a cane with no apparent purpose other than to be his constant companion. "You're telling me that you've been right here in the chief's yard and haven't cornered her with a passel of questions?"

Somewhere in Charles's vivid, and often disconcerting, imagination, he believed he was a private detective; more accurately, the owner, president, and sole full-time employee of CDA—Charles's Detective Agency. What's more frightening, he thought that I was a part-time employee of his imaginary business.

I took a sip of wine and shook my head while in the back of it I was conflicted by what Mel had told me. I knew if I shared it with Charles, he would have us going off half-cocked and in warp speed trying to solve a murder that was none of our business. I also knew that if Charles learned that I knew something related to the death of the young man, I would need an emotional suit of armor to deflect his wrath. The party was becoming less festive.

"Come on." Charles headed toward Cindy and waved for me to follow.

Cindy was talking to Dude who had arrived while Charles was complaining that I wasn't doing my job and leaving valuable information about the murder on the table. Dude, an expert on all things celestial, both astronomy and astrology, was telling Cindy about her astrological sign and what fate had in store for her. I didn't hear all of her response, but it sounded like she didn't give an "ass's ass" unless it involved losing thirty pounds.

Dude's head moved like a bobble-head doll. "Nope, Chieftress."

Charles squeezed between the aging hippie and in her mind the thirty pound overweight police chief. "Don't mean to interrupt."

"Did to," Dude said. "Me be jawin' with Chieftress. You be steppin' on my words." He folded his arms over his glow-in-the-dark florescent tie-dyed T-shirt. "Word book say that be meaning of interruption."

Charles looked at Dude. "Sorry, you're right." He then turned to Cindy who had stepped back to see the outcome of Dude versus Charles. "Chris wanted me to ask what you know about the murder."

I looked at Charles out of the corner of my eye and shrugged in Cindy's direction.

The chief rolled her eyes. "Listen good, Charles. This is all I'm going to say." She hesitated and waited for him to acknowledge her statement. He gave a slight nod. "The ME says that the victim was killed between seven p.m. and midnight the night before he was found. Death caused by BFT, blunt-force trauma, weapon unknown. The end." She smiled. "Now, party hardy."

Charles tapped the cane on the patio. "Who was he?"

Cindy took a sip of the beer that she had been liberally consuming. "What itty-bitty part of *the end* did you not grast—grasp?"

"Me got it," Dude said even though he wasn't the intended recipient of Cindy's question.

Cindy held out her hand, palm out, in Dude's direction. "See?"

"Yeah, so who was he?" Charles asked, unfazed by Cindy's comment.

"Okay Charles, you win," the chief said. "Here's the skinny, if you tell anyone, I'll deny saying it." Charles leaned closer to Cindy. "I have absolutely, positively no idea who he was. There, you dragged it out of me." She took another swig of beer.

Dude turned from Cindy to Charles and then back to Cindy. "Enough dead-speak. Where be MM?"

Cindy got a puzzled look on her face. "MM?"

"Mad Mel, Mel Evans," I said and was pleased since it was one of the few times that I could translate for Dude. I was usually the recipient of Dude-speak translations.

"Oh," Cindy said. "Guess he's not here because I didn't invite him. Why?"

Dude said, "Gregorian calendar say he be member of zero club. We be partying for zero honorees."

I looked at him with new respect. First because he knew what the Gregorian calendar was and second because it was one of the longest statements I'd heard him make.

"We don't know Mr. Evans that well and didn't know about his birthday," Cindy said. "Sorry. How old is he?"

"MM be the big 780 full moons last week," the surf shop owner said.

I glanced at Charles who said, "Sixty."

"Oh," Cindy said. "If we'd known we would have invited him. Again, sorry."

"Chieftress forgiven," Dude said. "Put MM B-day on calendar on wall to invite to next zero party."

"Good idea," Cindy said.

It was a good answer since Cindy hadn't been around Dude as much as Charles and I had so she didn't know if he was serious, and I doubted that she had a Gregorian calendar on her wall that went out another decade, 130 full moons to Dude.

The aging hippie seemed pleased that he had accomplished his mission, excused himself, and headed across the patio to Larry who was looking toward the road, probably waiting for pizzas.

Cindy watched Dude go and shook her head, a common reaction to my surfing buddy.

"I'm bar bound, want to amble with me?" she asked.

Instead of waiting for an answer, she put her arms around Charles and me and led us to the bar.

"Cindy," Charles said and took a beer out of a tin garbage pail filled with ice and cans of Budweiser, Bud Light, and Coors. "Didn't Brian Newman turn 70 this year?"

She took a gulp of Bud Light and looked at Charles. "That would be a big yes siree."

Charles looked around the patio. "Couldn't he make it?"

"Don't know. He *be* in the same group as Mel: uninvited."

"Why?" Charles asked before I could.

"I didn't invite anyone I work with. I couldn't see an upside of having any of them around in the unlikely, highly unlikely, event that I have some sort of out-of-body experience and do something stupid tonight. Catch my drift?"

Charles raised his can of Budweiser in the air; I did the same with my white wine; and Cindy followed with her Bud Light. We toasted her wise decision.

With fresh drinks in hand, the Eagles singing "One of These Nights" from the outdoor speakers, the *zero* party in full swing, minus Mel and Brian, and with the increasing anticipation of food arriving, it was turning out to be a good night.

That was until Cindy said, "Speaking of Mel, why did you want to know if he'd talked to me?"

Charles's head jerked in my direction. "Yeah, why?"

I ignored him and said to Cindy, "Nothing. He said he wanted to talk to you and I wondered if he had.

"Nope," she said and looked at Larry who was paying the pizza delivery man.

Charles tapped his cane on my foot and glared at me. He knew there was more to my question; after all, he was a faux-detective.

I whispered, "Later."

He stabbed the cane into my foot as the sounds of the Rolling Stones mumbling "Brown Sugar" filled the air. "Count on it."

Arrival of the pizzas made Charles forget Mel and why I wanted to know if he had talked to the chief. Cal, Cindy, Larry, Charles, and I had gathered around one of the never-used, expensive patio tables that Larry had conned another vendor out of so we could feast on hockey-puck, cremated hamburger replacement pizzas. Good fortune, and a lack of chairs at our table, had sent Brad and Hazel Burton to the other table to break pizza bread with Brandon, the Muensterman's, and Dude. I'd be surprised if that combination wouldn't inspire the Muensterman's to put their house on the market.

"Prince, or his name de jour, was singing "Purple Rain," a slight breeze was keeping the temperature comfortable, and Woody's pizza was ten times better than whatever Larry could have produced from the grill.

"Ya'll hear about the .5 club?" Cal asked after we'd refreshed our drinks.

"The what club?" Larry asked and then sipped his martini.

I thought it was an excellent question.

"Point 5," Cal said as if it was self-explanatory. "You know, point like a dot and five like the number on the other side of four and shy of six."

"So what the chicken turd does it mean?" Cindy asked.

She crudely spoke for all of us.

Cal leaned back in the chair and tilted his Stetson up and away from his eyes. "Walkin' group."

I was beginning to think that he was taking anti-verbosity lessons from Dude.

"What about it?" I asked.

"You know old man Carr, don't you?" Cal asked.

"Chester Carr?" I said.

"That's the one."

Chester Carr was a friend who was a Folly Beach native. I talked with him a few times when he had worked at Bert's Market, the beach's iconic grocery that never closed, and then we got better acquainted when he befriended Melinda Beale, Charles's aunt who had moved to Folly two years ago, bringing with her unbridled spirit, a refreshing sense of humor, a thirst for adventure, and terminal cancer. She left us a year ago and I'm certain that she's now spreading her unique sense of joy to her fellow heavenly residents.

"Walking group," Cindy said. "Chester Carr. Isn't he like 137 years old?"

"Not ninety yet," Cal said. "Besides, the group is a bunch of seasoned citizens Chester's herded together. They ain't going to push his speed to heart attack miles per hour."

"What about the group?" I repeated.

Cal looked at each of us. "Thought since some of y'all are aging a bit, you might want to take a gander at joining."

Cindy jabbed Larry in the ribs. "That means you, dear. You could use some good exercise besides lifting boxes of nails and hardware-do-hickey things."

"Two questions," Charles said. "Who's in the group?" He held his thumb in the air. "And," he added his index finger to his raised thumb, "what in decimal-world does .5 mean?"

Cal removed his Stetson and set it on the table, wiped sweat off his forehead, and said, "For one, I'm in the group. Then there's Theodore Stoll, Harriet Grindstone, then there's Chris's bud William Hansel, and a new guy named Potsticker or something like that, and four or five others whose names these beers have removed from my memory." He tilted his Coors in my direction.

I had known William Hansel since my second week on Folly when he had been my neighbor until a peeved murderer torched my rental house with me in it. William was one of the few African Americans who called Folly Beach home and earned a paycheck as a professor at the College of Charleston. I wasn't familiar with the others Cal had mentioned.

Cindy chuckled. "Theo Stoll?"

Cal nodded.

"What's so funny?" Charles asked.

Cindy said, "If Theo's in the walking group, .5 means they walk .5 inches a week. A lump of coal'd turn to a diamond quicker than he can cross Center Street. Sure it's the same Theodore Stoll?"

I wondered how many Theodore Stolls there could be on the island.

"Plum sure," Cal said.

Larry had his elbows on the table. "You said some guy

named Pot something."

"Yeah," Cal said. "Potstick or Potting soil or something."

"What's his first name?" Larry asked. He had given up on Cal remembering the last name.

"Abe, I think. Why?"

"Just curious," Larry said. "More drinks, anyone?"

Charles raised his hand and Larry pointed to the bar. What a great host, I thought.

We spent the next five minutes speculating about the origin of the group's name before Cindy stuffed the last bite of pizza in her mouth and muttered that she'd better check on her other guests. She said that she needed to see if Dude had confused them into a stupor or if Brad Burton was telling them how awful all of us at our table were. Charles said he'd go with her in case she needed an extra set of hands to strangle Burton.

Then Larry leaned over and asked if I could stop by his store in the morning. He said he had a problem and may need my help.

If that didn't pique my interest, nothing would.

Chapter Five

Pewter Hardware was in a seashell-pink, concrete block building with four parking spaces in its tiny lot. The building, located next to the post office, would fit in the lighting section of Home Depot, but if you were thin, and didn't have to pass anyone in the aisle, you could get to most anything there you could need.

I was more than curious why Larry wanted to talk to me, so I was at the store as soon as it opened. Scattered storms were predicted so I drove. That's the excuse I used; the truth was that I was too lazy to hoof it. Brandon greeted me before I'd had a chance to look around and shared that he had a great time at the party but that his head felt like "fifty pounds of cement in a forty pound sack."

I didn't have any hardware store analogies, so I said that I understood and asked where Larry was.

"The boy called as I was unlocking the door. He'll be here shortly." Brandon smiled. "Get it? Larry, shortly."

Larry's diminutive size not only would have been perfect for a jockey but had been perfect for climbing up gutter downspouts and trellises and entering second-story windows. His previous career had been as a cat burglar but he'd given it up at the urging of the Georgia Department of Corrections when as incentive they'd given him free room and board for eight years. That world was behind Larry, but his lack of altitude hadn't changed and provided fodder for jokes—attempts at jokes—from Brandon and others.

I frowned but Brandon had already turned and started straightening water hoses on the endcap near the entry.

I heard Larry before I saw him. That wasn't a short joke. He had opened the door but hadn't stepped in. "Thanks for coming to the party last night," he said and peeked inside and yelled to Brandon, "Can you handle the crowd for a few minutes?"

I was the crowd.

Brandon was in back and yelled that he thought he could. Larry jerked his head in the direction of a small, Folly River Park across the street. "Let's check out the view."

Larry's house backed up to the river and he had plenty of time to check the view, so I assumed it was his way of getting out of earshot of Brandon or the crowd that might descend any moment. We walked up the slight incline into the park and Larry said, "Did you see a semi run over me last night?"

I said no and that I would have noticed and he said that he felt like something gigantic had traversed his head. From my extensive study of this morning's condition of last night's attendees, I think I can conclude that beer retailers had a serious spike in sales the last twenty-four hours.

Larry plopped down on the closest seat at the picnic table. I sat across from him and remained silent. This was his story and I didn't want to clutter his alcohol-jumbled brain with extraneous chatter. He closed his eyes and squeezed the bridge of his nose.

"Have you run across someone named Abraham Pottinger?" Larry asked as he slowly opened his eyes. "He's been here about three months."

"Don't believe so. Who's he?"

"Blast from the past."

My head didn't hurt as much as Brandon's or Larry's, but that was a bit too cryptic. "Explain."

"I met him in Atlanta in the eighties." Larry stared at the river and seemingly into his past. "I was between careers." He hesitated and then smiled. "Giving up my job at the chop shop after three police raids and transitioning to burglary."

I was one of only a handful of people on Folly who knew about his left-of-legal past before his stint in prison and his move here. To his credit, the first person he told when he had arrived was then chief of police, Brian Newman. He'd said he wanted Newman to know so if anything bad happened on Folly the chief would suspect and want to talk to Larry and that the newcomer would understand and cooperate. At that moment, Larry gained Newman's respect which went much further than Larry's size and they'd become friends.

I said, "That was a long time ago."

Larry nodded. "I ran into Abe at a scuzzy diner that catered to some of the city's lowest lowlifes. He always wore the latest fashions and talked like an English professor."

Larry paused again and continued to gaze into the past.

"What brought you together?" I asked.

"Money."

"Explain," I said a second time.

"Abe's a con man, a damned good one. He could con the tats off Kid Rock. I'd seen him a couple of times in the diner and one day he stopped at my table, said that he needed a partner in a business deal he was working on. I asked him why he was talking to me and he said that he needed someone who appeared to be unsavory and little." Larry smiled. "Half of that, the little part, rubbed me wrong and I told him so. He went in sweet-talk mode and before he was done had me convinced that my size was the next best thing to penicillin. Told you he was good."

"Business deal?"

"He had business cards that said *Abraham R. Pottinger and Associates, Theft Risk Consultants*. He'd approach mid-sized businesses, the ones with some money but not big enough to afford full-time security like mom-and-pop jewelry stores, high-end appliance stores. He'd tell them 'for a one-time, affordable fee' he would conduct a thorough analysis of the business and provide the owner with a foolproof, written plan to prevent theft from outside and from employees."

"Why'd he need you?"

Larry smiled but the lines around his eyes didn't cooperate. "He told me that he was doing okay, but wanted to be able to introduce me to the store owners as one of his associates. He'd point to me and tell them I was a reformed burglar and would be able to bring my expertise to Abe's *thorough analysis.*"

"What happened?"

"It sounded good. Hell, I even started believing it. The man could con the Pope into becoming Muslim. Anyway, Abe's affordable fee was up in the thousands and may have been worth it if the service was legit. We sold the proposal to a dozen businesses. Exactly zero of them received a plan."

"I suppose for their fee the businesses learned not to buy a security analysis," I said.

"Good point. Some of the businesses reported the scam to the police and Abe disappeared from my life as quickly as he entered it." Larry rubbed the bridge of his nose again and looked me in the eyes. "Until last week."

"What happened?"

Larry pointed toward his store. "He walked through the door sporting a big, con-artist grin, bent down and gave me a hug, and said how great it was to see me. I nearly threw up; my past stomped on me like a combat boot on cricket."

"What did he want?"

Larry pounded his fist on the table and took a deep breath. "He said he'd heard that I was here and wanted to stop in and see his *old friend*. He said he'd turned his life around and was now as straight as a laser. Said he'd moved to the beach and bought a house and planned to spend the rest of his life enjoying the simple things."

"You didn't believe him."

"Not for a nanosecond," Larry said without hesitating. "Once a con man, always a con man."

I didn't remind Larry that he'd turned his life around and wondered if Abe could've done the same.

"Have you seen him since then?"

"No, thank God. He said we needed to get together sometime over a drink and talk about old times. I thought right, *when hell freezes over.*"

"What do you want my help with?" I asked, remembering what Larry had said last night.

Larry looked at the table, toward his store, and then back at me. "Remember last night when Cal was talking about the walking group?"

I said that I did.

"Remember when Cal was saying who was in the group? He said that some guy named *Potsticker or something like that* was in it."

I remembered.

"That's mighty close to Pottinger. If it's him, it means nothing but trouble. Trust me."

I'd known Larry for a long time. If he said it meant trouble, it did. "What do you want me to do?"

"Don't know, thinking this up on the fly. Maybe you could join the group and figure out what Abe's up to."

I nearly laughed when he said that I could join a walking group, but realized that if the group was headed by Chester Carr, there couldn't be much walking involved.

"Why me?"

"I trust you Chris. You're good at sniffing out bad stuff and don't jump off the pier until you see it's safe below. If you need to, you can take Charles with you. Will you help?"

No, no way, please no, I thought.

"Of course."

Chapter Six

A knock on the door distracted me from thinking about Larry, his nefarious history, and a guy named *Potsticker or something like that* who could be Larry's past coming back to haunt him. The disruption was okay with me since I had no idea what to do about Larry's situation. It was okay until I opened the door.

"Are you Christopher Landrum?" asked a tall gentleman, in his mid-thirties, sporting a buzz cut, a starched-white shirt, slacks with a sharp crease, spit-polished shoes, what appeared to be a new navy blazer, and a frown.

No one outside the Department of Motor Vehicles had called me Christopher in the last fifty years, but I said yes.

He handed me a card that indicated that he was Detective Kenneth Adair with the Charleston County Sheriff's Office. "May I come in?"

I figured it would have been rude, and rather unproductive, to have followed my urge and slammed the door in his face. I stepped aside, waved him in, and asked if he wanted anything to drink. He declined, and I asked what I could do for him.

"I have a few questions, Mr. Landrum. Purely routine."

Unlikely, I thought as I suggested that we would be more comfortable in the kitchen, and offered him a seat at the table.

"Do you know Mel Evans?" he asked.

As I looked in the detectives penetrating stare, I decided that it was time to adhere to Dude-mode. "Yes."

Being the astute detective that I suspected him to be, he

realized after a few seconds of silence that I was finished.

"Were you with Mr. Evans last Thursday on his boat, the ..." Adair took a notebook out of his blazer's inside pocket, flipped through a few pages, and continued, "*Mad Mel's Magical Marsh Machine?*"

"I was."

"What was the nature of your excursion?"

"Mel had taken a group on a, umm, picnic, the night before and it got too dark to see what they may have left on the beach, so he asked if I could help him make sure the site was cleaned up."

I was following the old television detective show line: "The truth, the whole truth, nothing but the truth." Yes, I was skipping *the whole truth* part. I also realized that he was looking at me like he didn't believe a word I was saying.

"Where was this so-called picnic?"

"Out at the end of Folly, an area often referred to as Boneyard Beach."

He leaned forward. "Did you find anything unusual when you got there?"

Like a dead body, I wondered. "Only a few empty beer cans."

He wrote something in his notebook although I doubted that he would have forgotten *few empty beer cans*. I asked again if he wanted something to drink and again he declined. I was failing to win him over with kindness.

"How long were you there?"

I smiled. "Until the sky opened up and a torrential downpour soaked us."

His scowl indicated that he didn't see the humor in us standing in the rain. "So how long were you there before the rain?"

"No more than fifteen, twenty minutes."

"And then you returned to the marina?"

"Correct."

"Did Mr. Evans indicate that anything unusual happened during the picnic?"

I was now back *to the truth, nothing but the truth*. "No." Mel had told me that nothing unusual had happened *during* the picnic. "Why?"

He returned the notebook to his pocket and leaned back. "You've been dating one of our detectives."

I didn't hear a question so I sat silently.

His frown broke, but his expression was still professional and didn't disclose anything. "I don't know her well," he said, "but I hear that Detective Lawson thinks highly of you, and that over the years, you've been tangentially involved in some investigations."

I still didn't hear a question, but nodded anyway.

"I wouldn't give this much information to someone I was questioning, but because of your, umm, relationship with Lawson, I'll share that our office has received a missing-person's report about someone who participated in Mr. Evan's excursion."

"Did the person go missing during the trip?"

Detective Adair shook his head. "That's where it gets vague. The person filing the report knows that the alleged missing person, a male, college student, was on the trip but thinks that he wasn't on the boat when it returned to the dock."

"Did anyone else notice him missing?"

"No. I believe that as a result of alcohol consumption, the others wouldn't have noticed even the strangest occurrence."

Adair would have already known about the body on the beach, so he was playing games with me. I wanted to ask if the body had been identified as the student but that would have opened a door that I thought needed to remain closed.

"Who told you that I was with Mel?"

Adair's frown returned. "Sorry, I can't say." He stood. "I believe that's all the questions," he hesitated and then added, "for now."

"Have you talked with Mel?"

"Yes," he said in a tone that indicated that it was all he was going to say. I walked him to the door and he thanked me for taking time to talk and said for me to say hi to Detective Lawson and to call him if I thought of anything else.

Until recently, I had to leave the house to find myself in trouble. It now seemed that trouble came knocking. I was on the phone to Chief LaMond before the detective was out of the drive.

"What now, Chris?" she said.

I hated caller ID. "Wondering if you know the name of the murder victim?"

"Drew Casey. Bye."

"Whoa. Anything else?"

"Oh, thought you asked his name."

"You know better, Chief LaMond."

She giggled. "Sorry, you're just too easy to fiddle with."

I heard her sigh and then she said, "He was a junior at the College of Charleston. Lived by himself in an apartment off-campus. His family's out west somewhere but they've been estranged since he graduated from high school. Reason unknown and no one knows how to contact them. Mr. Casey must have money since he paid cash for his tuition and didn't give the college information on his parents when he enrolled. The name and number he gave for the person to contact in case of an emergency came up a dead end. There was no such number and only about a zillion people in the country with the common name. Seems strange, doesn't it?"

"Yes."

"So, that's it. I'm getting this third hand. As usual, the high-and-mighty sheriff's office is shutting out us little-ole-town, dumb-fuzz folks."

With roughly twenty-five employees, the Folly Beach Department of Public Safety wasn't tiny, but was charged with providing police, fire, medical, and rescue services to the island that can swell to sixty thousand people during peak season; a daunting task that often overwhelms the department's ability to meet its varied obligations. Nevertheless, considering the challenges, Cindy's department performed admirably. There is not always an amiable working relationship between her department and the sheriff's office and information was seldom effectively communicated, causing more conflict.

I thanked her for what information she did have and asked if she could let me know if she found out anything else.

"Chris, you know I live to share confidential public-safety

information with you," she said, in her East Tennessee sarcastic tone.

"That's why you're my favorite law enforcement officer on Folly Beach," I said.

"Moose manure." She hung up.

Who told the police that I had been with Mel on his boat? Did the police believe Mel killed the student? Did they suspect that I was part of it?

What have I gotten into?

I was less successful with my next call. Mel's answering machine informed me that he was unavailable and that if I left a number and a brief message that he *might* get back with me. I left him a Dude-like message saying, "Chris here, so was detective. Call," and hoped that would have been enticing enough to get his attention.

I called Charles and was less successful than with my call to Mel. Charles, to add to his list of idiosyncrasies didn't own an answering machine or cell phone. I listened to his phone ring a half dozen times and gave up.

My stomach began to growl; skirting questions from a detective and two unsuccessful phone calls made me hungry. My cupboard was in its usual state of bare, so I headed to the Lost Dog Café for a late breakfast. The Dog was a few blocks from the house and I could have walked but instead rationalized several reasons why I should drive instead of admitting that laziness trumped them all.

The Dog was a block off Center Street and the most popular breakfast spot on Folly Beach. I expected a long wait after driving around the block twice trying to find an empty parking place. I lucked into a space two blocks from the restaurant and realized that I wasn't much closer than if I'd left the car at home. The Dog was located in a former Laundromat, but you would never have known that the colorful restaurant had ever been anything but the place to get good food, stimulating conversation, and gossip galore. My luck changed when I saw Charles seated on the front deck.

He reached down and picked up his cane and pointed it at

the seat on the other side of the small table. He scooted his coffee mug, *Folly Current* newspaper, and Tilley hat over to his side of the table to make room for me.

I said, "Good morning," like most normal people I had known before moving to Folly would have done—remember, remarks like *good morning, hi* or *hello*, appeared to be borderline rude.

He said, "Mel, what's the deal? Larry, what'd he want? Dead guy, what do you know?"

I rest my case. I delayed having to answer the master inquisitor when Brittany, one of the Dog's more cheerful waitresses, noticed me and asked if I was ready to order. I looked at Charles's half-eaten French toast, and said the same. She gave me one of her high-powered smiles, said she'd take care of it for one of her "more handsome" customers, and delivered the check to the table behind us.

"Enough foodie talk," Charles said before Brittany had time to put in my order. "What's up with Mel?"

"Why do you think something's up?"

"You asked Cindy if he'd talked to her and when I asked you about it you said you'd tell me later." He looked at his wrist where most normal people would wear a watch. Charles, not a full-time resident in the world of normal, didn't own a timepiece but didn't hesitate to imagine one like he imagined so many other things. He pointed his fork at me. "Later just arrived."

Charles was like darkness chasing sunset. At times it took longer to catch it, but it always did. There was no reason not to tell him everything; and perhaps he could shed light on what had happened. I began with Mel arriving at my door and our trip to Boneyard Beach. Charles gave me dirty looks twice and interrupted to castigate me for not calling him and taking him with us. I overlooked his whiny criticism. I proceeded to tell him about the visit by Detective Adair and how I limited my answers to the specific questions he had asked and even then being as brief as possible.

Charles looked around the patio and then back at me. "Thomas Jefferson said, 'The most valuable of all talents is that of never using two words when one will do.'"

Another of Charles's quirks was quoting United States presidents. I had never known if the quotes were real, never cared enough to check, but did know that with the quantity of books he had in his apartment and his proclamation that he had read them all except the cookbooks, his presidential utterances could be accurate—or not.

I finished describing Detective Adair's demeanor and how I skirted *the whole truth* in telling the detective why Mel wanted to return to Boneyard Beach, when Brittany arrived with my breakfast. I managed a couple of bites before Charles started with the questions.

"Learn anything about the body?"

I shared what Cindy had told me about Drew Casey.

Charles huffed and leaned toward me. "And when were you going to tell me this?"

My impatient friend thought that I should tell him about anything that I ever learned that he didn't already know within seconds, or less, of learning it.

"Just did. And, for the record, I called you as soon as I got off the phone with the chief. Guess who didn't answer?"

A large construction truck drove past and the sound of its engine wiped out most of his words. I heard, "Excuses, excuses … forgive you this time."

I let him mumble as I watched a group of vacationers waiting in front of the restaurant for a table. I avoided eye contact with three different couples who kept looking our direction and wondering if we were ever going to vacate the valuable piece of real estate. Brittany returned with coffee for Charles. The fragrance of freshly brewed coffee filled the air around the table and I continued to avoid eye contact with the antsy diner wannabes.

"So what did Larry want to talk about?" Charles asked, finished for now with Mel's story.

"Seems an acquaintance from his past has come to Folly," I shared what Larry had told me about Abraham Pottinger.

"Is he about Larry's age, wears fancy duds, and looks a little like George Clooney will when he's sixty?"

"Could be. All I know is that he's about the same age as Larry and wore good clothes back when Larry knew him. Why?"

"Seen a stranger around town a few times. The fellow's out of place. Who here wears pressed khaki shorts?"

"Could be," I told Charles that Larry didn't trust Pottinger regardless of what he had professed about changing from his life of crime.

"Larry doesn't think leopard-Abe can change his spots?"

"You got it."

"Does Larry remember that he changed his?"

Charles was one of the few on Folly who knew about Larry's past and his life-altering transition to a well-respected business owner.

"Sure, but Larry can spot a problem a mile away. If he has a bad feeling about Pottinger, there's something there."

"Then," Charles tilted his head and nodded, "what does Larry want us to do?"

Us, I thought, but didn't say it because it would have been a waste of a word.

"Cal told me that one of the members of the .5 group's name was something like 'Potsticker.' Larry thinks it's Pottinger." I took a sip of coffee and continued, "If it is, Larry is convinced that he's not in the group for exercise. He's out to con members out of their false teeth, as Larry put it."

"And we're supposed to do what about it?"

"Larry asked me to join the walking group to try to figure out what Pottinger's up to."

Charles chuckled. "You in a walking group. Didn't know Larry was that funny."

I smiled and told Charles that if the group was headed by Chester, I wouldn't have to worry about too much walking.

"Sounds like what the group needs is someone to do some detectin'. When do *we* start?"

Chapter Seven

The .5 group gathered at the crack of dawn every other day at the Folly Pier. Their dedication impressed me until Chester confessed that "crack of dawn" was nine-o'clock, or two and a half hours after sunrise. Today would be the group's next walk so Charles and I decided to stroll by Chester's house around the time they should be finishing.

My crack of dawn arrived hours earlier than Chester's, and I had time to kill and used my culinary skills and fixed a bowl of Cheerios, and wondered what Charles and I were getting into. What were we supposed to do if the newcomer in the group was Abraham Pottinger? I could picture Charles sideling up to him and saying, "Abe, good buddy, how're you planning to rip off these geezers?"

Charles may not be that direct, but he wouldn't burn too much daylight before finding a way to interrogate Abe. If he was as good at the con as Larry had said, Pottinger would see through Charles's questions and if he had a less than legitimate motive for being here, he wouldn't have to search far to learn that we were friends with Larry. The weather forecast called for scattered showers, so maybe I would luck out and it would rain on Chester's parade and I wouldn't have to face the alleged con artist.

The rain gods had forsaken me and the sky was clear and the temperature mild as the walkers' *crack of dawn* had come and gone. Chester lived on West Ashley Avenue, a block off Center Street, the location of most of the small island's retail establishments, restaurants, and bars. I met Charles in front of St. James Gate, one of Folly's newest restaurants, where today he wore an orange University of Texas San Antonio long-sleeve T-shirt with something that looked like a bird's head on it, blue shorts with ravels on the legs, florescent-red tennis shoes, Tilley hat, and his cane. I was attired in my Folly summer uniform of a faded golf shirt, shorts, canvas Crocs, and a Tilley similar to the one he had that I had given Charles a few years back.

He pointed to the logo on his shirt. "Get it?"

"Get what? That bird's head?"

"Chris, oh Chris," He leaned against his cane. "I figured that since you're a college graduate you'd know that it's a roadrunner." He smiled. "Walking group. Roadrunner."

I nodded, not because I cared, but to get him to shut up. I changed the subject. "I figure they've had time to get to Chester's. Ready to stroll by?"

"See if I get the plan." He pointed his cane toward our destination. "We're going to say, 'Hey group, you look like you've been out for a walk. Can we stop and jabber a while? Oh, hi stranger, you look like the crook Larry said was over here swindling the life savings out of old folks. We're here to make sure you get locked up for the rest of your dirty, rotten, lying, stealing life."

I bit my lip and tried to keep a straight face. "You've got it."

"Then lead on."

Moments later, Charles and I were strolling by Chester's house when Charles glanced over at the screened-in porch where several people were gathered.

He turned to me and in a stage whisper said, "Look, there's Chester." He then turned toward the porch. "Hey, Chester, how're you doing?"

Not inconspicuous, but better than yelling, "Hey, Chester, who's that crook with you?"

"Yo, Charles, Chris. Come join us."

So far our well-thought-out, highly-detailed plan was on track.

Chester opened the screen door and waved us in. He was five-foot-six, mostly bald, chunky, his shape complemented by Coke-bottle-thick glasses, and in the words of Charles's late aunt, "a spittin' image of Mr. Magoo."

"Say hi to our little group of walkers," Chester took a deep breath and gestured toward the five others. Sweat rolled down his face.

"Wobbly Walkers," said a short, attractive lady in a wooden rocking chair nearest the door.

"Silly girl," said a man leaning on the back of the woman's rocker. "We're senior strollers." He leaned his head back, the bill of his black USS Yorktown ball cap pointed toward the ceiling. His way-off-white, sleeveless T-shirt slid off one shoulder as he tried to act insulted by the wobbly walker remark.

"That's ET," Chester said by way of introduction as he pointed to the man who looked about 117, but was no older than 85.

ET shuffled over and shook our hands. "Name's Theodore Stoll, Theo to my friends."

"ET to everyone here," interrupted the rocking-chair lady.

Theo looked at her and said, "Huh?"

She smiled at him and repeated what she had said. When he turned back toward us, the lady cupped her hand around her ear and nodded. Got it, Theo's hard of hearing.

Theo nodded and continued. "A term of endearment, after the loveable movie alien." He pulled up his black, knee-high support stockings that now reached his shiny, green jogging shorts.

The lady held her hand in front of her face and giggled.

Theo pointed to the rocking chair. "That's Connie DeWalt. Cute as a button, ain't she?"

Connie was in her mid-sixties but still had the figure of a fifty year old. She nodded in our direction, said "it's a pleasure," and winked at Theo.

"Excuse our condition," Chester said. "We just finished our longest walk ever."

"Where'd you go?" Charles asked.

Chester wiped sweat off his left arm. "Started at the foot of the pier. Too many steps to start on the pier. Walked all the way up to city hall and back here."

It was a distance that could better be described in yards rather than in miles.

"Come meet the rest of the group," Chester said. He stepped around the rocking chair and led us to the wicker chair leaned against the window frame. "Meet David Darnell, he's new to Folly. Moved here and opened an insurance agency."

David unfolded himself from the chair and towered over us with his six-foot-five or so frame and gave each of us a firm, insurance-salesman handshake, told us that he and Alice, his wife of forty years, had moved to Folly to get away from the rat race and frigid winters in Boston.

"So what do you two do?" he asked.

Charles told him that he was retired, and that I owned the island's best and only photo gallery, but that it was open two days a week, and that quicker than a blink of the eye I was going to close it and deprive the photo-buying public of getting any more pictures. It wasn't how I would have introduced myself but Charles didn't give me time to answer.

I saw a head peak around the talkative insurance agent.

"A couple more to meet," Chester said. "Harriet Grindstone, these are my friends Chris and Charles," as if she hadn't already heard our names three times in the last five minutes.

Harriet managed to slip past David and firmly shake our hands. She was thin but had a strong grip for someone whom I judged to be around 70. I suspected that her walking clothes doubled her weight.

"The weather's terrible today, isn't it?" she said as way of introduction.

I thought the weather was perfect but I agreed. Charles, the chameleon, also agreed with her, Chester shrugged, and David who was standing behind her rolled his eyes.

"Your friends William Hansel and Cal Bellew are usually with us along with two more irregulars. Life must have gotten in their way today," Chester said, and led us to the other person on the porch we hadn't met.

"Fellows, meet our newest member, Abraham Pottinger."

Bingo.

"Pleased to meet you gentlemen. Call me Abe, like Honest Abe," Pottinger said, and rushed to shake our hands.

At five-foot-seven, he was three inches shorter than me, not fat, not thin, had a full head of dyed black hair, and Charles was right, had a strong resemblance to an older George Clooney.

"Believe I've seen you around town," Charles said.

I didn't tell Pottinger that Charles had remembered him because of his non-Folly attire, which today included Tide-white Nike tennis shoes, pressed khaki shorts, and a white, Brooks Brothers' polo shirt. He looked as out of place as a Maserati at a moped rally.

Abe turned to me. "Thought you looked familiar. Walked by your gallery a few times. I'll stop in the next time I'm that way."

"That's all of us," Chester said, and scooted closer to Abe, Charles, and me. "Want some Kool-Aid? It's our drink of choice. Got Fig Newtons too." He leaned closer and whispered, "Prevents constipation, you know." He pointed to a small round table between the door into the house and a rocking chair.

"Think I'll have some," Charles said. "Abe, can I get you more Kool-Aid or cookies?"

Charles was already on the hunt.

Abe declined and Charles made his way to the refreshment table. Chester reached for four chairs that were folded and leaning against the wall, unfolded two of them and said for us to take a load off.

Abe's chair was closest and Charles asked him how long he'd been on Folly. He said a couple of months, and then Charles asked, in a way only he could, "Why?"

"Good question, my friend," Abe said, clasped his hands behind his head, and leaned back. "I was in the theft-risk consulting business out west. Sure, I made plenty of money working with businesses helping them prevent theft from employees and outsiders, but it got old. Before that I was in financial planning and wealth management, still dabble in it." He paused and looked toward the ocean. "Found out that I had a friend or two in the Charleston area and decided to shred my business cards and move here and soak in the fresh salt air, sunshine, and fine people like the walking group here." He waved his hand around the porch.

Harriet and Connie were talking but kept glancing at Abe. If they missed anything he said, it wasn't much. Theo and David were in a stimulating conversation about their leg problems, swelling and aching, and the best brand of support socks.

Chester moved his chair closer to Charles but didn't interrupt Abe as he told us more than we could understand about how the price of silver futures in India affected gold in the United States. Charles's attention drifted and I was surprised that it was more than he, the ultimate trivia collector, wanted to know.

Charles turned to Chester. "So tell us about your group?"

"Charles, I owe it all to your dear aunt. When that sweet and sexy, if I might add, Melinda came into my life last year, I was about ready to check out." He shook his head. "I was in the final stretch of time in this world. My wife, Rosie, God rest her soul, was already with our maker. We were childless, and if I was honest with myself, I hadn't contributed one little kidney bean to society. I was ready to go."

Charles leaned over and patted Chester's knee. "Now Chester, don't be—"

"Hold on, Charles, I haven't finished."

Charles sat back and pointed his palm at Chester. "Sorry."

Chester looked at me and then at Charles. Abe was still leaned back in his chair and taking in everything. "As I was saying, your aunt barreled into my life full of energy, humor, and despite her terminal disease, more hope and positive outlook than anyone I'd ever known. To use a word that was popular before most people were born, I was smitten."

Charles hesitated and then said, "Aunt M. sure liked you."

Chester's face turned red. "Shouldn't tell you this seeing that you're her nephew, but if I'd been a few years younger, I think she and I would have had more fun on the Serta than sleeping, if you know what I mean."

I didn't think there could be any doubt, and neither did Charles who said, "I understand."

"Eww!" Harriet said.

I didn't think that she and Connie had missed much.

Chester coughed and leaned closer to Charles. "Anyway, Melinda recharged my batteries, she convinced me that I wasn't nearing the end, but was only beginning to enjoy my twilight years, and that I needed to get in shape and smell the roses." He chuckled. "And smell the rose, the wine kind, if you get my drift."

"So," I said before Charles did, "the walking group is to help you get in shape?"

He reached down and patted his calf. "She said with a little work, I'd once again be a chick magnet and sexier than ever."

"Eww!" Connie and Harriet said concurrently.

They scooted their chairs closer to Chester. Our conversation was more interesting than whatever they had been talking about.

"Tell them your silly-ass rules," Harriet said. She had no trouble finding things to complain about.

Chester frowned at her. "They're not silly, they're thorough." He turned back to us. "I started the group as a New Year's resolution and promise to Melinda, well, to her spirit since by that time she was already up there charming God." He pointed to the ceiling, but I suspected he meant to heaven rather than Melinda and God hanging out on the roof. "Members must be at least sixty to join; don't want any of those young whippersnappers horning in and trying to make us marathon runners."

I glanced around the room. There wasn't a gnat's chance in a bat cave of that happening.

"I lied about my age to get in," Connie said. She had scooted her chair even closer.

"No she didn't," Chester said. "That's why I made up a two page application and had each applicant show proof of age. Even her." He pointed at Connie.

"Yeah," Theo said. He moved closer to the expanding group around Charles and me. "At first he said a driver's license would do and then anal Chester said it was too easy to forge so he made us show a passport or an original birth certificate. Know how hard it is for folks our age to come up with an original birth certificate?"

"You know that's not the reason, Theo," Chester said. "Two of you don't have driver's licenses any more, and one of you, whom I will not identify, had your license yanked by the police after you ran down three stop signs and the next day drove your car down the boat ramp into the river."

"Whatever," Harriet said. "The point is why in the hell do we need to go to all that trouble to walk around Folly Beach? You wouldn't find any of these silly-ass rules back in Montana where I grew up," she groused. "We didn't need rules and silly-ass papers to fill out. Yep, I remember back when this was a free country."

Theo showed more energy than I had noticed when he pointed outside. "And then foreigners came and stole it from the Indians."

"You would know," Harriet said. She winked at Theo. "You were there."

"I want to make sure our group stays within the defined parameters," Chester said.

Harriet raised her hand and was acknowledged by Chester. "Tell the boys about the last statement on your silly-ass application."

Chester shook his head. "All it says is, 'The .5 Club will not be liable for members who fall and break a part of their body or drop dead during any group-organized walk."

"Wise addition," Abe said. "Good risk management."

Harriet exhaled. "Legal gobbledygook, bull-hockey if you ask me."

Chester leaned forward and glared at her. "I didn't ask you."

How could I not want to be a part of this fun group, I wondered.

"So where'd the group's name come from?" Charles asked.

Chester shook his head. "Sorry Charles, that's a secret. Only official members of the group are privy to knowing."

Harriet mumbled, "That's the next to last statement on the

silly-ass application."

Chester ignored her, or perhaps didn't hear her. "I've got an idea," he said, snapped his fingers, and looked at Charles and then at me. "You two boys might be old enough. Why don't you join us?"

"Only if you can find your original birth certificate or passport," Harriet said. "Martians and illegal aliens don't need to waste time applying."

"Wow, that's a great idea," Charles said.

Great, since that was the reason for walking by Chester's house. I also suspected that Charles was enthused because he would learn what .5 meant.

Chapter Eight

The next morning, I was sitting at my kitchen table, sipping coffee and filling out Chester's two-page application chock-full of questions and "silly-ass" rules. I wondered why he needed my shoe size, but if I wanted to be a member of the .5 group, whatever that meant, I had to play by his rules. I was also thinking how positive an impact Charles's aunt had on Chester. Even after her death, she'd touched many lives.

I refilled my coffee and questioned what I could learn about Larry's nemesis by strolling around Folly. Abe seemed like a nice enough guy, he asked more questions than I was comfortable with, but appeared interested in the others, and wasn't asking anything too personal. If he had an ulterior motive, it wasn't apparent; then again, that's what defined a good con artist.

Someone pounding on the door interrupted my peaceful morning; something that was happening way too often. Mel was on the screened-in porch, looking like he did the last time he'd disrupted my morning, except today he wore a camouflaged fatigue cap with *Semper Fi* on the crown.

"Don't take this old Marine more than once to know where there ain't food," he said, and shoved a box from Dunkin' Donuts at me and squeezed past me into the room. "You're not out of coffee, are you?"

He was already in the kitchen and looking for a mug. "Speaking of food," he said although I didn't recall talking about the subject, "why the hell wasn't I invited to the big shindig the other night? I turned the big 6-0 this year."

"Don't know. I didn't make the guest list."

"Oh well," Mel said, "it's water over the damn dam. Probably had something to do with me hardly knowing that little-squirt, hardware store guy."

I nodded like I thought that minor detail might have been the reason he wasn't invited.

"Don't think it's because I'm queer, do you?"

"No. Most likely it was because Larry and Cindy don't know you well enough to appreciate your charming, warm, and friendly personality."

Mel stared at me; his often-displayed frown deepened. "You making fun of me?"

"Yep." I opened the box and offered him first donut.

"Thought so," he mumbled because his mouth was already full of the bigger portion of a chocolate glazed goodie. He then smiled. A crumb slipped out of his mouth.

"I don't suppose you're here to feed me and let me make fun of you," I said and took a bite of a sugar-coated cholesterol builder.

He finished the first donut with one more bite and grabbed another.

"Cop came to talk to me again last night."

"Have you talked to Chief LaMond?"

"Umm, no."

There went that advantage, I thought. "Who was it?"

Mel snarled. "Detective Asshole."

"Adair?"

"That's what I said."

"What'd he want?"

"Asked if I knew someone named Drew Casey. I asked him if that was the body they found. He said something like 'I'm asking the questions,' I refrained from smacking the crap out of him, and told him that I didn't think I knew anyone with that name."

I shared that Casey was the dead student.

His frown deepened. "Chris, I'm afraid this Casey person

may be gay. It's starting to hit a little close to my crib."

"Did Adair say Casey was gay?"

"No, but he asked me if I'd ever been to LeBar." Mel sat back in the chair and appeared to lose interest in the donuts.

"Where's that?"

"Downtown Charleston, half block off North King."

"Never heard of it."

"No surprise. It's a hole-in-the-wall neighborhood gay bar. You straight folks lead such a sheltered life, never get out, never experience the joys of the world."

And he said all that with his patented frown. "What'd you tell him?"

"Told him that I'd been there a few times. Maybe twice with Caldwell; a couple of times by myself. I wasn't a regular."

Caldwell Ramsey and Mel had been together for several years and lived in a small house on the outskirts of Charleston. Caldwell, at six-foot-five, towered over Mel, had played basketball at Clemson in the mid-eighties, had a quick smile, something that his partner had never mastered, and was African American.

"Did Adair ask if you were gay?"

"Shit no." He reached for another donut. His appetite had returned.

"Did you tell him you were?"

"Negatory. No ask, no tell. Didn't figure it was any of his freakin' business." He paused, looked at the depleting collection of donuts, and then back at me. "I don't hide my sexual preference; at least not since I was mustered out of the not-so-gay-friendly United States Marine Corp." He held his arms out to the side. "As you can tell from my non-pastel wardrobe, I don't flaunt it either. It's a part of me the same as my cheerful disposition." He winked. A glimmer of humor showing through. "I don't give it much thought."

"Did you get the impression that the detective was implying that Drew Casey was gay?"

"No doubt. I gave it a lot of thought last night, couldn't sleep, and Caldwell's in Nashville this week so I couldn't talk to him about it. I don't have gaydar, can't tell if a fellow's gay just by looking at him, but the more I thought about it, several of the kids on the excursion just might have been of my persuasion."

"Why?"

"Most of my college groups are opposite-gender attached—guy-gal, gal-guy, couldn't pry them apart with a crowbar. This group was different, but I didn't think about it until after asshole detective left last night. The group was all-friendly like but didn't seem hitched-up M-F. It could also have been my imagination running wild after the kind of questions assho—Adair kept asking."

"How did Adair leave it?"

"He ran out of questions. He asked me some things about others in the group and I told him that I didn't know anything more than what I told him the first time." Mel paused and looked at the ceiling and started to reach for another donut, but pulled his hand back. "He said we might need to talk further."

"That's it?"

"He told me not to leave town."

I'd watched enough television to know that it's seldom a good sign when the cop tells you not to leave town. I pointed that out to Mel and he agreed that it was not the ending for their conversation he would have desired. It took me fifteen minutes to convince him that contacting an attorney would be in his best interest; three more minutes for him to decide that he didn't know any attorneys; and, another minute for me to remind him that he did know one, an attorney who owed him a big favor.

Sean Akers was one of Folly's four practicing lawyers and had been a friend for as long as I had lived on the island. Sean had been half of the law firm of Aker & Long until Long was murdered and the police had fingered Sean as the prime suspect. During those traumatic few days, Dude had introduced me to Mel and with the captain's help and his Magical Marsh Machine, we were able to find the killer and come within a hair of losing our lives in the process.

***

The weather was still nice so Mel and I walked three blocks to Sean's second floor office on Center Street two doors from City Hall.

"Morning, Marlene," I said to the receptionist as Mel and I entered the office of Sean Aker, Attorney at Law.

Marlene had been holding her pet Shih Tzu on her lap and sat her canine companion on the floor and looked at her watch. "Chris, what brings you out so early?"

It was ten, but that was early for anyone to be visiting the law office that handled mainly DUIs, criminal defense, family practice law and estate law and more mundane wills. Many of Sean's clients didn't get out of bed, or meet bail, until afternoon. I asked if she remembered Mel and she smiled and said "of course," and then I asked if the boss was in.

Marlene smiled and looked at Sean's closed door. "He's here, been on a call, off the phone now and asleep if you ask me. Let me check." She dialed his extension. Sean answered and she told him who was here and he said he'd be right out.

Sean opened the door with a hand-painted parachute over it, reflecting one of his hobbies—skydiving, not painting. He glanced at me and moved to Mel and gave him an exaggerated hug which clearly made the former Marine uncomfortable. Sean was in his mid-forties, about my height but weighed a zillion pounds less, and had short, curly hair. His white, Ben Silver polo shirt, khakis, and deck shoes on sockless feet were in strong contrast to Mel's battlefield attire.

Sean stood back from Mel and looked at me. "What trouble are you two bringing me this morning?"

He signaled us into his office. "Marlene, hold all my calls."

She giggled. "As if you're going to get any this early." She picked her dog up and placed it where it had been when we had entered.

The office had a schizophrenic feel to it. There was an orange surfboard leaned against the wall in the far corner and a packed-parachute in the other corner. Then there was a foot-high bronze statue of Lady Justice on his desk. One side of her scales held paperclips; the other red jellybeans. The candy had been there so long that I suspected that it would be as chewy as the paperclips. Three law books were piled beside the statue and a dozen legal folders were stacked on top the legal tomes.

This was Mel's first visit to the skydiving, surfing, scuba-diving attorney's office. Mel filled one of the side chairs in front of Sean's desk. He looked around the office and focused on the parachute, which I admit, was not a normal law office accessory.

"Planning on jumping out the window?" Mel asked.

Sean turned toward where Mel was looking and chuckled. "Considering some of my clients, I've thought about it a few times, but that's not why it's here. Some buddies and I are going skydiving this afternoon. I didn't want to leave it on the motorcycle."

"I jumped a few times when I was in the service," Mel said. "Gotten smarter in my old age, wouldn't do it again if a damned Sauroposeidon was chasing me off a cliff."

"A what?" Sean asked before I could show my ignorance.

"Big-assed dinosaur. Enough about you. Chris here," he hesitated and pointed his thumb at me, "thinks I need a good attorney. I didn't know any good ones, so we came to see you."

Sean leaned back in his chair and winked at Mel. "Not the way to start; showing how stupid I am by embarrassing me in front of Chris by talking about a *sopodun*, or whatever you called that dino-thing, and then saying that I'm not a good attorney."

"See," Mel said. "There you go again, all about you. Can you use your law school learnin' and help me?"

Sean pulled a yellow legal pad out of his top drawer and grabbed a pen from under today's Charleston *Post and Courier*. He put on his lawyer's face. "Okay, what's up?"

"This poker-up-his-ass detective from Charleston hinted that I killed some stupid college kid. He didn't arrest me but came back again and—"

"Whoa," Sean interrupted. He glanced over at me, and tilted his head, as if to say, "What have you brought me now?" He turned back to Mel. "Start from the beginning."

Mel and I started tag-teaming Sean with everything we knew about the death of Drew Casey, Mel's fateful excursion to

Boneyard Beach, the call Mel had received about a missing member of the group, a detailed description of Detective Adair's two visits to Mel's house, Mel and my visit to the spot on the beach where the party took place, and the detective's visit to my house and his questions.

During our recitation, Sean jotted notes that looked like a cross between the lost art of shorthand and a two-year-old writing the Gettysburg Address. Mel and I had gotten to the point where I suggested that he contact an attorney, when Sean dropped the pen and said, "Duh!"

Mel looked at me and turned to Sean. He leaned forward and put his ample elbows on Sean's desk. "Sean, Chris, I didn't kill anybody, especially not some college squirt. I didn't do anything wrong except take a bunch of drunk college kids to the beach and let them party and let off steam."

Sean leaned toward Mel. "Mel, I don't doubt you, but does the word irrelevant mean anything to you?"

"Sure, so what?"

"It means that it doesn't matter one atom, or one whatever-is-smaller than an atom, if you killed that kid. If the police believe that you did, you're in, and here's a legal phrase for you, deep Dalmatian dung."

Mel shook his head. "What do I do?" he asked in a low voice.

"First," Sean said, "give me a buck, and I'm your lawyer."

Mel reached for his wallet. "Didn't know lawyers came that cheap."

"We don't. That's the retainer. The comma and extra zeros come later."

Mel looked down at the desk. "All I've got is a boat and a Camaro, both upside down. Sean, I can't pay—"

Sean held his hand, palm toward Mel. "Mel, I owe you my life. We're okay for now. If you're charged with murder, I'll need to bring in someone who handles that level of defense and we'll have to figure something out."

"I didn't do it, Sean."

"Remember irrelevant?"

Mel shook his head, flipped a dollar bill on the desk, and said, "What now?"

"If the cops contact you, do three things." Sean pulled open a desk drawer, took out a card, and handed it to Mel. "First, say these six words, 'I need to call my lawyer,' second, dial my cell phone, and third, don't say another word until I get there. I mean it, Mel, not a word."

Mel looked at Sean, over at me, than at the parachute in the corner. "Crap, maybe I could go with you this afternoon and jump without one of those things."

It wasn't a bad idea.

Chapter Nine

On the walk to Mel's car I tried to reassure him that he had nothing to worry about; a poor attempt at best. From what the tour guide had told me combined with the type of questions that Detective Adair had asked, Mel was more than a blip on police radar.

Instead of going in the house and worrying, I drove off-island to the Harris Teeter to do some irregular grocery shopping. My grocery list was short and I could walk next door from the house to Bert's and pick up what I needed, but I had realized that my cupboard was one bag of Cheetos from bare and I needed a major grocery trip.

"Ah, Mr. Landrum," came the deep voice of William Hansel from behind me. "I see you've found it necessary to increase your stock of canned goods and cleaning supplies."

Only William, a tenured professor of hospitality and tourism, could describe a grocery cart holding two cans of sliced peaches and a can of Comet Cleanser in a way that could sound like a master's thesis on American consumerism. Regardless of his professorial way with words, he was one of my favorite people and I had spent many summer days sitting beside his garden enjoying ice tea that he had insisted on delivering on a silver platter and discussing the various issues of the day and his frustrations with the staid world of academia.

"And you as well," I said and peeked in his cart containing three boxes of tea, and four ears of corn.

"Did you hear about the college student who tragically lost

his life on the far end of our island?" he asked.

I pulled my cart out of the center of the aisle. "Drew Casey," I remembered that he was a student at William's college. "Did you know him?"

William moved his cart behind mine and out of the traffic pattern. He was my height, lighter in weight, much darker in color, and as usual, well-dressed. William shook his head. "Not only was I aware of who he was, Mr. Casey was a student in two of my classes. His demise was tragic."

"Do you know much about him?"

He sighed. "Unlike many of my colleagues who feel that they must befriend their charges to effectively communicate classroom material, I espouse a more detached pedagogical paradigm. I present the prescribed material, explain and repeat where necessary, and trust it to the students to assimilate the information. I choose to not share laughs, libations, or personal histories as means of inculcating classroom information into the brains of my impressionable charges."

No would have sufficed, but that would have been too Dude like. I would have been wrong.

William continued, "But I must say, Mr. Casey provided a different construct."

"What's that mean?"

"You have been well-enough acquainted with me over the years to know that I harbor no biases or prejudices against anyone based on physical or mental differences."

That was true. He had never spoken negatively about anyone since I had known him. Being African American, he had a ringside seat to racial tensions; he had experienced an emotional breakdown four years ago; and on a less-serious level, I had watched him stuffily navigate the more laid-back vocabulary of many Lowcountry residents. He could have been called the master of differences.

"I agree."

He looked around the aisle to see if anyone was close enough to hear. No one was. "Mr. Casey was a homosexual. I, you understand, am not making judgments. Some of the finest and most creative people throughout history were reported to have shared that proclivity: Lord Byron, Oscar Wilde, Walt Whitman, Leonard Bernstein, Michelangelo, my heavens, even Leonardo Da Vinci. You do understanding I am sharing what Mr. Casey had shared with me."

I nodded and thought that *he was gay* should have covered it; but again, William was William.

He tapped the handles on his cart. "Mr. Casey chose not to wear his sexual inclination on his sleeve. Even though I had given no signs of being interested in his life outside my classroom, he had a way of pulling one in. I must confess that while I had no interest in his lifestyle choices, he, in a quiet and endearing manner, shared with me his estrangement from his family. He kept to himself and didn't appear to take up friendships with his classmates. He seemed to be a kind and gentle young man."

"Did he say why he was estranged from his family?"

"He never shared that fact or supposition."

"Did he have enemies?"

"I was not able to detect anyone who would have harbored ill will toward him. Then again, I wasn't able to observe any of his interactions outside the lecture hall or my office."

"Do you think his murder had anything to do with him being gay?" I was reaching for straws.

"I would have no way of knowing, but if I was forced to speculate, I would have to believe it could have been a contributing factor."

"Did you know the other students on the outing?"

"I have not seen a list of the participants, so it is possible, but no one has said anything about being with the group." He shrugged, "I have no further knowledge of the situation."

"Changing the subject," I said, after realizing that William couldn't shed additional light on Drew Casey, "I hear you're in Chester's walking group."

William smiled. "That would be accurate. My teaching is continuing to keep my mental faculties clear, and buoyantly sharp. But since I surpassed the three score mark three years ago, my physical limitations are escalating."

I assumed he meant that he was getting old and out of shape and said, "Me too, although my mental faculties have never have been as clear as yours."

He chuckled. "Ah, you underestimate yourself. Nevertheless, I felt that joining Chester's group would provide me with the incentive to work on improving my physical condition without resorting to joining a physical improvement facility or embracing yoga." He chuckled again at what I guessed was the thought of a sixty-three year old, male college professor twisting his body in the shape of a pretzel in front of a room full of trim, youthful soccer moms.

"Isn't Abe Pottinger's in the group?"

"That would be correct. Why?"

"Nothing really," I said—more accurately, lied. "I met him at Chester's yesterday and heard he was new here. Just curious about your take on him."

"He and I have only walked three or four times together. I had a doctor's appointment and missed yesterday's stroll."

"What's your first impression?"

"Mr. Pottinger appears nice enough. He comes with a sales background. He is curious and asks questions about each of the members. He hasn't attempted to sell me anything, but I wouldn't be surprised if that changed at some point."

"What does he sell?"

"I have no idea." William gave me a sideways glance. "I am curious about your line of questioning. Please don't get angry for me saying this, but your interest appears on a deeper level than mere curiosity."

"Not really," I lied again. "I believe he's someone Larry LaMond knew years ago in Atlanta and was wondering why he was here. I'll ask the next time I see him."

"I would think that would be an expedient way of soothing your curiosity."

Not really.

Chapter Ten

It had been months since I had opened the gallery on weekdays, but I still stopped by a couple of times during the week to make sure the ancient air conditioner was still working and that no one had broken in and stolen anything. Deep down I believed that my photos had exceptional worth and a thief with good taste and an eye for outstanding art would find it hard to pass up stealing them. I also believed that one day I'd get a metal detector and find a zillion dollars' worth of doubloons in front of the Tides Hotel. We all have fantasies, or so I told myself.

It was a couple of hours after my visit with William when the bell over the front door jingled and Charles yelled, "You open to handle the rush?"

I was in the back room and realized that I wasn't the only one with fantasies.

"Dream on," I said and waited for him to come around the corner.

He tapped his cane on the wood floor in rhythm with his steps as he came through the gallery and into the back room. He wore a long-sleeve, orange Buffalo State College T-shirt, ratty cargo pants that he wore nearly as often as the sun had come up, his Tilley, and a larger-than-usual smile.

"Why so cheerful?" I asked as he walked to the small refrigerator and grabbed a Diet Pepsi.

"I'm meeting Heather at the Surf Bar at seven."

Heather Lee and Charles had dated for four years and had

been engaged for a short time last year. Everyone who knew them was convinced that they were destined for each other, but Charles had confided that he doubted that he was the "marrying kind." He was probably right. The reason that he had proposed was to honor the dying wish of his aunt. Though Heather and Charles had not been joined in holy matrimony, they were joined in similar interests, potent feeling for each other, and quirkiness.

It was a little after five so I didn't think he answered my question, but knew that if he did it would be on his terms and timeframe.

Charles looked at his bare wrist. "Got two hours before I'm meeting Heather, want to go over with me? I'll let you buy me a beer, or two."

How could I refuse such a generous offer? The Surf Bar was less than a block off Center Street and across the street from the Folly Beach Department of Public Safety. It was also fewer than a hundred yards from the gallery so we walked. Two surf boards, one red, the other yellow, were attached to the fascia over the door of the faded blue bar. The inside dining area was packed with a smattering of what appeared to be college students bemoaning how hot it had been on the beach; two tables of construction workers were in mismatched chairs at the mismatched tables who could have told the college students what it was really like to be hot; and five vacationers were taking in the ambiance of the surf memorabilia that dotted the walls, ceiling, and bar.

It was loud so I pointed toward the patio and Charles followed me outside where there were three tables that hadn't been invaded by diners and drinkers. We grabbed one in the corner as far away from the noise as possible. A large-screen television adorned one wall and was playing a video of surfers maneuvering waves of a size that had never been seen at Folly. Luckily, the sound was muted.

A harried bartender rushed over and took our order while telling us that two waitresses were late and if we needed anything else to come inside and yell. He left and I asked Charles if there was anything special about tonight since it was rare for him to take Heather out. She was a massage therapist and plied her trade at

Millie's, a popular Folly Beach salon. About the only time Charles and Heather frequented eating establishments was when she attended open-mic night at Cal's Country Bar and Grill and occasionally charmed her way into the weekly gathering of the Folly Beach Bluegrass Society. In addition to her paying gig as a massage therapist, Heather prided herself as being a psychic and a rising, country-music star. Her psychic skills were questionable, but there was no question about her singing ability—she had none. That had never stopped her. If she hadn't doted over Charles and brought such joy to his life, and was fun to be around, I would have strangled her long ago, in the middle of her nearly-unrecognizable rendition of "Crazy."

The bartender brought our drinks and set them down so hard that chardonnay sloshed out of the Ball jar and Charles's beer nearly tipped over. It appeared that the waitresses still hadn't arrived. Our silence came to a halt when four men arrived and grabbed the table nearest us. Mel was one of the four and saw me, smiled, as much as Mel ever smiled, and moved around to take the chair closest to our table. The other three chairs filled and the occupants started looking for a server.

I leaned back and told Mel that they were short on help and if they wanted drinks before sunrise, someone would need to go inside. He passed the information along to the man sitting to his right, who jumped up and headed to the bar. The two men on the other side of the table were in deep conversation about pollutants in the marsh and something about wanting to find a lawyer to sue someone. Mel ignored them and put his hand to his mouth and whispered, "Marsh tour captains. I'll introduce you when Robbie gets back with the real reason we're here. Beer. Oh yeah, we're also celebrating Timothy's announcement that he's tying the damn knot with his better, much-better, half."

Charles nearly fell out of his chair leaning to hear what Mel had said. I nodded to Mel and shared with Charles who the group was and why they were here.

Robbie returned with his hands wrapped around four bottles of Miller High Life and set them on the table. The others grabbed the bottles as if they were winning lottery tickets.

Each captain took a quick sip and then Mel stood and pointed to our table. "Guys, want you to meet my friends." He pointed at Charles. "The one with the stupid shirt's Charles Fowler." He turned to me. "The boring looking one's Chris Landrum, he owns that photo store on Center Street. Don't know what the hell Charles does except get in trouble."

I was disappointed that none of Mel's colleagues asked what kind of trouble; I'd have been interested in hearing Mel's version. They didn't pretend to be interested in who or what we were.

Mel continued, "Chris, Charles, this here's Folly's leading, and damned near all of its, marsh tour boat captains." Mel hesitated and looked around the patio. "We get together every month to talk about how cheap vacationers are, bitch about government regulations, talk about stupid things that happen on our charters, share what we've scheduled, and to fix prices. Today we're celebrating Timothy's announcement that he's committing single suicide, ending his forty-three years of freedom, happiness, and all that other crap that goes with being unhitched." Mel took a sip and pointed to the chunky, long-stringy-haired man who looked like the stereotypical boat captain.

Timothy chuckled, held his bottle in the air. "At least I'm marrying a woman."

Mel frowned and I thought he was going to leap across the table and grab Timothy's throat but instead he faked a smile. "Right. Anyway, he's marrying above his raisin'. Y'all might know her, Samantha, she waits tables at Loggerheads."

The name wasn't familiar so I smiled at Timothy and said, "Congratulations."

"Robbie's the ugly cuss stuck sitting next to Timothy," Mel said. "He owns the company that has those god-awful, glow-in-the-dark kayaks you see flitting around the river like water bugs. He's got a shiny-new boat like mine, and's big in that ecological bullshit people talk about in the marsh."

Robbie stood, all six foot two of him, with his shaved head covered with a FB ball cap, and held his bottle up to Charles and me. "Pleased to meet you," he said. "If you ever want the *best* tour of the marsh or to rent a kayak, I'm your man."

Mel waved his hand in front of Robbie's face. "Down Robbie. This ain't no damned marketing meetin'."

Robbie smiled and sat.

Mel put his hand on the shoulder of the person sitting next to him. "Little twerp's Nathan."

I remembered him from Mel's dock the day we went to Boneyard Beach.

"Friends call me Nemo," the little twerp said as he looked up from his bottle and managed a hint of a smile. He had on a *Hard Rock Café, Toronto* T-shirt, and his long, black hair was pulled in a ponytail and held with a child's, multi-colored rubber band with a plastic blue butterfly attached.

"Nathan," Mel said, establishing that he wasn't a friend, "has an old beat up fishing boat and cons people into hiring him to take them on e-co-logical, natural, environmental, blah-blah-blah trips to the hinterlands. Throws out all sort of highfalutin' words to prove that he earned his PhD in eco-crap. Impresses the hell out of librarians and AARP wobblies."

Nathan smiled and pointed his bottle at Mel. "Jealousy rears its ugly head, again."

Note to self, I thought. *Don't invite myself to any of these happy, cheerful meetings.*

Before I could figure out something to say, Timothy snapped his fingers. "Now I remember. You two caught that killer a while back; the one who had something to do with the beach church."

Robbie piped in, "Yeah. Mel said he may be in a bind with the cops about a kid getting himself killed last week. Said you're helping him."

I looked at Mel. He shrugged.

Robbie continued, "Think you'll catch the killer like you did the church guy?"

Charles sat back in his chair.

I flinched.

A college-aged waitress bounced up to the table and announced that she was "Randi with an *I*," and took a second round of drinks order from the captains and a second beer for Charles and chardonnay for me.

"If the boss man comes around, y'all be sure and tell him how good a job I'm doing," she said and winked at Mel. "He's already chewed my ass for being late."

Her wink was wasted on Mel, but he fended a smile from his underused smile muscles and Randi, with an *I*, headed inside.

Mel turned to Robbie. "I don't need no damned help. Didn't do anything wrong and don't know nothing about that dead kid."

Robbie looked at Nemo and then at Timothy before turning back to Mel. "You said the cops talked to you and asked if you'd been to that queer bar in Charleston. Mel, you know we've got your back, but you're gay and it sounds like the dead guy was too. It's your business, not mine, but it sounds like you need all the help you can get."

Charles cleared his throat. "Ronald Reagan said, 'We can't help everyone, but everyone can help someone.'"

The captains turned to my friend. Robbie nodded; Timothy tilted his head and looked at Charles like he was a warthog; and, Nemo's face mutated into a snarl.

Mel pounded his hand on the table knocking over an empty bottle in front of him. "Told you I don't need any damned help. Period!"

"Doesn't sound that way to me," Nemo said.

"It's none of our business," Robbie said. "Mel will do what he has to do."

Timothy leaned against the table. "It sure as heck is our business. If someone gets killed on one of our charters, it'll hurt us all." He paused and looked around the table. "Whether you admit it or not, business sucks. There's too many of us doing the same thing. I don't know about you, but Samantha and I need all the money we can pull together to get off to a good life."

Nemo said, "I agree with Timothy. No offense Mel, but with you running college students out in the middle of nowhere to get drunk, that sure as hell don't bode well for the environmental tours the rest of us are doing."

I would hate to hear what it would sound like if Nemo meant to offend Mel. I gripped the edge of the table and waited for Mel to explode.

Randi returned before Mel could use his military training and break every bone in Nemo's body. She set the drinks on the table, told us how delighted she was to be waiting on us, and was oblivious to the increasing tension between Mel and Nemo.

Randi left to spread her charm to other customers and Robbie said, "Come on, Nemo, there's enough room for all of us. The economy's in a lull but I hear it's picking up. We need to support our friend. We know Mel didn't have anything to do with the kid's death."

"Do we?" Nemo said.

Mel took a deep breath, flung a five dollar bill on the table, stood and stormed off the patio. I hated to see him go, but considering the alternatives, his departure could have saved him from being arrested for assaulting a marsh tour captain, or two, or three.

Charles watched Mel leave and stared at three hand-painted wooden signs near the exit. Each had an arrow and one said, *Hawaii 5,550 miles*, another read, *Baja, California 1,854 miles*, and the third, *Folly Beach 2 blocks*.

"Think that's as a crow flies or as a car drives?" he said.

Over the years, Charles had been accused of being a nut, a fruitcake with too much whiskey in it, and as flaky as a croissant. Granted, these were accurate, but he was a master at saying or doing something outlandish to diffuse a difficult situation.

"Hell if I know," Nemo said.

Robbie said, "Better be a crow. You'd have a hard time driving to Hawaii."

Timothy shrugged and took a long draw on his beer.

And I silently repeated what Nemo had said when Robbie proclaimed that we knew that Mel hadn't killed the college student. "Do we?"

Chapter Eleven

Heather passed Timothy, Nemo, and Robbie as they left through the same outdoor exit that Mel had huffed and puffed through. Timothy whispered something to her and patted her shoulder as they passed in the doorway; the other captains ignored Charles's girlfriend.

Charles glanced at his watch-less wrist as Heather arrived at the table.

"Don't give me that I'm-late-if-I'm-not-early look, Chucky," Heather said as she gave him a peck on the cheek and shook her head at the same time. Charles detested being called anything but Charles. Only Heather could get away with calling him Chucky; further proof that love was blind, or deaf. She pulled out a chair and moving one of his empty beer bottles to his side of the table looked at me. "What's up with you two and Timothy?"

"Why?" I asked.

Heather pointed to where she and Timothy had spoken. "He said something about y'all wading in deep trouble." She frowned. "Said if Chucky here drowns, Timothy'd have a shoulder for me to cry on." She held her nose. "Ewe!"

Charles asked, "Do you know Timothy?"

Can't slip anything by my friend, I thought.

"Not really," she said. "Know Samantha better. She's his fiancé, you know."

We didn't an hour ago, but Charles sat back and said with much confidence. "Sure, we knew that. How do you know them?"

"Samantha's a regular at Millie's, comes in each week." Heather rolled her eyes. "She spends every penny she makes waitressing on her locks, her fingernails, her toenails, and for me, massages. Yeah! Timothy's been in a few times to fetch her after her remodeling. Not sure about him."

Randi, with an *I*, noticed the addition to our table and came to get Heather's order. "Better lay menu's on us," Heather said. "I'm starved. You joining us, Chris?"

I glanced over at Charles and he shrugged, so I said, "Sure."

Heather held three fingers in the air. "Three menus, and I suppose these boys'll want more giggle-juice."

"On the way," Randi said without asking for a translation.

Charles watched the waitress walk away and turned to Heather. "Why aren't you sure about Timothy?"

I knew he wouldn't forget. Charles is a dry sponge for rumors; he'll suck up more of them than the nearest two competitors combined.

"Samantha's having second thoughts about tying the knot."

"Why?" Charles repeated.

"She didn't say, but I think it has something to do with him being closed-minded."

"About what?" I asked.

Randi returned with Heather's Budweiser and three menus. Heather asked her to come back in a few minutes so she could catch up with our drinking. She took a gulp and turned to me.

"Think maybe her fella's a bit shy on tolerance for those who're different," Heather said. She then took another drink.

"For example?" I asked and figured if I asked the same question as many ways as possible, we'd get an answer.

Heather looked around. The table the captains had occupied was empty and no one was within fifteen feet. "I didn't want to say it out loud, but Samantha told me that Timothy said he couldn't stand fags, A-rabs, and blacks, but he didn't say blacks, you know."

I suspected that we did. "Samantha had trouble with that?" I asked.

Heather continued to look around. "One of her best friends from high school is black and that she was planning to invite her to the wedding but was afraid Timothy would say something that'd cause a ruckus."

"Sounds like he's more than a bit intolerant," I said. "Think she'll call off the wedding?"

"Probably not, but she's also worried about money. Said Timothy's business ain't quite paying the bills and he's always complaining about it. Said there're too many boats chasing too few customers, or something like that. Said the bank's ready to come a callin'."

"She say anything else?" Charles asked.

"Gee, Chucky, do I look like a psycho-chiatrist or a reporter?"

Randi returned and asked if we were ready to order. Heather said she didn't know about the "two old men" but she was. Fish sandwiches all around plus an extra order of fries, and more beer and wine, seemed to satisfy Randi's quest.

"Who's the bald one?" Heather asked before Charles tried to pump more information about Samantha. "He looks familiar."

Charles acted like he'd known it forever. "Robbie."

"Has he got an older sister?" Heather asked.

"Don't know. We just met him. Why?"

Heather closed her eyes wiggled her freckled nose. It was like she was conjuring up an image. "He looks like a younger, taller, and balder version of one of Millie's clients. Her name's Connie DeWalt. Thought that may be why he looked familiar. Connie's always bragging about her brother, how he's a self-made, successful entrepreneur, but I don't recall her saying what he did to be so successful. I'm often working in another room and don't hear everything Millie's clients say."

"Is she attractive, in her mid-sixties but looks younger?" I asked.

"Sounds like her."

"We met her at Chester Carr's house," I said. "She's in his walking group."

Heather nodded. "Think I heard her say something about

being around a bunch of geezers."

Charles leaned forward in his chair and pointed his finger at Heather. "You're looking at two of those geezers, so watch what you're saying."

"It's a walking group that Chester started," I said. "He credits Melinda for getting him started down the road to health, and Charles and I think it would be good for us. Besides, it would support Chester."

Heather turned to Charles and grinned. "Now Chucky, don't get yourself hurt out jogging."

"Walking, Heather."

"Whatever, just don't get hurt." She pointed at the table that had been occupied by the captains. "Who else was in that group?"

"Mel was, but left before the others," I said.

"Rumor around the salon is that the dead college student was on Mel's boat and that a cop was talking to him about it—talking to Mel, not the dead college student. Could he have something to do with it?"

Charles and I both said no.

"And the other guy?" Heather said.

She was falling under Charles's nosy spell.

"Nemo," Charles said.

Heather grinned. "The missing clownfish in that old movie?"

"Don't believe it's the same one," said Charles, as if Heather would have confused the two. "Nemo's Latin for *nobody* or *no one*, you know."

Now that one I didn't know, and wondered why Charles did.

Heather said, "Oh."

Chapter Twelve

Free parking near the pier was always at a premium, so most of the group parked at Chester's and then he drove them the whopping two blocks to the foot of the pier where the walks began. I said we would meet them there. The "early morning" trips began at nine o'clock so Charles, of course, expected me to be there at eight thirty. I had the completed two-page application and had slipped my passport in my pocket in case Chester was serious about seeing proof that I had been around more than sixty years.

It was a cool day with a low cloud cover. Charles greeted me in the pier's parking lot and was wearing tan shorts, a green and gold long-sleeve T-shirt with a large T and Arkansas Tech in smaller print underneath.

He pointed his cane toward Charleston. "Ready to stroll to the Battery?"

Charleston's historic Battery was eleven miles away and the longest walk that Chester had mentioned was about the length of seven football fields so I assumed my hyperbole-prone friend was teasing.

"If you are, I am," I said and sat on the bottom step to await the arrival of the group.

A half hour later, Chester rolled in the lot and seven people rolled-out of his thirty-year-old, baby blue Mercury Grand Marquis land yacht. Chester maneuvered himself around the group, flailed his arms, and herded everyone over to Charles and me. He would have made a sheep dog proud.

"A near-record crowd today," Chester said with a big smile on his face. He was proud of his creation.

The near-record group included Theo, William, Harriet, David, Honest Abe Pottinger, Connie DeWalt, the group leader Chester, and the two soon-to-be newest members, Charles and me.

Chester held out one hand at me and the other at Charles. "Applications?"

Charles had folded his application to the size of a postcard and handed it to Chester while I unfolded mine and handed it over. Chester read our responses and asked for proof of age—honest, he did.

Harriet was standing behind Chester and mumbled, "Oh Christ-on-a-stick, Chester. Can't you see they're way over sixty?"

I wasn't happy about her description, and it did nothing to speed Chester's review of the documents. He scanned my passport and Charles's original birth certificate, looked at me—probably to see if my face was the one on the document—and said, "Can't be too careful."

A terrorist crossing the border from Mexico carrying an AK-47 would have received less scrutiny, but this was Chester's club and rules.

"Can we got on with it?" Harriet asked.

David asked, "Where to today?"

Chester looked at each member of the group. "Thought we'd head up Arctic then over to Bert's before heading to the house."

"How about down Arctic?" David said.

"Think we need to go up Center Street; maybe make all the way to Woody's," Harriet added.

Chester rolled his eyes, a magnified sight behind the bottle-thick glasses. He leaned close to me. "This is a debate we have only every other day."

Chester raised his hand above his head and pointed up Arctic Avenue. "It's my group. That way."

"Dictator," Harriet mumbled.

David said, "You win."

Chester moved a foot from Theo's ear and screamed the destination.

"That far?" Theo yelled as if Chester couldn't hear any better than he could.

Chester's proposed route was no more than five long blocks and I figured even Theo could make it.

"Guess the Battery's safe from this group today," Charles whispered, even though a whisper wasn't necessary.

Chester gave another herding motion and we slowly, I emphasize slowly, headed east on Arctic Avenue.

After thirty yards, Abe was already ten paces ahead of the rest of us, revealing that he was not accustomed to being in a walking group. He looked at a street address on one of the small condo buildings on the ocean side of the road and said, "How come it's called Arctic Avenue? Shouldn't that be in iceberg country?"

It was a fair question and one that I had naively asked my first week on the island. I gave him the same answer I had been given. "Heck if I know?"

Abe looked at Charles who shrugged. And, he was the one who had known what nemo meant in Latin. The rest of the group was struggling to make the "exhausting" walk, as Harriet bemoaned, and hadn't heard the question.

We were half way up the block when Theo yelled from the back of the pack, "Where are we going, Chester?"

Chester was fifteen or so strides in front of Theo and stopped and walked back to the man bringing up the rear. Chester put his arm around him, leaned close to his ear, and repeated our flight plan. Harriet had also slowed to let Theo catch up with her. She smiled and gave him a kiss on the cheek and said something like she was glad he was with us.

Chester moved beside Charles and me. "Theo's getting worse."

"Memory?" Charles asked.

"Afraid the guy's losing his mind, like really losing his mind," Chester said. "Alzheimer's I suspect but he won't see a doc about it."

Charles looked back to Harriet and Theo. "What's his story?"

"Sad one," Chester said. "He invented a replacement-window system that uses a highfalutin gas between the glass panes that keeps cold air out in the winter, scorching heat out in the summer, and noise out all the time. Started his own company and sold it three years ago to that humongous window company that I can never remember the name of. He pocketed several million dollars. He and his wife moved here and she up and died six months after moving into their dream house on the marsh. They'd been married fifty-two years. Sad."

I looked back at Theo and Harriet. "Looks like she's taken him under her wing."

"She really has," Chester said. "Some of the others make fun of him behind his back because he's so slow. He thinks they call him ET as a compliment. It means Energizer Turtle. He keeps on going, going, going, but at a speed that would take time-lapse photography to detect movement." Chester looked toward Abe leading the group and said that he'd better catch up with the leaders so they didn't miss the turn to Bert's.

Charles looked at the frontrunners—walkers—and then back at the rest of the group. "This bunch is almost as much fun as the boat captains."

Chester had caught up with the leaders and turned them in the direction of Bert's. I turned and watched Theo laughing at something that Harriet had said, and wondered about Larry's request and how I had planned to get the slightest idea about what, if anything, Abe was planning to do to rip people off.

I sighed, stretched out my arms, and turned to Charles. "True, but look how much exercise we're getting."

I wondered if that was all we'd get by following Larry's hunches.

$$***$$

"Well, well," exclaimed Eric, Bert's Market's amiable clerk and man with the most-recognizable beard on Folly Beach. "What brings such a distinguished group in this morning?"

Calling us distinguished said a lot about other customers

who frequented Bert's at all hours of the day and night, but I let Chester answer. He moved to the front of the group, pulled his shoulders back, and, with great pride, said, "Eric, this is our walking group. We start at the pier and head out in different directions a few times a week."

"Welcome," Eric said. "What can I get for you after such a long excursion, Chester? Water, candy, oxygen?"

Eric had known Chester since the group's leader had worked part-time in the store and felt comfortable teasing him. Besides, I agreed with Eric about oxygen since Chester now leaned against the counter and was trying to catch his breath. David and Abraham appeared full of energy and antsy to continue, but Harriet and William had followed Chester's lead and leaned on the nearest horizontal surface.

"Funny," Chester said and wiped sweat off his forehead. "We needed to cool off, we're about at the mid-point of our longest walk yet. After the group jabbers a bit and cools down, I'm going to buy each one an ice-cream sandwich."

I moved away from Chester and Eric and spotted Abe in the back corner of the store huddled with Connie and Harriet. Their body language screamed something more intense than talking about the walk, so I moved over one aisle and as close as possible without appearing to eavesdrop. I picked up a jar of pickles and studied the label like it contained a map to the fountain of youth.

Abe had an arm around Connie but was talking to Harriet. "Incredible deal for us more mature adults." He lowered his voice and all I could make out was, "…simple as that … few papers and the money starts rolling in … turn your house into cash today …"

Harriet glanced over at me but must have figured that I wasn't close enough to hear or didn't care if I overheard. She turned to Abe. "It's called a reverse mortgage?"

"Sure is," Abe said. "All the smart people in California, Florida, and New York are jumping on the bandwagon. You get to stay in your house as long as you want, and the company pays you a lot of money each month for as long as you live."

He said something about how much they would get after their house was appraised, but I didn't catch the details.

"And you're the exclusive agent for the company in the Charleston area?" Connie asked.

"Sure am." Abe noticed me and my fascination with the pickle jar. He smiled at me and motioned for the ladies to move closer to him.

Harriet asked, "Are other companies selling it?"

"Oh yes. It's the hottest thing in wealth management."

"So why should I go with your company?" she asked.

Excellent question, I thought.

"Excellent question," Abe not only thought but said. "Here's the best part. My company has a huge international conglomerate behind it. It's so hush-hush that I'm not even at liberty to divulge the name, but rest assured, you've heard of it. They're wanting to corner the reverse mortgage market. They've got deep pockets and don't mind paying more, much more I might add, for the houses now so they can flush competitors out." He mumbled something else I couldn't hear and then said, "For the next forty-five days, they're paying a twenty percent premium to people who take advantage of their already great deal. I put my house in the program and am getting way more than anyone else offered and lifetime security."

Connie looked at the floor and back at Abe. "Interesting."

They moved farther down the aisle and would have known that I was listening if I followed. I heard Abe say something about getting together with the ladies later when Chester interrupted and asked us to gather around the ice-cream freezer.

That was when I learned that Theo could move faster than a glacier. He was the first to the freezer and the others followed. Chester said that since this was the longest hike to date, he was buying everyone a treat. No one applauded, but they were pleased.

The distance to the ending point of the excursion from Bert's was a long block and a half along the second busiest street on the island, so Chester's treat provided not only a cool refreshment but enough sugar to keep the group energized. We were in the homestretch, albeit a long one, walking single file since there were no sidewalks and we occasionally had to step on the busy street. Charles was in front of me tapping his way with his cane on the gravel berm and William was a step to my rear. Abe walked in front of Charles and had his left arm around Connie. Between the sounds of cars roaring by, I caught Abe sharing more about the miracle product, reverse mortgages. Harriet was behind Connie and seemed more intent on complaining about us walking too fast, the dust we were stirring up along the way, and the nerve of Chester making the group walk so far.

On a more pleasant note, William walked behind me and was humming "What A Wonderful World." From anyone else, it may have been a pleasant sound; from one of the best singers that I'd ever heard, it was a delight.

The mood turned less pleasant when William tapped me on the shoulder and asked if I had learned anything more about the murder. He said that after our conversation, he'd heard that several of his students had known the dead man and were "bummed." I told him that he knew as much as I did, and he said that he hoped that the authorities had a better understanding than the two of us. I agreed.

"Chris, allow me to ask you another question." He continued before I agreed to allow him to ask. "Are you familiar with a financial product known as a reverse mortgage?"

I had received a brochure in the mail a year or so ago from a finance company in Columbia touting the benefits to the elderly of getting one. I was not in a financial bind and deposited the colorful brochure in the trash with other junk mail. I had made the mistake of asking Bob Howard about the product, something that I had only learned about through the brochure. He began one of his Bob Howard patented rants about how reverse mortgages are the worst thing since mosquitos and Twitter and how they took advantage of the elderly and something about the downfall of the global economy. I had asked him what was wrong with them and all I got, or could understand, was that they were high-interest loans against the house and that the fees were, in his words, "damned astronomical," the heirs may not get the house, and all the house expenses still fell to the person getting the reverse mortgage. Bob conceded, in a whisper as I recall, that for some people they could be a good thing. He didn't say the same for mosquitos and Twitter.

"William, I'm no expert, but from what I've heard, they need to be looked at closely before going down that road. Why?"

William pointed to the front of the group. "Abe called last night to talk to me about them. It seems he represents a company getting into the business of selling the product and was touting the advantages. I, as you are well aware, am quite conservative and look askance at anything new, particularly when it comes to my economic wellbeing."

"Wise," I said.

"I told Abe that I would contemplate the opportunity. I wish I'd replied in the negative. He told me that he was also a financial advisor and that if I wished to look at investment opportunities that far exceeded the index funds, he would be glad to review my portfolio."

"What'd you say?"

William chuckled. "I informed him that I was a college professor and that to me a portfolio was something that I had my students prepare to showcase their work and that I would never be financially 'loaded,' as my students say, enough to need a financial advisor. He shook his head and said 'you never know,' and for me to keep him in mind if I ever needed assistance with my wealth-management plan."

From comments that he had made over the years, I knew that William was more financially secure than he would let on, but was relieved that he didn't let Abraham know it.

"Did he say anything else?" I asked.

"Not much. He did indicate that he was working with Theo and since everyone in the group knew that Mr. Stoll was well off, that should tell me something about Abe's financial-management savvy."

Knowing Larry's history with Abe and his concerns about Abe's arrival on Folly, I was afraid that it told me too much.

Chapter Thirteen

The group walked, crawled, up three steps to Chester's screened-in porch on his faded-yellow cottage. We looked more like we had traversed Pennsylvania barefoot rather than the five-block-long walk with an ice cream break in the middle. Harriet complained about having to move one of Chester's plastic chairs off the walk; Connie said that she may have pulled a muscle in her calf while crossing Center Street and sat in the lawn chair that Harriet had griped about having to move and rubbed her leg. Theo yelled "What?" at Connie, and went on to say that he may be suffering sunstroke; and, David didn't say anything because he was gasping for breath. Charles and I followed David's lead and didn't say anything, not because we couldn't breathe but because we had nothing to say. Abe put his arm around Theo and said, "Refreshing!" William smiled and said something pedantic that meant that it was fun, and Chester said, "Lemonade anyone?"

That got everyone's attention except Connie who was sitting in front of the house when a rusting, silver Nissan Maxima skidded to a stop in the gravel along the side of the road. I was on the porch and saw Connie rise from the chair, warily put weight on her leg, and limp to the passenger side of the car. The windows were tinted and the passenger window was partially down so I couldn't get a clear look at the driver but he looked vaguely familiar. Abe was helping Chester with the plastic cups he was filling from a sailing-flag covered, glass pitcher that he brought from the kitchen. Harriet remained true to her complaining self when she said, "It's about time." To Abe's credit, he smiled and thanked her for being patient. Con artist or consummate salesman?

The Nissan was thirty feet away and I couldn't hear what was being said, but Connie was flailing her arm around and had the windowsill in a death grip with her other hand. Saying that she was agitated would be mild. She pushed away from the car and it spun its wheels in the gravel as it pulled back on the street. Connie turned and stormed toward the porch; her calf injury having miraculously recuperated. She yanked on Chester's screen door so hard I was afraid that it would pull off its hinges, took a deep breath, and grabbed the last cup of lemonade. The rest of us pretended that nothing had happened and even Abe didn't try to comfort her.

Chester cleared his throat, and failing to get everyone's attention, clapped his hands. All but Theo stopped talking and looked at the host. Harriet tapped Theo on the arm and pointed at Chester.

Chester increased his volume and said, "Folks, our humble walking group added two new members today."

Everyone but Charles and I clapped, feebly, but an effort nonetheless. I attributed the lack of enthusiasm to the exhausting excursion.

After the non-thunderous applause died down, Chester said, "Now that Charles and Chris are full-fledged members, we can tell them the genesis of our name." He nodded and looked outside, probably to make sure that no television crew or international spy ring was eavesdropping on the soon-to-be revealed secret. "The lofty goal of our group is to walk from where the old Coast Guard station began at the end of East Ashley Avenue to the end of the island where we can have a view of the glorious Morris Island Lighthouse."

Harriet interrupted. "It'll never happen."

Chester ignored her. "The distance from the stanchions at East Ashley to the end of the island is a quarter of a mile, and the return trip an equal distance."

Harriet, oozing sarcasm, said, "Who knew he was a mathematician?"

Chester shook his head. "Anyway, the full walk will equal a half mile. Now, you know all those oval stickers you see on young people's cars that say 13.1 or 26.2?"

Chester stared at me until I nodded. "Well, that's the number of miles that those young, fit folks run, in a mini-marathon or a marathon."

I wondered if Chester thought Charles and I didn't know that, but I decided to remain silent and nodded, again.

"So, in case you haven't figured it out, the .5 stands for a half mile, the distance to the lighthouse view and back. There you go, now you know the secret. Cool, huh?"

"Stupid," Harriet said.

Charles said, "Cool."

And Connie remained quiet on the other side of the room. She stared out at the road and rubbed her forehead. Charles was talking to Chester about where he could get a .5 sticker to put on his bicycle, so I took the opportunity to get more lemonade and moved to the vacant chair beside Connie.

"You okay?" I asked.

She continued to stare out the screen window but said, "Yeah, he drives me crazy."

"Who?"

"My brother," She tilted her head toward the road. "That was Robbie out there while you all were pretending you didn't see us arguing."

"Does he run marsh tours?"

Connie finally looked up at me. "Yeah. You know him?"

"Not really. I met him last night at the Surf Bar. He was with some of the other captains."

"That's probably where the trouble started."

"Trouble?" I asked.

"Yeah, his buddy Timothy's getting married to a nice gal who works at Loggerhead's."

I told her that that's what I'd heard.

"Seems that Timothy's long on ignorance and short on cash and asked Robbie if he could *borrow* two thousand dollars to help get through the wedding expenses. Robbie's got two thousand bucks like this is my natural hair color and I have all my teeth. You can guess what my stupid brother pulled up to ask for."

"Money."

"He had the audacity to ask me if I'd lend Timothy two thousand dollars. Can you believe that?"

I said I thought that was unreasonable.

"You bet your cute tush it was," she said and shook her head. "Now don't get me wrong, I want Timothy and Samantha to be happy. Sam seems like a nice gal, but I don't know what she sees in Timothy. He's a moocher, always griping about how bad business is and thinks there are too many captains doing the same thing out there and Folly'd be better off if one or more of them disappeared." She paused and shook her head again. "Oh well, love beats all. If I had it, I'd lend the money to Sam but never to Timothy. Don't matter anyway, I don't have it to give, excuse me, to lend."

I asked if I could get her more lemonade and she said that would be nice. Charles, Chester, and now David were in deep conversation about the stickers; William had excused himself and headed home; and, Abe was in the corner whispering with Harriet.

I returned with Connie's drink. She took a sip and then said, "Looks like Timothy might get his wish about getting rid of one of the captains."

I asked what she meant.

"Rumor is that a guy named Mel killed one of his passengers, some college kid."

"Why do they think he did it?"

Connie looked around and leaned closer. "Now this is rumor, you understand."

I motioned for her to continue.

"Robbie likes Mel, even though Mel's gay; says he lives with a man, and get this, the man he lives with is black." Connie looked at the ground and shook her head. "What's the world coming to? Anyway, rumor has it that the dead college kid was gay and that Mel made a pass at him and the college kid who was decades younger than the captain rebuked him."

I waited for more, but Connie seemed to be at the end of

her story. "They think that Mel killed the young man because of that?"

Knowing Mel, it's farfetched, but I also knew that nothing spreads faster than a rumor, regardless how valid or ridiculous it may be. It hurt to think this kind of thing was being said about a friend. I had no idea what had happened the night of the party, but knew that Mel would not have killed the kid for that reason.

"Connie, I've known Mel Evans for years. I would trust him with my life, in fact I did trust him with it a year or so ago. I can't believe he killed the student."

"I'm just telling you what's going around. Somebody killed him, Mel was responsible for the group, and I hear the police have interrogated him."

"That may be so, but that doesn't mean he had anything to do with it."

"Tell you what." She looked at the street, and back at me. "I'll take your word about Mel and if anybody asks my opinion, I'll say I don't know anything. Fair enough?"

I told her that it was, but I still had a sour feeling in my stomach. Regardless how I had defended him, Mel was responsible for the group and opened himself up to suspicion because he did a poor job of accounting for members of the group when they left Boneyard Beach.

Chapter Fourteen

Chester had run out of lemonade and everyone but Charles and I had drifted away, most likely to ice sore legs, feet, and to take an afternoon nap to recuperate from their longest walk yet.

Chester watched David as he walked to his car. "Fellows, could you spare a few more minutes? Got something to bounce off you."

Put like that, I knew that Chester wouldn't have been able get rid of Charles if he'd pointed a loaded copperhead at him.

"Think so," Charles said. He then glanced at me.

"Of course," I said.

Chester said, "Let's go in where it's cooler."

Chester's front door opened to a small living room with two oversized, dark-green, velour recliners facing a large-screen television that was the size of a bank vault. Chester hadn't entered the world of flat-screen televisions, but also hadn't deprived himself of the largest screen I'd ever seen in a floor-model set. Two lamps provided the room's illumination and everything was neat and uncluttered. A window air conditioner was loud, but the cool air felt good.

"How about something a bit stronger to sip on?" he said as he weaved his way around the recliners and television and stood in the kitchen doorway. "Got whiskey, wine, and beer. No dancing girls or peanuts."

I said wine and Charles said, "Beer. Sure there're no dancing girls?"

Chester laughed and went to get our drinks.

Charles pointed to a photo beside an old-fashioned, clunky, black telephone, perched on a small table under the window. In stark contrast to the phone, there was a high-tech digital answering machine. The photo was sepia and from the clothing, I would guess it had been taken in the 1940s. Chester returned with our drinks and caught me looking at the picture.

"Wedding day, June 3, 1944," he said and handed me a glass of white wine. "That's my blushing bride Rosie. An angel, a true angel."

Charles took the Budweiser from Chester. "You were quite a fetching couple."

I wouldn't have been that generous. Chester's glasses in the photograph were smaller than those he wore today, and he had more hair, but I can say that his appearance has improved with age. Rosie's nose was pinched and out of proportion to her face; and if she had a chin, it was well hidden. They had big grins and appeared happy, and that's what mattered.

"Thanks. She's been gone eleven years and until your aunt came along, I had never thought of another woman. Charles, I do miss Melinda."

Charles was seldom at a loss for words, but this was one of those moments. He smiled. I suspected that a trip down memory lane wasn't the reason for Chester asking us to stay.

"What's up, Chester?" I asked.

He had lowered himself on the vacant recliner and took a sip of beer. "This is kind of hard for me to talk about. I don't know anything for sure. I'm guessing. Gee, I don't know, maybe ..."

Charles interrupted. "Spit it out."

Chester looked down at his bottle and then up at Charles. "Since you're a detective, I thought I'd talk to you about this."

I started to debunk Chester's assumption about Charles being a detective, but had come to realize that it would be useless. Charles thought he was, some others actually believed him, and truth be known, he and I had solved some crimes, enough to lend a touch of credence to Charles's claim.

The impatient, alleged detective, said, "About what?"

"It's about Abraham Pottinger, you know, from .5."

We had just walked roughly .2 with him and spent an hour on Chester's porch talking to him, so I was pretty certain I knew which Abraham Pottinger Chester was referring to.

"There's something fishy about him," Chester continued. "He sort of drifted into the group. Hadn't been here long."

I asked, "Who brought him in?"

"That's the funny thing. I was in Mr. John's Beach Store talking to Paul, the owner, you know? I wanted to get one of the new Folly Beach T-shirts with the big red FB on the front, think they're cool looking. Anyway, he came up and introduced himself, said he was new to the beach and had heard about my group. He said he needed some exercise and wondered how he could join. He was dressed all formal like and looked out of place."

Chester paused. A mistake around Charles. William had once said that Charles had *horror vacui.* I had no idea what it meant so I used Charles's trivia-collecting technique and asked. William said it was Latin for fear of empty spaces; said it usually referred to visual space, but could also describe Charles's inordinate need for words to fill silence. I had said, "Whatever."

"What happened?" Charles asked.

"First, he didn't look like he met our stringent age requirement, so I asked to see his driver's license. Low and behold, he was over sixty, sixty-one in fact. I gave him an application, always carry a few extras around with me, and told him where and when we meet. He showed up the next day with his completed application in hand and joined us for our walk up Center Street."

"What's fishy about him?" I asked.

"Now I could be one-hundred percent wrong, so don't take this as gospel, but I'm beginning to think his motives are not pure and he's not that interested in exercise."

"Why?" Charles asked.

"The way he's latched on the gals in the group. Don't think it's a hanky-panky thing, although they're mighty attractive. Anyway, my hearing's not the best, but I am able to catch smidgens of his conversations and he's always talking about ways they can make oodles of money."

"Reverse mortgages?" Charles said.

Chester smiled. "See, I knew you'd figure it out. Did you catch all that today?"

Charles reached over his shoulder and patted himself on the back. "Sure did."

I asked, "What do you think's wrong with him talking to them about reverse mortgages?"

Chester looked back down at his bottle and then nodded. "I know there's such a thing, but he's always talking about how he can offer such a better deal than other companies. How's that possible? Just seems fishy."

"What do you want us to do?" Charles asked.

A great question, I thought.

"Hold on, Charles," Chester said. "There's more."

"And?" Charles asked.

"It's about my buddy Theo." Chester shook his head. "Don't know if you noticed, but he's, how shall I say it, he's in declining mental health. Probably Alzheimer's, he's forgetting things. The other day he forgot where he lived."

I was beginning to wonder about Chester's "mental health" since he'd told us the same thing about Theo other day, but I let him continue.

"I'm afraid Theo is low-hanging fruit for scam artists. We old folks are more susceptible to that kind of thing. I read in a magazine where there's something in the brain that gets a bit scrambled as we get older. It's not only folks with Alzheimer's, but all of us. I think it said we believe more of the scams than we would've when we were younger. Scary. Want more to drink?"

We declined.

"Think Abe is running a scam on Theo?" I asked.

"Don't know. That's what I want you to figure out."

Charles said, "Why do you think he might be?"

"Theo's old, Theo's rich, Theo's losing his mind. And, oh yeah, Abe's been huddling up with him more each walk and before you got here today, Abe asked Theo to lunch tomorrow. Fishy."

And so it seems, particularly after what Larry had told me. Chester said that was all he had, so I asked him if he wanted us to walk with him to the pier so he could get his car. He said no, that he'd get it after a nap.

"Why didn't you tell Chester about Abe and Larry?" Charles asked after we had left the cottage. Charles had to make a delivery for the surf shop and I told him that I'd walk there with him.

"I couldn't think how to tell him without divulging more than he knows about Larry's past. Plus, I didn't want Chester's feelings of 'fishy' to be clouded by Larry's suspicions."

"Good point." We'd reached Folly's only stop light. "What's your take on what Chester said?"

"I didn't hear all of it at Bert's, but Abe was pushing his reverse mortgage idea on Connie and Harriet. Theo's wealthy so he wouldn't have interest in it."

Traffic stopped and we headed across Center Street. "Theo'd be a lot bigger fish to fry if Larry's suspicions are accurate," Charles said as we reached the sidewalk.

"You can say that again," I said. We were now at the steps in front of the surf shop.

Charles paused on the first step. "So what are we going to do . . .?"

My cell phone interrupted the rest of his rather predictable question. The screen read *Mad Mel*.

"Morning Mel," I said.

"Damned caller ID!"

I agreed.

"What are you doing for lunch tomorrow?" he asked.

Mel's normal voice was about as loud as a drill instructor so Charles didn't have to lean close to hear.

Abe hadn't invited me to his lunch with Theo, so I said, "Nothing, why?"

"Meet me at the Crab House, eleven hundred hours."

Charles moved a step back and pointed his index finger at his chest.

"Can Charles come?"

"Could I stop him?"

"Probably not," I said.

"Then why in the hell did you ask?"

"Being polite."

"You failed!" Mel blurted.

"We'll be there."

"On time?"

With Charles, there's no other way, so I said, "You bet."

The line went dead.

Charles seemed to forget his trip to the surf shop and ushered me to a patch of shade around the side of the building. "What's that about?"

"Don't know. You heard as much as I did."

Charles leaned against his cane. "Mel doesn't invite people to lunch unless he's got a powerful reason. And why drive to the Crab House when it would've been easier to meet us on Folly."

"He's embarrassed to be seen with you," I said.

"Funny. He said Crab House before you asked him if I could come."

"We'll have to wait and find out. Speaking of waiting, isn't Dude waiting for you to deliver a package?"

Charles nodded and pointed his cane at the surf shop. "United Parcel Charles to the rescue." He waved bye as he scampered up the steps.

Despite the comment by one of the walkers that he was having a sunstroke, the temperature was mild for May, so I decided to walk to the end of the pier instead of heading home. Folly's iconic pier was more than a thousand feet long and stuck out into the Atlantic and served as the figurative center of the island's coastline. I often ventured to the far end of the structure when I needed to think, or when I wanted to have a good view of the beach, or if I wanted to take a nap in the shade under the diamond-shaped, elevated second deck. This would be a good time for all three.

A dozen or so fishermen were spread out along the rail, a flock of seagulls circled overhead, and the smell of filleted fish filled the air. The vacation season wasn't in full swing so the beach wasn't as crowded as it would be in a few more weeks, and the end of the pier was deserted so I had my choice of benches.

Instead of falling asleep, my mind wandered and tried to assimilate everything that'd been happening the last few days. The death of the college student was tragic, and even though he'd been on Mel's charter, it was difficult to believe that he had anything to do with it. So, why had the rumors of his involvement been spread so quickly? Granted, Mel was gay and apparently so was the student. But so are many others, here on Folly and elsewhere. Was the bias against gays so strong that people automatically jumped to conclusions? And then there's Abe Pottinger. Was Larry right about Abe's less-than-stellar reason for being here? Or, since Larry knew Abe and his sordid past, was my friend biased against him? How did that differ from how people viewed Mel?

Chester didn't know anything about Abe and Larry's relationship, and yet he thought something was fishy about the newcomer. How much credence could I put into Chester's suspicions?

And now both Larry and Chester want Charles and me to see what we can learn about Abe. How are we supposed to do that? Add to all that, Mel wants to meet me—and of course Charles—for lunch. Something told me that he didn't just crave our company.

And then I fell asleep.

Chapter Fifteen

The Charleston Crab House was eight miles from home and on Wappoo Creek, a waterway that branches off the Ashley River on the west side of the city. We arrived on-time by Charles's Standard Time, or thirty minutes before Mel had said, and were ushered to a table on the outdoor patio overlooking the scenic waterway. While we waited for Mel we were treated to a float-by from two small sailboats and three dolphins frolicking near the dock. So far, the day was perfect.

Mel headed our way and I doubted that the day would stay perfect. His normal sour expression looked festive compared to the look on his face, and I suspected that a storm was nearing. The former Marine didn't disappoint.

"They're out to get me," Mel groused as he yanked the chair out from under the table and plopped down.

Charles glanced toward the door; probably to see if he meant it literally.

"Who?" I asked, assuming that the time for civil greetings had passed.

Mel glared at Charles and then at me. "Damned if I know."

It was time for me to keep my mouth shut and let Mel tell us whatever it was.

Charles, to no surprise, didn't adhere to that philosophy. "How do you know?"

Mel took a deep breath. "I've taken fire in combat. I've been in more bar fights than I can count. And, I'm pretty good at catching people bad mouthing me behind my back. I can damned sure tell when someone's got me in their scope."

"Humor us and say why you think you've been targeted," I said.

"Yeah," Charles said. "I haven't been shot at, I know I haven't been in many—okay, no—bar fights and would bet money that Chris hasn't either. We're not as good as you at knowing when someone's out to get us."

Mel stared at Charles and then waved for the waitress who had been talking to three customers at the next table. She looked over and Mel shouted for her to bring him the "strongest brew in there." He pointed toward the bar so she'd know where they kept the brews.

Mel glanced at a passing sailboat and turned to me. "That detective called yesterday."

"Adair?" I asked.

"Yeah. Said he had some 'routine' follow-up questions, and all casual-like said, 'Remind me how often you visited LeBar.' Well, I reminded him that I'd said a couple of times with Caldwell and maybe a couple of times by myself."

Charles rubbed his three-day-old beard stubble. "So?"

Mel picked at his paper napkin and leaned back in his chair when the waitress brought his drink and asked us what we wanted. Charles said a beer and that he didn't care how strong it was, and I ordered wine. The waitress left and Mel leaned forward and put his elbows on the table.

"I sort of underestimated the number."

"Sort of?" Charles said.

"Yeah, more like a dozen times by myself. Never counted because I didn't see any damned reason to. Who knew somebody'd be keeping score."

"And you didn't tell Adair anything different than you did the first time?" I asked.

"No. Stupid not to, but no."

I would agree it was stupid to not tell the detective the number of visits, but I was having a hard time seeing why that made Mel think someone was out to get him. Again, I waited to let

Mel's story unfold at his pace.

The waitress returned with Charles and my drink and, to his credit, Charles sipped his beer and didn't ask Mel what he'd meant.

"It gets worse," Mel mumbled. "Adair asked me if I was sure that I didn't know the dead kid. I said no, I didn't remember him."

"But?" Charles said.

Mel glared at him. "A few times I was there I may have gotten a bit snookered. LeBar's small and often it's ass-to-ass, steppin'-on-toes packed. Every once in a while, a lost straight person stumbled in, but it's rare. The regulars have the queer factor in common, but they're varied after that: tall, short, bi, trans, black, white, old, and young, like college students."

A light was coming through the cracks in Mel's story. "College students like Drew Casey?"

"Adair asked if I met Drew Casey in LeBar."

I wanted to scream, "Did you?" but waited.

"I told him no, but to be honest, I could have."

Charles said, "Could have?"

"I was a few generations older than some of the folks in there, and with my handsome looks and charming smile, several of them recognized me." Mel grinned to let us know he was kidding about the looks and smile. "Anyway, I was a conversation piece, maybe even some kind of challenge to a few of them, and they sort of flirted."

I prayed that I was wrong about where this seemed to be headed, but asked anyway. "Was Casey one of the college students?"

"I don't know, I really don't." Mel shook his head and looked down at the table. "There was always a bunch of them, it's dark, and I seldom had a shortage of beers. Guys, he could have been."

"What about the kid who rented the boat and who blew the whistle on you?" Charles asked.

"Charles, did you miss the part where I said I was pickled, in the dark, and packed in like sand in concrete. I don't freakin' know!"

"Did you leave the bar with any of them?" asked fearless Charles.

"Shit no!" Mel slammed his fist down on the metal table. "Why would you even ask that? Caldwell and I are committed to each other, have been for years, always will be. You know that!"

Charles held up both hand, palms facing Mel. "Didn't mean to insult you. You know cops'll come at you with that."

"Have you told Sean any of this?" I asked.

"I've got a meeting with him this afternoon. Wanted to see what you thought before spilling my guts to an attorney."

I shook my head. "I don't know what the police have or if someone's trying to frame you, but from Adair's questions, he thinks you're more involved than taking the group to the beach."

Charles picked his cane off the deck and pointed it at Mel. "Don't know what Sean will say, but my unprofessional, untrained legal advice would be for you to keep your trap shut and let your lawyer do the talking."

Food arrived and we ate in silence with a few bursts of frustration, anger, and whether he'd admit it, fear from Mel mixed in. I reinforced what Charles had suggested about Mel keeping his mouth closed and letting his attorney do the talking. Mel said that he would, but his personality and direct approach to a problem would make it hard. He had looked at his watch a couple of times and finally said that he needed to get to his meeting with Sean. He thanked us for listening to his ramblings and said he'd get lunch. That was a new experience for me but I managed to handle it without reaching for the check. Charles, as usual, managed to sit on both hands during the awkward check-grabbing portion of the meal. Mel stood, saluted us, started for the exit, and turned and said that we could get the cumshaw. Charles saw the confused look in my eyes and whispered, "Marine-speak for tip."

Mel was gone, I had enjoyed a nice meal, prayed that he would follow our, and Sean's advice, added another word to my vocabulary, and listened to Charles say that we needed another drink. I succumbed.

"What do you make of it?" he asked after the waitress delivered our drinks.

I took a leap and decided that he was talking about Mel's situation. "He's playing with fire lying to the police. Asking Mel a second time about his trips to the bar, tells me that Detective Adair knows that it's more than two visits without Caldwell."

"You betcha."

"But, nothing I know about Mel tells me that he would pick-up, or be picked-up at a bar by a college student."

Charles tilted his head to the left. "Even if he was snookered."

"I doubt it. Trouble is, if Adair has a witness who claims that Mel was there with Drew Casey, and Mel's already on record lying about the number of times he was there and denying that he knew Casey, he's twisted himself into a knot. That's a knot that'll take more than Sean to untie."

Charles rolled up his napkin and tried to tie it in a knot. "That macho-Marine could be in a minefield of trouble."

We sipped our drinks and Charles scooted his chair around so he had a better view of the creek.

"Umm," he said and shook his head.

"What?"

"Nothing."

I'd spent countless hours with him over the years. If I'd learned anything, it was that *nothing* was never nothing. I lowered my head and looked at him with my upturned eyes. He caved.

"Okay, okay," he muttered. "Speaking of knots, think Heather and I should tie one?"

That wouldn't have been on my top twenty list of what "nothing" had meant. Before she left us with only memories, Charles's Aunt Melinda had made a deathbed wish that Charles would get married. Melinda had lived in a small apartment across the hall from Heather and they had talked about how much Heather wanted to become Mrs. Fowler. At an impromptu memorial for his aunt, Charles proposed, but in the months since then, he'd told Heather that he couldn't go through with it. He told her he had proposed more because of Melinda. Heather had been hurt, angry, and had felt rejected. But they had continued to date.

I wondered why he had brought it up again. "Do you want to?"

Charles stared at the creek like he thought a mermaid was about to leap out of the water and say yea or nay.

"Remember when we first met," he said, and continued to stare at the water.

"Sure."

"I told you that people thought I was gay because I'd never had a girlfriend."

I smiled, which was wasted on him since he continued to look at the water. "You said you weren't gay but that you couldn't afford yourself much less a girlfriend."

"Good memory. Did you know people are saying that again?"

"Why?"

"Umm," he hesitated but never wavered from watching the fascinating creek. "Umm, they're saying that since I hang around with you so much, we must be lovers."

That threw me. "Think I should tell Karen?" I used humor, or attempts at humor, as my main defense against things that made me uncomfortable or when I didn't know what to say.

Charles turned away from the creek, shook his head, and looked at me. "Suspect she already knows you're not gay." He shook his head again. "Chris, you know I'm not gay, and most of the time it doesn't bother me about what people think, but it got me to start thinking again about getting married."

"Any conclusions?"

"Most people my age have settled down, married—some two or three times—and have a passel of kids, and mortgages, and IRAs, and, patios and patio furniture, and, well, bunches of stuff. Seems like I should be settling down before it's too late." He sighed. "I know Heather wants to and Lord knows, I couldn't find anyone better. It was about the last thing Melinda said to me." He paused and then turned back to wait for the mermaid.

That's what Melinda wanted and what Heather wants. "What does Charles want?"

He fiddled with his glass and folded his napkin into the shape of a sail. I didn't think he was going to answer, but he said, "I've lived alone my entire life. I eat what I want to eat when I want to eat, go where I want when I want, do what I want when I want, wash my underwear once a month whether it needs it or not. Chris, I don't know if I could change." He paused. "Don't know if I want to."

That was more than I wanted to know, but it was good he was talking about it.

"What's your gut tell you?"

"Most of the time I start pondering this, my guts too busy with heartburn to tell me anything."

That should tell him something. "You need to listen to your heart, head, and your gut and if they all say yes, that's your answer. It should come down to what you want, and only what you want."

"Easier said than done."

I nodded. "Yes."

"Okay, now that we have my future figured out, how about you? When are you and Karen getting hitched?"

It was my turn to stare at the mesmerizing creek.

"Good question, my friend; good question."

Chapter Sixteen

I dropped Charles at his place after eight miles of talking around his question about my matrimonial plans. It wasn't that I was avoiding answering; it was having to answer the same question that I posed to him at the Crab Shack. Avoidance was another one of my defense mechanisms that I had perfected over the decades, so instead of further pondering the question that I had no answer to, I turned my attention to Mel.

I was pulling into the drive and remembered that William had the murder victim in two classes. I backed out of the drive and drove five blocks to the professor's small, well-kept house. William was in the garden when I pulled in behind his car. He looked up from tilling the soil, or whatever you do to work garden-growing magic. He smiled and leaned the hoe against the oak tree that shaded the back half of the garden.

He waved me to two shaded chairs. "You've come to give me a temporary respite from this laborious task."

I smiled. "And to give you a break from hoeing."

"Shall I fetch ice tea?" he said.

"Sounds good, can I help?"

"Unnecessary, I'll return momentarily," He took off his sweat and dirt-stained gardening gloves and headed to the house.

I had spent several summer days under this tree during my first year on Folly. Gardening was William's passion and he had said that it was his way of escaping the demands of his students, his idealistic yet unrealistic administrators, and the petty bickering that takes place in most work environments. I had spent many years working in a large, bureaucratic company and had shared similar stories with him. I'm not certain that misery loves company, but it made for interesting conversations.

William returned with a silver platter holding two large glasses of tea and a silver ice bucket. I thanked him and he said that it was the break he needed. Of course he used more multi-syllable words to say it.

"While I appreciate your appearance," he said, "I suspect that this visit is for more than providing me with a chance to catch my breath."

"Guilty as suspected," I took a sip of tea. "I was wondering if you remembered anything else about Drew Casey or his classmates that could help figure out what's going on."

William took another sip and nodded in the direction of the house that I had lived in when I first moved to Folly; more accurately, the house that replaced my house, since mine had been torched with me in it by a murderer who thought that I was getting too close to learning his identity. "Am I detecting that you're having more than a passing interest in the tragic death of my student? Have we, meaning you singularly, forgotten the fatal result one can face from becoming ensnarled in police business?"

"You're right, of course. I know what I'm doing can be dangerous, but as you have figured, I don't take kindly to people accusing my friends of things they didn't do. I've known Mel Evans for going on two years. I've trusted him with my life, and I've never seen anything to indicate that he could have harmed that kid. For that reason—"

William raised both hands. "Chris, no need to continue. I can only hope that I have as good a friend as you if I find myself in such a difficult situation."

"You do, and you're looking at him."

"I'm humbled. In return, allow me to respond to your initial query. As I said the last time you broached this topic, I make it a practice not to become involved in my students' lives outside the classroom. But I knew that you had an interest in Mr. Casey's death, so I put my classroom-only practice on hiatus and paid particular attention to what students were saying about the young man's demise."

"Learn anything?"

"I did, but I don't know what to make of it. Perhaps it will provide you with some enlightenment. And to be honest, I had heard some of this long before Mr. Casey's death, but I was hesitant to talk about such matters."

I motioned for him to continue.

"A month ago, I asked him how he was doing. It was a benign enquiry and I often ask students the same thing. Their typical response center on classes and majors." He hesitated and tilted his head. "Mr. Casey's answer was outside those parameters. He shared that he had been teased relentlessly by some classmates."

"About what?"

"His sexual orientation," William said, almost in a whisper. "He wasn't one to hide his homosexuality and was paying the price for his openness."

"Did he say who was teasing him?"

"He didn't share names, and I didn't ask. He said he didn't want to make a case out of it and dropped it thereafter."

William may have thought that was critical information, but I didn't hear anything that could be helpful. "Was that it?"

"That's only prelude to what I shall now disclose."

He stopped making eye contact, and was uncomfortable with the topic. I again asked him to continue.

"The day before yesterday, I overheard two students who had been on the fateful excursion. One of them, Dawn Henderson by name, said to Peter Mellon that she was glad that, and this is her quote, 'the queer' got what he had coming to him. I've had the impression that Ms. Henderson was, how shall I say it, pre-judgmental when it came to African Americans. I suppose those feelings could also apply to homosexuals, but I'm not certain. She went on to say that she knew that the 'queer boat driver' had killed him."

"She said she knew?"

"Those were her words, but here's the part that I believe to be most significant. Mr. Mellon chided his classmate when he told her that she didn't know that the, umm, homosexual boat captain killed Mr. Casey. Mr. Mellon said that all she knew was that Mr. Casey, along with more than one other gay individual, landed on Boneyard Beach with the group, but she did not recall seeing him get off the boat when it returned to the dock."

"Why not?"

"Because, according to Mr. Mellon, he and his fellow adventurers were so inebriated that they wouldn't have known if Santa Claus and his reindeer had exited the boat upon return to its mooring."

"What did she say to that?"

William chuckled. "She gave him a look that I was pleased that she had not directed at me, and said that she 'knew what she knew,' whatever that meant."

"What did her classmate say?"

"They walked away and I felt it unwise to follow."

"One more question. My understanding is that one person booked the excursion and that Mel didn't get the names of the others, so I doubt any of them knew Mel or anything about him before they had met on the dock."

"Appears logical."

"Then how did Dawn Henderson know Mel was gay? That would have been the last impression I would have had when I met him for the first time. He looks and acts every bit the ex-Marine that he is; he dresses macho, rants-and-raves macho, and unless pushed, never says anything about his personal life."

"That would be my assessment."

"Do you recall anything that either of the students said that indicated they knew?"

"No."

William kept glancing at the hoe and at the garden. I had pushed him out of his comfort zone, both by talking about Mel's sexual orientation and his sharing that he had been eavesdropping. It was time to change the subject, so I asked him what he had planted for the growing season. He smiled, exhaled, and went into a monologue about the various vegetables that were planted, what he would be planting next, when they would be ready to harvest, what kind of salads he made with some of them, and how he prepared the meat that he featured with each veggie. He said a lot more, but with my total lack of interest in gardening and cooking, I tuned out somewhere around how the zucchini would be ready in the next couple of weeks, but he would have to wait until the fall for the parsnip, or maybe it was catnip.

I thanked him for the tea and conversation. He thanked me for stopping by and allowing him to take a break. I told him that it was my pleasure, and he told me not to get myself killed.

I agreed that that would be a good idea and left him with a smile on his face. I wasn't as cheery.

Chapter Seventeen

I pulled in the drive and Chief Cindy LaMond pulled in behind me in her unmarked Crown Vic.

I met her in the yard between the two cars. "What'd I do wrong now, Chief?"

"Several things, I'm sure." She shook her head. "But, that's not why I stopped."

I started to make a smart comment, but waited.

"I'll stop playing police chief around seven; can you stop by the house after that? I promise Larry won't try to fix supper."

"Having a zero-plus-a-few-days party?"

She frowned. "Nope. You're the only guest, unless you want to bring your new-best friend Brad Burton."

"Right. What's up?"

"Later."

"I'll be there, sans Burton."

I had a couple of hours to ponder Cindy's invitation. It only took me five minutes to realize that I had no idea what it was about, so I took the remaining time to take a nap, and prepare a healthy supper of peanut butter on Ritz crackers; okay, not healthy, but my refrigerator was plum out of zucchini and parsnip.

Charles wasn't with me, so I was able to arrive at the LaMonds at seven rather than early. Cindy greeted me and said that Larry was on the patio. We stopped in the kitchen on the way, she grabbed a can of Budweiser, poured me a glass of Chardonnay, and I followed her.

Three patio chairs had been pulled in a tight triangle on the crushed-shell surface and Larry occupied the one facing the marsh. A small glass-topped table beside his chair held an opened pizza box from Woody's, two beer cans, and Larry's Pewter Hardware ball cap. He heard the door open and jumped up, turned, and greeted me with a smile. His Pewter Hardware logoed white polo shirt had a dirt stain on the shoulder and was pulled out of his khaki slacks. He wore tennis shoes but they were untied. It looked like he had spent the day wrestling uncooperative sheets of plywood.

He shook my hand; his smile was intact but seemed forced. "Have a seat. I'll be back." He headed into the house.

Cindy pointed to the pizza box and asked if I wanted a slice, glanced at the door, and whispered, "Larry wanted to fire up the grill and fix burgers. You and the fire department should be thankful that I talked him out of it."

I told her that I had already eaten and thanked her for the offer. Larry returned and flopped down in his chair. The plywood must have won the battle. Cindy took the remaining chair and asked if I was certain that I didn't want pizza. I again said I was certain, and she said, "Good, more for me."

Larry took a long draw on his beer, glanced at Cindy, and back at me. "Guess you're wondering why we asked you over."

I didn't want to appear too shocked at the invitation seeing that we're friends, but I'd only been at their house a few times and they were more spontaneous for gatherings like the zero party.

"Had me wondering."

"It's about Abe Pottinger. Have you met him?"

"Yes, in fact Charles and I are now official members of the .5 club. It would have been easier if we tried to drop in on the president at the White House than getting past Chester's membership requirements."

Cindy smiled and Larry shook his head.

"Anyway," I continued, "we took our first walk with the group the other day and spent some time talking to Abe. I think you're right, Larry, he's up to something. He was pushing reverse mortgages to a few members. I'm no expert, but he was touting a much higher monthly payment to his 'clients' than other companies offer. I don't know if he's gotten any of them to sign up, but I wouldn't be surprised if he wasn't close."

"No surprise," Larry said. "That's Abe."

"Do either of you know Theodore Stoll, goes by Theo?" I asked.

"By sight only," Cindy said.

Larry nodded. "Yeah, he lives up the street; big house facing the marsh."

Cindy looked at Larry. "How do you know where he lives?"

"He's been in the store a few times. Nice gent, but forgetful. He bought WD-40 for a squeaky door. Came in a week later to buy WD-40; said he had a squeaky door. He told me all about his house." Larry shook his head. "Not that I didn't want to sell another can of the stuff, but I asked him if it was the same door he'd been in earlier to get something for. He said yes, and that he must have forgotten that he already bought a can. How do you forget something like that?"

"Why'd you want to know if we knew him?" Cindy asked.

I told them about how some in the group were worried about his "forgetfulness" and how Abe had been talking to him about his finances. They were afraid that Theo may be vulnerable and since no one knows much about Pottinger, they were worried.

"Good reason to be," Larry said. "But that's not, umm, not the reason we asked you over."

Cindy said, "Let me get you a refill." She popped out of her chair and headed toward the door. From the way they were acting, I thought she was right about me needing more wine.

Larry mumbled something about the weather and how bad today's traffic had been, evidently stalling until Cindy returned.

Cindy handed me my glass. "Where are we, Larry?"

"Waiting for you."

Cindy took her seat and looked at her husband. "Tell him."

"Well, umm," Larry began, hesitated, and continued. "Abe came in the store yesterday. He asked me if I could spare a few minutes. There weren't any customers and Brandon was there if any came in. I said yes and escorted him to the side yard." He took another gulp of beer.

"Get on with it sweetie. Chris doesn't have all night."

I wanted to hug her, but instead focused on Larry.

"Abe started talking to me all friendly. Said he'd heard that my wife was the police chief. Said that he was proud of me for owning Pewter Hardware. And since it was the only hardware store on Folly, it must be a goldmine."

Cindy interrupted. "Little does he know."

Larry continued, "He slobbered on about how he was so glad that I'd made a legitimate living and life for myself. If I didn't know him like I do, I'd have felt good about what he was saying. I kept waiting for the other shoe to drop. He blabbered some more goody-goody stuff and then he got around to why he was there. Need more wine? I'm getting another beer."

I said no and he headed to the kitchen.

Cindy watched him go inside and turned to me. "This is rough on him, please be patient. He'll get to the end of his story. Before daylight."

Larry returned and looked at Cindy and she motioned for him to continue.

"Then Abe threw some shit at the fan and it smacked me in the face."

Figuratively, I hoped.

"The damned crook leaned against the side of the building and said something like, wouldn't it be terrible if the citizens of your quaint island learned that you're a thief, and here you are married to the police chief. He then said, and I think these are his exact words, 'Her career would be in the crapper, and you'd be run out of town on a rail quicker than you can say cat burglar.'"

Larry's whole torso shook, his hands clutched into fists, and he glared at his beer can.

Cindy leaned over and patted his arm. "It's okay hon, we'll get through it. Why don't you tell Chris what Pottinger wants?"

Larry looked up from the can. "Abe looked at me and said, 'You're a good friend, Larry. I've always liked you. I can make this problem go away.'"

"The problem that Abe had just created," I said.

Larry nodded. "He said that he'd driven by our house and could tell that I made a good living and with a wife whose chief, money must be rolling in. He said for a mere fifty-thousand dollars he'd find a way for my *secret* to stay that way."

"What did you tell him?"

"I told him to get his crooked, blackmailing, freakin' ass off my property."

"Good. What'd he say?"

"He gave me his smarmy grin and said he'd give me a week to think about it before everyone on one small island in South Carolina learns about me."

I looked at Cindy who sat stiffly, showing no emotion, and then back at Larry. "What're you going to do?"

"First, I don't have fifty grand lying around. Second, if I did, I wouldn't be caught dead giving him a cent of it. Beyond that, we're at a loss."

Cindy leaned forward in her chair. "I told Larry what happened in Atlanta's ancient history. It's none of anyone's business and to let that slime bucket tell whatever he wants to anyone he wants to tell it to. It's probably a bluff anyway."

"You're wrong, hon," Larry said, his voice calmer and his hands more relaxed. "It could cost you your job if people learned it from Abe who would make a big deal out of it and try to imply that I'm still a crook and that you're corrupt."

Cindy patted his arm again. "Larry you know—"

Larry squeezed her hand. "Wait, I've kept it secret too long. It's time, past time, to tell everyone and take our chances. The mayor already knows and he's your boss, even promoted you to chief. Chris and Charles here know and neither of them has shunned us, at least as far as I can tell."

Cindy held Larry's hand and turned to me. "What do you think, Chris?"

"I agree with you, Cindy; it's been many years and is none of anyone's business."

Cindy nodded and started to speak. I held my hand up. "But, you know as well as I do, probably better, that there are some who would take the information, spread it, embellish it, and use it to derail any of your efforts as chief. They're good at working behind the scene. They won't directly attack you because they know it would look petty. Whether what Larry did decades ago is anyone's business or not, or that it's ancient history, won't matter. Perception is reality, and the perception of those who don't know him, can be devastating if they hear it from Abe."

Larry raised his hand like he wanted to ask his teacher a question. "Here's what I was thinking. Abe said he wouldn't do anything for a week, so I'd like to ask him to reconsider; tell him we don't have the money; and throw myself on his mercy. If he says no, I'll tell everyone before Abe can."

Cindy shook her head. "Larry, that idea's about as good as two broken crutches. Why in holy hotdogs would he show a glimmer of mercy? Maybe I could talk to him, being chief and all."

"No way," Larry said. "I've got to try."

I waved in their direction. "Let me throw in my two cents worth."

They turned toward me.

"Larry, I don't think he would pay attention to you. He's already said what he would do, and won't believe that you don't have money." I turned to Cindy. "The police chief can't approach him. That could get you in more hot water than anything that Abe can say about Larry. You need to stay above the fray."

"You're right," Cindy said. "So what do we do?"

"I'll talk to him."

Cindy jerked her head toward me. "Hell no!"

Larry leaned toward me. "No way."

I held out both hands and pointed a palm at each of them.

"Hear me out. It's a longshot, but think about it. I've met him so he knows who I am. He's heard Chester Carr and Cal Ballew say that I'm friends with the mayor and am dating a detective from Charleston. That gives me some creds. I can tell him I know you are in hock up to your shingles with the hardware store and this house and you couldn't come up with five-hundred dollars much less fifty grand. He would have no way of knowing it's not true. And I can tell him the mayor and other 'key officials' already know about you. Again, he has no idea who knows. And I could say that you've already planned to come clean."

Larry looked over at Cindy who said. "I need another beer. "Larry? Chris?"

We each said yes. And I took a deep breath.

Cindy returned with the drinks and we stared at the marsh. My thoughts were going in circles and I couldn't imagine what was going on in their heads.

"Guys," I said, "me talking with him would give you deniability and a way to stay at arm's length from any volatile reaction. I'm not saying it'll work, but it's worth a try."

Larry said, "I don't like it. I'd rather just blow his brains out, if he had any."

Cindy put her hand on Larry's arm, again. "Now hon, it's really not that bad. You've made countless friends here. Regardless of your past, they will continue to support you, and for my job, hell, I'm police chief." She chuckled. "I'm supposed to be unpopular."

Her comment was intended to lighten the mood, but I suspect as far as Larry was concerned, it had failed. I know it had for me.

After more discussion, we agreed that my plan was weak, probably would fall on its face, and was possibly dangerous, but no one had a better idea. Larry gave me Abe's number, told me where he lived, and wished me luck.

I started to head home, stopped, and turned to Cindy. "Got a favor to ask."

"Gosh," she said, with mock astonishment, or I assumed mock. "Why in the world would I do you a favor? All you're doing for us is confronting a sleazy blackmailer." She nodded. "Okay, I'm all heart. What is it?"

"Use some of your police resources and see if Abe is licensed to sell reverse mortgages, and if he is, what's the reputation of the company, and if he's a financial advisor. I'm worried about members of the .5 group and Theo in particular."

"You've got it. And Chris, thanks."

I hoped that she would be able to say that in a few days.

Chapter Eighteen

After a night of tossing, turning, and second, third, and fourth guessing my offer to talk to Abe, I called him and was now driving to his house. The good news during my morning call was that he was curious enough to want to meet; the bad news was that he said he would be in Charleston until nine tonight and I could meet him then. That meant that I had all day to worry and wonder, and I had used every minute of it. I had called Larry and told him the plan so in case no one ever heard from me again, they would have a starting point to begin the search for my body. Larry had said for me to stop teasing about something like that; I said I wasn't teasing. He wished me luck and asked that I call as soon as the meeting ended.

Abe lived five blocks from the center of town and across the street from the city's tennis court. The plan to talk to him made more sense when I was sitting with two good friends in the safety of the LaMond's back yard. Asinine was the only word that came to me to describe it as I parked a half block from Abe's house.

He greeted me on the porch of his attractive, post-Hugo, two-story brick house, one of the few brick homes on the island. He answered the door in a dark-gray suit, white shirt, with a red-and-blue rep tie loosened at the collar. I shook his hand and teased that he looked quite un-Folly-like. He gave me a salesman's, hundred-watt smile and said that he agreed but that he just got home from conducting a wealth-management seminar for a group of attorneys. His story sounded good, but I had my doubts about it, and from his breath, if he had conducted a seminar, it was held in a bar.

He invited me in and offered me a variety of alcoholic beverages. I said that water would do. He smiled and said that with the water tower fewer than a hundred yards from his door he figured that he could find a glass of it. I nearly gagged on his charm while he went to find my drink.

He returned with my water and a glass of an amber-colored liquid, probably bourbon, far from his first of the night. I sat on a soft-leather couch and he pulled a matching chair closer to me and took a sip.

He set his drink on a chrome-and-glass table beside the couch, leaned forward, and said, "Let me guess. You heard me talking to Connie and Harriet about the lucrative and lifetime-security I can offer through a reverse mortgage." He smiled and nodded. I almost had to shade my eyes from the sparkle from his capped teeth. "And, you want to learn how I can ensure your financial future." He leaned back but continued his syrupy smile.

I returned his smile with equal insincerity. "Not exactly."

"Then what brings you out on such a lovely night?" he asked, and took another sip.

"You may not know, but two of my best friends are Larry and Cindy LaMond."

His expression didn't change but I noticed a slight twitch in his cheek. "Oh, I believe—"

"Wait," I interrupted. I couldn't let him throw off my rehearsed introduction. "I was having a conversation with them last night and they shared some disturbing information. I hear that you and Larry go way back. He said that you had some, umm, less-than-legitimate dealings."

Abe leaned forward. "That's not—"

"Stop! Let me finish."

He reached for his glass but didn't lift it from the table, and then leaned back in his chair.

"Larry also shared that you had approached him with what he called an *untenable offer*. Now I don't know if you were serious or teasing your old friend, but let me tell you a few things you might not know about Larry and Cindy."

I threw in teasing to give Abe an escape hatch if he chose to take it, but I couldn't tell from his expression where he would go next, so I continued with the lesser-rehearsed portion of my pitch.

"Larry moved to Folly after serving a stint in prison. The first thing he did when he got here was approach Brian Newman, the police chief, to tell him about his past. That police chief is now mayor. And in those more than eighteen years there has not been a single accusation made against your former colleague. Not only does the mayor know about his past, Larry has told members of the city council, and the Charleston County Sheriff. What you think is a secret is old news to everyone who needs to know." I hesitated and took a drink of water. "Now in the next couple of days, he's going to tell everyone who comes in the store who doesn't already know."

Abe's faux-smile disappeared somewhere along my comments and his right arm began to fidget. "Mr. Landrum, you have no idea what you're talking about. To think that I would threaten my friend is ridiculous."

He reached for his glass, squeezed it so hard I was afraid it would shatter. I took the break to continue and I ignored his comment. "Now to your blackmail attempt."

"Blackmail!"

I thought he was going to leap out of his chair. I resisted the urge to run and stayed seated. "I hate to break the confidence of a friend, but let me tell you about Larry and Cindy. Yes, his hardware store appears to be successful, but ... crap, I hate saying this but you need to know, Larry's in hock up to his roof shingles. He owes a ton of money on the store, he owes countless vendors for inventory, and he's upside down on his house. He couldn't come up with five-hundred dollars, much less fifty thousand. I'm afraid you're fishing in an empty pond."

Abe stood and snarled. "And you want me to believe that pile of shit?"

"Believe what you want," I said as calmly as possible while my insides churned. "Larry doesn't know I'm talking to you; if he did he would have stopped me. I'm doing it because you need to know and if you have half the sense that I believe you do, you'll drop your plan."

I wanted to confront him on his reverse mortgage scheme and whatever con I suspected that he was running on Theo, but I didn't want to hit him with everything at once. I also didn't have evidence to make those accusations.

He reached out, grabbed my elbow, and tried to pull me out of the chair. I yanked my arm back and stood.

"It's time for you to leave before I do something you'll regret," he said and staggered to the front door.

I beat him to the door, grasped the handle, began to jerk it open, and then turned to him. "I hope I made myself clear, Mr. Pottinger. Believe me, it won't turn out in your best interest if you try to pursue your half-baked scheme."

I wasn't about to turn my back to him, so I opened the door the rest of the way and stepped backward.

"You're going to regret coming here." He took a step in my direction and shoved me out.

My foot missed the step and I fell backward. My back hit the small concrete porch and a sharp pain radiated down my arm. I looked up and saw Abe standing in the doorway. He glared at me with a smug look of satisfaction on his face.

He gave me another one of his high-wattage smiles. "Don't you forget—"

I never heard what I wasn't supposed to forget. What I did hear was what sounded like a firecracker exploding across the street behind me. What I saw was horrific. Abe's smile turned to abject fear. His chest exploded. The center of his white shirt turned crimson. And, he flopped backwards as if he'd been clobbered by a sledgehammer. He was dead before his body hit the highly-polished wood floor.

My first thought was total disbelief, followed by, *Am I next?* I rolled to my left and off the porch. I tried to maintain a low profile as I turned to look where the shot had come from. There were two security lights on in the small children's playground across the street but the shadow of the pavilion shaded the three-foot-high wooden picket fence from the light. I caught movement beside the tennis court but it was too dark and too far away to make out anything other than there was someone dressed in dark clothes walking toward the next street over.

I was still afraid to stand and knew I couldn't help Abe. My phone had slipped out of my pocket when I hit the porch. I grabbed it and was relieved to see that the keypad illuminated when I tapped the phone icon. I was shaking and it took two tries to punch 911. I told the dispatcher what had happened but couldn't remember Abe's house number so I said it was across from the tennis court. The calm voice on the phone said that was all she needed and for me to stay on the line.

A large dog stirred up by the gunshot was going berserk a few houses away. The next sounds I heard were from at least two patrol cars and the distinct siren from the city's Fire/Rescue pick-up truck—all screaming my direction.

The Fire-Rescue truck arrived first and two firefighters who doubled as EMTs rushed up the steps to the unmoving con artist. Medical training wasn't necessary for them to tell there was nothing to do for the body splayed in the doorway. One of them turned to me as I stood on the porch and stared at my yellow polo shirt and asked if I had been hit. It was the first time that I'd noticed blood spatter on the shirt. I caught my breath and told him that I was okay. Officer Bishop, whom I had met only a few months earlier at the scene of another death, jumped out of the first patrol car and rushed over to Abe, assessed the situation, and then turned to me. Next to arrive was Officer Allen Spencer, whom I had met my first month on Folly, and had established a good relationship with him over the years.

I described what had happened, and what I had seen across the street. Both officers looked toward the tennis court and asked if I had seen the vehicle the shooter left in. I said no and that the person had gone around the corner and I couldn't see anything. Bishop radioed to the only other patrol officer on duty to stop any vehicle moving in the general vicinity. Spencer walked to the fence to see if he could see anything. I figured it would be futile.

I was surprised to see Cindy's unmarked police car arrive next. Like Officer Bishop, she walked over to Abe, spoke to the

EMT, and said something to Officer Bishop before coming over to me.

She looked at my bloody shirt. "You okay?" Her face was expressionless but she looked like she had aged ten years since last night. She turned and looked toward the tennis courts.

It was warm but I was shivering. I said I was okay and she asked me to join her in her vehicle. She offered me a bottle of water. I accepted.

"What happened? Don't leave anything out."

I began from when I arrived through when I called 911. She asked me to repeat what Abe and I had talked about and what I saw across the street after Abe had taken his last breath. She mumbled a half-dozen profanities and then called Detective Adair. She slammed her hand on the steering wheel and stared at Abe's front door. I wished that I had a steering wheel to pound.

Chapter Nineteen

I was still in the chief's car when the Coroner's van inched around us on the narrow road and stopped in front of Abe's house. Five minutes later, a white, unmarked Chevy Caprice pulled in behind the coroner's vehicle and Detective Adair stepped out, buttoned his navy blazer, and glanced around before walking up the steps and looking at the late Abe Pottinger. Adair looked as fresh and unruffled as if he had just stepped out of a clothing store ad as he talked to Officer Bishop and he looked back at us before walking to Cindy's window.

"Good evening, Chief," he said in a tone that didn't imply that there was anything good about it. He then leaned down and stared at me. "You again."

Cindy gave him a staccato, police-speak version of what had happened and Adair asked if Cindy and I could join him in his car. It was one of the last things I wanted to do, but didn't take it as a request. We followed with Cindy taking the passenger's seat and I slid in back.

"Mr. Landrum, why were you at the victim's house?"

I had hoped we would ease into that question, but Adair didn't seem able to ease into anything.

I nodded toward the house. "I met him a few days ago when I joined a walking group that a friend had started. Abe was a member of that group." *All true*, I thought, and continued, "He had been talking to the others about something called a reverse mortgage that he was selling. I wasn't knowledgeable about it and wanted to find out more." All true, but not quite—not even approximately—all the truth.

Cindy leaned up in the seat and turned toward me but didn't say anything.

"Why were you meeting with him this late?"

A marginally good question, I thought. "When I called him he said that he would be at a meeting in Charleston and wouldn't be home until nine."

"And your curiosity about reverse mortgages couldn't wait another day during normal business hours?"

"Could have, I suppose."

Adair jotted a note in a small notebook that he had taken from his inside coat pocket and turned back to me. "Hmm, okay," he said, and frowned. "Walk me through what happened."

This is where it's going to get tricky. I told him that we had finished our conversation about reverse mortgages and I was leaving when Abe was shot.

I looked at Adair and looked at Abe's front door. "I was going out the door and Abe was holding it for me, then the shot." I looked at Adair like that was it?

He stared at Abe's door. "Were you facing the street? Did you see where the shot came from?"

Careful Chris. "No. I was facing Abe." I glanced down at the blood spatter.

The detective followed my gaze, and then looked at his notebook. "Were you beside him in the doorway, in front or behind him?"

I knew where he was headed. "I was sort of in front of him, almost on the front porch, sort of turned sideways, I guess."

He looked at the front door and then across the street at the fence and the tennis court. "Mr. Landrum, is there anyone who would have wanted you dead?"

Other than Abe Pottinger, I thought. "No, why?"

Adair rubbed his chin, glanced at Cindy, and back at me. "From how you described what happened, it looks like you could have been the intended victim and the shooter missed. You were between Pottinger and the shooter. Why would someone have taken a shot at him with you in the way?"

"Good point," I said, knowing that if the forensic services techs were as good as I thought they were, the pattern of blood spatter on my shirt would tell a different version, would tell that I was flat on the porch when the shot was taken. How would I explain that?

Adair squeezed the bridge of his nose and stared at me. "You're certain you don't know anyone who had it in for you?"

"Not to my knowledge."

He jotted another note. "Okay, now when you were in there," Adair nodded toward Abe's house, "did he seem nervous, say anything about being in danger, or anything out of the ordinary?"

"Not really. I'd only talked to him briefly before tonight, so I couldn't tell if he was acting strange. He seemed fine."

"Did you notice anyone in the area when you arrived?"

Like someone with a rifle lurking around the house, I thought. "No."

Adair turned to Cindy. "Chief, did you know the victim?"

And I thought my answers were touchy.

"Umm," Cindy said, and then she paused. "I never met him."

"Okay," Adair said. "Back to you Mr. Landrum. You told Officer ..."

"Bishop," Cindy said.

"Right. You told Officer Bishop you saw someone running away by the fence." Adair looked toward the two officers who were waving flashlights back and forth lighting the ground beside tennis court fence.

"Not running, it was more like a confident walk. All I could tell was that the person was dressed in dark clothes."

"Man or women?" Adair asked.

"Couldn't tell. The person was too far away and it was dark."

He jotted another note and then looked me in the eyes. "Tell me one more time where were you were when he was hit?"

I repeated my fictionalized version. Adair looked skeptical, but he always did, so I couldn't tell if he believed me or not. He asked if there was anything that I wanted to add. I said no and he closed his notebook.

He asked Cindy to stay behind and told me that he didn't have anything else—for now.

Detective Adair hollered as I walked away, "Mr. Landrum, please give your shirt to one of the techs standing by the Forensic Services SUV."

I said, "Sure," as if there was a choice.

Five minutes later I was pulling into my drive, shirtless, sweating and still trembling from what had happened. I was thinking how things couldn't get worse, when my phone's ringtone startled me.

"Chris, this is Sean. Thought you'd want to know. The police arrested Mel Evans for murder."

I nearly dropped the phone. "When?"

"An hour ago. He called from jail. I'd told him that I wasn't the person he needed if he was arrested; I reminded him of that, hung up, and called my buddy, Martin Camp, he's one of the best criminal defense attorneys around. I caught him at a fund-raiser for a gubernatorial candidate. He griped about having to visit the jail in a tux, but said he would head over and see what he could do."

"What evidence do they have?"

"No clue. Mel didn't know."

Will I ever learn not to say that things can't get worse?

Chapter Twenty

I called Charles first thing in the morning to see if he wanted to meet for breakfast. I realized that I hadn't eaten since lunch yesterday, was starved, and needed someone to talk to about what had happened. More importantly, Charles would be on my case for weeks if I let much time pass before I told him everything. If he heard it from someone else, he'd make me regret not telling him not only for weeks, but for months, possibly years. Charles's memory would make an elephant look senile.

As usual, he was sitting on the front patio of the Dog and was quick to remind me that he had been there for a half hour, and that I was late because I had the audacity to arrive at the time we had agreed upon. After the last twenty-four hours, I was in no mood to banter, and ignored the comment.

"Did you fall off the wrong side of the bed this morning?" he asked as I lowered myself into the chair.

"If you only knew."

Amber stopped at the table after delivering breakfast to two couples at the next table.

"Coffee?" she asked.

I nodded and she headed inside. Amber and I had dated for a couple of years and we had still remained good friends.

"Then you'd better tell me what I should know," Charles said.

The patio was full and I leaned closer to the table so I wouldn't have to talk loud. "Mel was arrested last night for killing the student."

Charles reacted like he'd been hit by a Taser. "You're kidding."

"Sean Aker called me late to tell me."

I didn't want to say it was before eleven o-clock or Charles would have chided me for not calling him last night. I didn't look forward to sharing what else had happened.

"Why? What do they have on him?"

His questions were familiar since they were the same ones I'd asked Sean. I told him everything that I had learned, which wasn't much, and he asked what we could do. I said there wasn't anything until we knew more.

Charles took a deep breath, looked around to see if anyone was eavesdropping, and leaned closer to the table. "Could he have done it?"

Good question, I thought. "He has a temper; his military training probably taught him a dozen ways to kill; and, he has little sympathy for, as he puts it, 'the sniveling, spoiled, college brats,' that he ferries through the marsh."

"Christ, Chris, I hope you're not his defense attorney."

I shook my head. "Hold on."

Charles gestured for me to continue.

"With that said, I haven't seen anything to make me to believe he's guilty. He came to me as soon as he heard that someone may not have made it back from the party. He asked me to go with him to Boneyard Beach to see if we could find out anything about a missing student. Would he have done that if he killed the kid?"

"Not unless he was trying to deflect blame."

"What motive would he have for killing a sniveling, spoiled, college brat?" I asked.

"You said William told you that the kid was gay. Maybe he made a pass at Mel, or vice versa, and something went wrong."

I shook my head. "Can you picture Mel killing a kid over that?"

Charles looked down at the table and back at me. "No, but it doesn't matter a fig what I think. What do the cops think? They must have something more than a hunch or Mel wouldn't be in jail."

"We need to wait and see."

Amber returned with my coffee and apologized for taking so long. I ordered oatmeal and bacon.

"Got it." she said. "And what's this I hear about you being with that guy who got murdered last night?"

Charles jerked his head toward me so quickly that I feared that he'd sustained whiplash.

I looked at Amber. "I'll tell you later."

She started to object, but instead said she'd get breakfast started.

Charles had both hands on the table and looked like he was ready to leapfrog over it to get to me. "Spit it out."

I motioned for him to sit back and I began with my conversation with Larry and Cindy and regurgitated everything from that meeting to handing my shirt to the Forensic Services tech. Charles had asked me to repeat so much of it that my breakfast had arrived and was getting cold before I had to tell him for the second time what color shirt I had been wearing.

Charles let the information percolate. "So, if you hadn't stumbled, I'd be eating breakfast by myself."

"True, but only if I was the target."

"Other than me at this moment, who'd want to shoot you?"

"You're beginning to sound like Detective Adair, without the good clothes and starched-on frown." I shook my head. "I don't know anyone who would want me dead."

"Then who'd want Abe coffined, besides, I can't believe I'm saying this, Larry?"

I pushed the oatmeal around the bowl. "Larry thought that Abe was up to no good when he joined the walking group. Chester said the same thing. If that's true, any of the walkers could have a motive."

"You said you saw someone rushing away."

I nodded.

"Then scratch Theo."

I smiled. "True."

Charles turned serious. "Who knew you'd be there?"

I looked toward the street and the small group of people waiting for a table, and back at Charles. "Only Larry and Cindy." I hesitated. "Unless Abe told someone."

"And according to my source who waited hours, many hours, to tell me about the murder, Cindy was one of the first there after it happened."

I wondered what had taken him so long to "remind" me about waiting until this morning to tell him. Wondered, but didn't acknowledge it. "She was there almost immediately."

"So unless Larry was doing something like hosting a prayer meeting, he doesn't have an alibi."

"Odds are he was alone," I said.

"And he had one humongous clump of motive."

"Yes."

Charles leaned back in his chair and looked at me. "And it slipped your mind to tell Detective Adair about the real reason you were at Abe's?"

"I wouldn't say slipped, but I didn't tell him."

Charles's head bobbed up and down. "Because if you told him, Larry'd be sharing a cell with Mel."

"Adair would need more than that, but that's a valid point."

"Let's say that Larry did it, why would he shoot him when you were there?"

"Don't know, but Larry was mighty angry at Abe. Cindy was working so he was alone, and he knew when I'd be there, and could have figured that Abe would be at the door to meet me, or see me off."

Charles rubbed his left temple and gazed at a car parking in the small lot in front of the restaurant. "It would've taken a good shot from someone across the street to hit Abe. Does Larry even knows how to shoot a rifle?"

"Don't recall him saying anything. But that's not something that comes up in many conversations."

"So, we don't know if Larry was a good shot, but we do know that it doesn't take a whole hell of a lot of training for someone to take a piece of wood and smack a college student on the noggin'.""

My head began to hurt. In fewer than twenty-four hours one friend was arrested for murder and another good friend became, to me, the prime suspect in another killing. And, if I told the police what I knew, Larry would go to the top of the cop's suspect list. Could both Larry and Mel be guilty? They're headstrong, neither has an alibi, and if pressed under the right circumstance, they were capable of violence.

"Are you listening?" Charles said, jolting me out of my depressing thoughts.

"Sorry, what?"

"I said what are we going to do about it?"

Take three ibuprofen, get in bed and pull the covers up over my head, and wish it would all go away, I wished. "Find out what's going on."

"Right answer."

While Charles said it was the right answer, he also said he didn't have time to talk about it because he had to deliver some surf-stuff for Dude. Before he headed out, he said that he and Heather wanted to go to Crosby's Dock Party tonight and asked if Karen and I wanted to go with them. That was Charles-speak for could I drive. I reminded him that Karen was out of town, but that I'd go. He said great and asked for a ride. I said sure.

Chapter Twenty-One

I picked up Charles and then Heather at her tiny apartment in a former bed and breakfast that had been converted into apartments. Charles's aunt had lived there for the all-too-brief time that she had been with us on the island. Her death still hurt each time I saw the building and I knew it affected Charles, although having Heather there brought enough cheer to his life to neutralize some of his pain.

Crosby's Fish & Shrimp Co. was a family-owned seafood market by day, rented its dock and facilities for weddings and other special events, and, most every Friday evening, hosted a party featuring, to no one's surprise, fresh fish, beer, wine, and live music. The event had been a favorite for locals and enlightened vacationers for years, and garnered large crowds to enjoy the food, drink, and fantastic views of the sun sinking behind the water and marsh. I had attended a few times with Karen, and was surprised that Charles had wanted to venture this far off-island. On the mile-long drive over, I learned that attending was Heather's idea. She said that Charles needed to expand his horizons, and besides, she wanted to hear who her musical competition was. I thought, but didn't say, that no one could compete with Heather's vocal skills, although chalk scraping a blackboard would come close.

We arrived at five forty-five to find the gravel lot full even though the party didn't begin until six. I had to park along the road. Charles was quick to point out that if I wasn't late, we could have parked in Crosby's lot. I was equally quick to point out that he had said what time for me to pick him up. "Harrumph," was his articulate, clarifying response.

Not only was the lot full, but the dock was already packed and we had to stand in line to get drinks, and stand in a longer line to order supper. Charles sent Heather in search of a table, saying that she could use her charm and convince someone to move over and share the limited number of tables with us.

A thin, long-haired vocalist was under a covered portion of the dock singing "Sittin' on the Dock of the Bay" and accompanying himself on guitar. All the tables were full but by the time Charles and I had our food and drink, Heather had charmed two couples into sharing their table. Listening to the musician who had transitioned into "Leaving on a Jet Plane," hearing the sounds of the festive, Friday-night crowd, and watching the fishing boats bobbing in the water had the calming effect that I'd hoped for. The terror of the shooting and my worry about Larry and Mel were drifting away and I began to enjoy my shrimp, coleslaw, and hush puppies. A plastic cup of wine didn't hurt either.

The sounds of "Rainbow Connection" had ended and Heather noticed that the musician had taken a break and was talking to a young girl. Heather hopped up and said she needed to ask him something. She stood behind the curly-haired girl talking to the singer and Charles leaned close to me. "So, how're we going to figure out who killed the con guy and the student?"

There went my calm evening.

I looked at Heather who was now talking to the entertainer and laughing at something that he'd said. I turned back to Charles. "I'll call Sean Monday and see if he knows what Mel's attorney has learned."

"Why not talk to Mel's new lawyer?"

"He doesn't know me and wouldn't be able to tell me anything anyway. Mel's the client."

Charles thought a second. "What about Abe?"

"That's a tough one."

Before I could elaborate, Heather returned sporting a huge grin.

"That's Jerry." She pointed at the vocalist. "Jerry Crosby,

nice guy. I told him I was a singer and asked if he'd ever shared the stage with guest musicians."

If Jerry only knew, I thought, but kept my mouth shut.

Charles didn't. "What'd he say?"

"He said no, but he had a list of people who could sub for him if he couldn't make the weekly gig." She pantomimed writing on a large piece of paper and smiled even broader. "He said he would add me to the list. He was really nice." Heather air-strummed a guitar and returned to her seat and meal.

I prayed that Jerry had a long list as he started singing "Margaritaville."

If Charles's question hadn't put enough of a damper on my calming evening, a bucket of damper poured on my head when I saw Chief LaMond walking across the deck followed by two of her officers. I breathed a sigh of relief as she passed our table. She gave me a slight nod, and proceeded to the far end of the dock where some people were yelling and waving for her.

Charles dropped his fork on the plate and pushed away from the table. "Let's see what's going on."

I'd had enough police contact for the week, for that matter, for a lifetime, and declined, but that didn't stop my friend who followed Cindy and her colleagues to whatever was happening. I took a bite of shrimp but noticed that it didn't taste as good as it did before Cindy arrived. I felt bad about not telling Detective Adair the reason that I had been to see Abe and still had the nagging feeling that Larry could be connected to his murder. Heather was telling one of the couples who had given up part of their table to us that her new friend Jerry was going to call her when he needed a fill-in. She must have forgotten the definition of list.

Charles returned more quickly than I had anticipated. "No biggie. Some drunk was seeing double and walked off the second dock that was only in his pickled mind. He's soused and doused."

Heather laughed and I was relieved that Cindy hadn't been looking for me.

"Oh yeah," Charles said after he winked at Heather. "Chief LaMond wants to talk to you before she leaves."

There went my relief, as Jerry strummed the first notes of "Bye Bye Love."

The police "event" had ended and Cindy's two officers casually walked the drunk off the property; as casually as possible with a soaked, staggering, middle-aged, bald-headed gentleman being aided by two Folly Beach police officers as they inched their way through the crowd. Cindy moved to a more isolated section of the dock behind a small storage building and waved me over. I saw her motioning and she knew I saw her, so pretending that she didn't exist wasn't an option. Charles asked if he should go with me and I said no.

I smiled as I approached the unsmiling chief. "Have fun out there?" I pointed to where the drunk had been pulled out of the drink.

Cindy shook her head. "It's the beginning of the weekend. It'll only get worse."

She took me by the elbow and moved us farther away from the crowd and music.

"Chris," She glanced at the wood deck, "we've known each other since when?"

"Since the day you got here. What, seven years or so?"

"About right. You came to my wedding; you've had faith in me even when I didn't; hell, you were even a big supporter and encouraged Brian Newman to appoint me chief despite the griping of a bunch of Folly-freaks."

I nodded and wondered where she was going with the trip down memory lane.

"It's hard to be mad at a good friend." She continued to look down. "But Chris, you've done it." She looked up at my face and shook her head. "What in holy-hell were you thinking when you lied to Detective Adair?"

I had asked myself the same thing several times. I hesitated before answering, but said, "Technically I didn't lie. I did want to know more about reverse mortgages."

Cindy tapped her polished shoes on the deck and took a deep breath. "Did you talk to him about the mortgages?"

"No."

She smacked her fist on the side of the building. "Have you talked to Detective Adair since we were in his car?"

"No."

"You never told him that Larry had asked you to talk to Abe, or that Larry knew the con artist."

"No. I didn't lie about it. I just didn't bring it up." I knew it was a pathetic argument as I said it.

She gritted her teeth, her fists were clinched. "Damn it. Why not?"

I glanced at our table and Charles was motioning for me to "invite" him over. I ignored his gyrations. Cindy was angry and I didn't need Charles to either defend me or take Cindy's side.

I turned back to the chief. "Because it would have implicated your husband."

Cindy blinked, started to speak, and then looked away from me and toward the water. I waited and she turned back toward me. "Are you serious? Do you think Larry killed Pottinger?"

"Do you?"

"No." Her fists were still clinched and she shook her head. "You think he did, don't you?"

"Cindy, I don't think so. I've known him longer than I've known you. He's been up front with me about everything, and we've been together in tight situations. He's helped me out of a jam or two, and has even used his pre-going-straight skills to help me catch a killer. I also know he was awfully mad at Abe and worried that your career and reputation would be hurt if Abe carried through with his threat."

"I thought I knew you better than that, Chris. There's no way. No way."

"You do know me that well, Cindy, but leave me out of it for a minute. Look at it like this. Does Larry have an alibi? You were working when Abe was shot."

"Yes, but—"

"Hold it," I interrupted. "Would he have known how to use a rifle? Could he have hit Abe from across the street?"

Cindy looked down at the pier and mumbled, "He used to hunt deer, but ... but you know he wouldn't—"

I put my palm up to her face. "Cindy, I may know that he wouldn't have done it, but I still have doubts. How would this sound to a detective who doesn't know either of you? Larry had motive, a good one. He has no alibi. And as a hunter, he knew his way around guns, so he would have means."

"He didn't do it."

"I'm not saying he did, but think about it. You're a cop. What would you do if faced with a situation like this?"

"I don't have to think about anything." She glared at me. "Larry had nothing to do with the murder, and I damned well don't appreciate it that you even think that he might have. Thanks a hell of a lot, *friend.*"

She turned and jogged off the deck.

I gazed out over the water, and listened to Jerry Crosby sing, "Help Me Make It Through the Night."

I took a minute to calm down before returning to the table. I'd had a few minor disagreements with Cindy over the years, but nothing approached tonight's outburst. She saw it as an attack on Larry, and to be honest, it may have been. I had doubts about his innocence, and if Cindy looked at it objectively, she would have questions. I leaned over the railing and looked at the black water below and then closed my eyes and tried to visualize the person hurrying away from the fence at the tennis court. Could it have been Larry? I had nothing to help me judge the person's height, but my first reaction was the person wasn't tall, so yes, it could have been him, then again it could also have been countless other people.

Heather was mouthing the lyrics to "Me and Bobby McGee" as Jerry sang it from the bandstand, Charles's arm was draped over her shoulder, and the others at the table were enjoying the fine weather, friends, and music. I was miserable.

I returned to the table but instead of sitting, I said, "Ready to go?"

Heather looked at Charles and he looked up at me and at his wrist. "There's an hour to go. Why—"

I interrupted, "I'll walk home and get the car from your apartment in the morning." The last place I wanted to be was around a bunch of people having a good time. I grabbed my keys and tossed them to Charles. I headed for the road and home.

I hadn't walked more than a few hundred yards when my car pulled off the road in front of me.

Charles opened the driver's door and yelled. "Old people shouldn't be walking that far. Get in."

I started to argue and tell him to go back to the party, but decided that it would have been to no avail and instead climbed in the back seat.

Charles said that it was getting too cold to stay at the party. It wasn't. He said that Heather was getting tired of the music. Impossible. And as he pulled up in front of her apartment, he said that it was looking like rain and they decided to leave before a downpour arrived. There wasn't a cloud in the sky.

"So, what in the pluff-mud's going on?" Charles had returned to the car after walking Heather to the door. I had moved to the seat that Heather had vacated.

I told him about my discussion—argument—with Cindy.

"What did you expect? You were accusing her hubby of murder. That'd piss anyone off."

"I understand, but I wanted her to look at it from an outsider's perspective."

"Did you miss the part about Larry being her hubby?"

We were still in the gravel lot in front of Heather's building.

I hated it when Charles was right. "Probably."

Charles looked at the building and then at me. "You think he could've done it, don't you?"

"Don't you?"

"Yeah," Charles mumbled.

"I don't want to believe it. My heart says he didn't. I know Larry fairly well, but I know that if given enough motivation people are capable of things that would never enter their mind. Larry's protective of Cindy and he saw Abe's threats as an attack on her."

I looked over at Charles, miraculously, he remained silent.

"There's more," I said. "I know why I didn't tell Detective

Adair about my reason for meeting with Abe, but now what do I do?"

"You wanted to protect your friends. I would have done the same."

"But now what? Cindy was angry because I didn't tell him. But if I tell him, it'll put Larry at the top of the suspect list."

"What if he did it?"

A sharp pain developed behind my eyes, my legs felt heavy, and I wondered why I had moved to Folly. "Then he should be arrested," I whispered.

"Even if Abe was a con artist, blackmailing son-of-a-scorpion?"

"Yeah."

"Okay," Charles said. "Let's don't get the caboose before the engine. Let's say Larry was sitting in his house figuring how many toilet seats to order when the blackmailer became dead. Who pulled the trigger?"

"If Larry's right about Abe not changing his spots, there could be several people he's either ripped-off or tried to rip off before he ever crossed the Folly River. Even members of .5 could have motive. We don't know if any of them have already fallen for his reverse mortgage scheme or if Theo has invested his significant wealth in something that Abe was pushing. In addition to club members, there could be others here who feel that he took advantage of them."

"Wouldn't we have heard if any of the .5 group felt that he ripped them off?" Charles said.

"Probably. Those folks don't hesitate to gripe."

"And gripe, and gripe, and gripe."

I smiled, for the first time in hours.

"But," Charles continued, "would that be enough reason for one of them to shoot him?"

I nodded. "What are the two most common reasons people are murdered?"

"Love or money," Charles said without hesitation.

I nodded again.

"Same reasons people get married," Charles added. "Doubt

Abe would have been killed for love; who could love that viper?"
He hesitated and then tapped the steering wheel. "Hmm, money,
yeah. But doesn't that bring us back to Larry? Fifty-thousand
smackers is a hefty amount of motive."

"And he'd be protecting the love of his life—love and
money."

"Chris, you know how to ruin a perfectly nice evening."

We left the parking lot and drove the short distance to
Charles's apartment. I realized that tomorrow the—our—walking
group would be making another mini-excursion, and told him that
instead of opening the gallery, I'd meet him at the pier.

"Good. Then we can ask which one shot Abe."

On my way home, I decided that Charles's direct approach
would be unwise, and unproductive, but did start thinking about
the possibility that one of the .5 members did it. Was it wishful
thinking to get Larry off the hook? And what should I do about
telling Detective Adair the truth about my fateful trip to Abe's
house? My head continued to hurt and sleep waited until three
o'clock to arrive.

Chapter Twenty-Two

I met Charles at the foot of the Folly Pier. The morning was cool and there were already a dozen cars in the lot, and four men nodded to us as they pulled their fishing carts to the pier's ramp. Charles was decked out in a long-sleeve, UNLV scarlet and gray T-shirt, gray cargo shorts, gray tennis shoes, canvas Tilley, and his cane.

"A gray day?" I said.

"Semi-mourning for Abe. Thought the group would appreciate it, but couldn't quite go for black since he was a lying, cheating, blackmailing sleazeball."

I must have thought even less of Abe since I had on an orange polo shirt, unadorned with any marketing logos, my usual tan shorts, and Tilley; nothing gray except my mood.

"So," said Charles, "now that you won't let me ask the group who wiped out one of their members, what's our plan?"

"Charles, you claim to be the detective, what do you think we should do?"

"Other than asking who did it?"

I nodded.

"Hmm," He rubbed his chin. "Got it. A friend of mine, who happens to be standing in front of me, had been known to say, 'You learn more from listening than you do by talking.' I think he meant that we already know everything we say, but can learn from the other person."

I nodded again. "Good. You do listen at times."

"What?"

Charles had managed to get me to smile; the first of the day. I hoped not the last.

"What are we listening for?" he asked.

"Anything out of the norm."

He turned and watched Chester's Grand Marquis inch its way into the lot followed by Cal's classic 1971 Cadillac Eldorado. "With that group, we need to listen for something that sounds normal."

Harriet hopped out of the land yacht followed by David Darnell, Connie, and Theo. Chester slowly pulled himself out of the driver's seat by holding on to the door.

Chester watched Cal and William exit the Cadillac. "Those two beansprouts said there weren't enough cubic feet left in my car so they caravanned with us."

Cal tipped his sweat-stained Stetson toward Charles and me. In addition to a Stetson, Cal wore bright-red, shiny jogging shorts, a black T-shirt with *Amarillo by Morning* in silver script on the front, and his cowboy boots that had to be as old as his Stetson, which dated to the 1970s. I smiled and thought about Charles's comment about normal.

He also had a black ribbon tied around his upper arm, a ribbon identical to those worn by the other recent arrivals. Normal?

Chester held out two ribbons. "Let me tie these on you. I thought since we lost Abe, we should honor his memory and mourn the loss. He was a valued member of .5 and the first of our close-knit group to leave us."

"Crap," Connie said. "We didn't lose him; he's dead. Besides, we hardly knew the man. I, for one, don't plan to miss him much."

David put a hand on Connie's arm. "Now Connie, a loss of one is a loss for all."

"What the hell does that mean?" Harriet blurted.

Charles leaned over to me and whispered, "Normal must be taking a later bus."

William, who does better at avoiding the mundane and pettiness around him, said, "What will be our destination this fine morning?"

"After some debate on the ride over, we decided we would get adventurous and stroll west on Arctic Avenue to where it intersects with Third Street and then up Third to Cooper, over to Center, and back to the house. It will be our longest walk yet, another step in preparation for our goal of reaching Boneyard Beach."

Chester's "adventurous" and "longest walk yet" consisted of four normal-length blocks with two short blocks thrown in. It may be another step toward the goal, but only a baby step.

"Let's get going," Harriet said. "It'll take us all day at this pace."

Theo said, "Huh?"

Harriet put her arm around his bony shoulder and yelled into his ear. "This way, Theo."

Connie walked with Theo and Harriet toward Arctic Avenue. Harriet moved close to Theo and kept her arm around his waist.

The rest of us followed Theo and his escorts. Chester hung back with Charles and me.

"We're all bummed about Abe. I had trouble herding them in the car; they wanted to stand around and mope. Who would have wanted him dead?"

"Don't know," Charles said. "You have any idea?"

It was better than asking Chester if he killed him.

Chester looked ahead to the group that had Theo picking up the rear, still aided by Connie and Harriet. Chester leaned closer to Charles and me. "Between you, me, and the lamppost, I say good riddance."

There wasn't a lamppost within a hundred yards. "Didn't trust him?" I asked.

"I could be wrong," Chester said, "but I've been around the block a few times, and like I told you the other day, I had the feeling that he had a con or two in him."

"Anything specific?" I asked.

"*Too good to be true*, popped in my head when he started talking about those backward mortgages."

Always-correct Charles interrupted. "Reverse mortgages,"

"Whatever," Chester said. "If they were so good, why didn't other companies pay as much as his? Think he had the gals snowed." He hesitated and pointed toward Theo's escorts. "David was also asking him a bunch of questions like he was interested. Seems that since he's an insurance agent, he'd know all about that stuff. Maybe he was just curious. Oh well, just seemed strange."

"Anything else?" Charles asked.

Chester looked at the group that was already past the Oceanfront Villas, a half block ahead of us. "We need to step it up," Chester said. "Don't want them to think their leader is a slacker."

We picked up the pace and Charles picked up the questions. "Anything else?"

"Nothing in particular," Chester said. "Didn't like the way he was sucking up to Theo."

"How?" Charles asked.

"On the way over, Theo said something about investing in a good deal that Abe showed him. That's all I know. You could ask him, he seemed to want to talk but the only person who seemed to understand what he was saying was David."

We had caught up with Theo, Harriet, and Connie—not too difficult since they were barely moving.

Connie leaned close to Theo and yelled, "That's too bad. We'll miss him."

Theo lowered his head. "We were meeting today."

Charles moved beside Connie and walked laboriously slow with the trio. "Hey, Theo, who'd you say you were meeting?"

Connie stepped back so Charles could get closer.

"Had an appointment with Abe after today's walk. I had a check ready to give him so he could put me in a special stock offering he told me about."

Charles had to yell for Theo to hear him, and Theo shouted everything he said. The rest of the group was well ahead of us, but seemed to slow, almost stop, when Theo started talking about a check and meeting Abe.

Chester said, "That's what he was talking about in the car."

I moved closer to Theo. "What kind of investment?"

Theo looked over to see who was talking. "Hush, hush," he said. "New company, going public next week. Abe said it'd make Microsoft look like a lemonade stand. Said he'd triple my million dollars overnight. Showed me a prospectus and letters from big-wigs in the industry saying it'd be the biggest thing since the iPhone."

Harriet was still holding on to Theo's arm. "Now Theo, remember I told you to check it out before giving him the money."

He huffed. "I did. Read the prospectus and called one of the experts Abe told me about. Guy out in Silicon Valley. He was real knowledgeable about the stock. Said it was a sure thing."

Having a second person involved reminded me of how Abe had used Larry as his security specialist when he was conning businesses in Atlanta.

I asked, "Could I see the prospectus?" That was the first thing that Abe was hawking that could be verified.

Theo shook his head. "No way. It was so confidential that Abe took it right back. Said if it got in the wrong hands, it could squelch the deal."

That made no sense, but I didn't see an upside of telling him so. "How about the expert's phone number in California?"

"Abe let me use his phone and he punched in the number. Sorry." He looked back down at the roadway and shook his head. "And then someone went and killed him. Such a shame."

"Now, Theo," Connie said, "you don't need the money the stock would have made you. You'll be fine."

"I know, I know. Just hate to pass on a golden opportunity."

The leaders of the group had passed the public restrooms and were stopped at the corner of West Ashley Avenue waiting for a break in the traffic so they could cross one of Folly's main streets. Chester yelled, "Wait for us!"

David waved for us to hurry. "Then speed it up, ET."

Theo, aka ET, said, "What?"

"They're waiting for us," Connie said.

A rather generous translation, I thought.

"Have we learned anything useful yet?" Charles whispered

as we caught up with the frontrunners—frontcrawlers.

"No prospectus, no one to contact about the 'sure thing,' and Theo ready to hand Abe a check for a million dollars. That adds up to a con, regardless how you spin it."

Charles nodded. "Then who killed him?"

The entire group, excluding the late Abe Pottinger, was now standing beside West Ashley Avenue waiting for the traffic to thin enough for us to make it across the street, when the conversation took a troubling turn.

David said, "Anybody know the guy who owns the hardware store?"

"Sure," Chester said. "Larry."

Charles said, "Why?"

David took off his black NRA ball cap, wiped sweat from his forehead, and looked at Charles. "Since I'm the newbie, I was just wondering."

Just wondering would never cut it with Charles. "Why wondering?"

Chester yelled, "Go!" before David answered.

We made it safely across the street and the group gathered around David.

"Don't know if I should say anything." David then hesitated and looked at each of us.

"Sure you should," Charles said, afraid that David would clam up.

"Well, I was in Pewter the day before Abe, umm, passed away. With the house we bought, I'm afraid I've become a regular at the hardware store. Anyway, I was picking up some caulk for the shower and to see if they had .22 caliber cartridges and Larry and Abe were in the back. They didn't see me."

"And?" Charles said.

"And, they were in the middle of, how shall I say this, a heated discussion."

"Like a fight?" Chester said.

David had become the center of attention. "More like an argument, no blows were thrown."

"What were they jawin' about?" Cal asked.

"I feel bad saying all this, seeing that Abe's no longer with us." He glanced down at the black ribbon on his arm.

Charles tapped David with his cane. "It's okay."

"I didn't catch all of it, but Larry said something about Atlanta. And, Abe said prison, but I didn't catch what he meant. He said that Larry had better watch out."

I felt a knot tighten in my stomach. This was a topic I would prefer to have stayed buried.

Cal stepped closer to David. "What'd he mean?"

"Don't know. He could've been warning Larry about something." He hesitated and looked at the road. "Or I guess it's possible that he was threatening him."

Charles asked, "Was that all they said?"

"That's all I caught. That's why I was wondering if any of you knew Larry."

Harriet said, "You think Larry shot Abe?"

William looked at Harriet and then around to the rest of us and broke his silence. "Perhaps I am speaking out of turn, but I've known Mr. LaMond, Larry, for perhaps more years than anyone here, other than possibly Charles. I find him to be an upstanding, honorable, honest, and quite pleasant individual. I cannot even find it in my imagination to picture him assassinating Mr. Pottinger."

I could only imagine what William and the rest of the group would think if they knew what I knew about Larry. They won't hear it from me.

Cal said, "I agree with William,"

Chester chimed in, "Me too."

"I'm not accusing him of anything," David said. "I don't know anything about the man other than he's been pleasant and helpful when I've been in the store. I simply found their disagreement odd in light of what's happened."

"David," Chester said, "I think you should tell the police? It might help their investigation."

"I don't know. I don't want to get someone in trouble for nothing. I really didn't hear enough to say much."

Connie had remained quiet throughout the conversation, and I was surprised when she said, "I think you need to go to the cops. They were on the radio this morning asking for information. What you heard may not mean anything to you but you never know where it might tell the police."

"Connie's right," Harriet said. "We owe it to Abe. Anything that'll help find his killer."

Theo looked at Connie and then over at Harriet. "Y'all talking about that dead kid who was killed by the queer boat captain?"

None of us were, but that got everyone's attention.

Harriet moved closer to Theo and said, "What boat captain?"

"Melville, or something like that. Don't hear good sometimes, so I could have the name wrong. He's the que—, umm, homosexual who takes drunken kids out into the marsh to do who knows what."

Charles moved closer to Theo. "The captain's name is Mel not Melville. His name is Mel Evans. What makes you think he killed the student?"

"Everyone knows he did," Theo said as he looked around the group.

"That's what I heard," Connie said. "Didn't you hear it, Harriet?"

"Yeah, but I didn't pay no mind to it. Rumors are as thick as gnats around here."

Cal stepped closer. "Gall darn it," he took off his Stetson and waved it toward the others. "Let's don't go off believing everything we hear. Let me tell you something, I know Mel and he's a fine man. He's rough around the edges. Some of you already know that. He saved my life a while back with the help of these youngsters here; almost got himself killed in the process." He pointed his Stetson at Charles and me. "He's a good man, yes he is."

"But he is gay," Chester said.

"A big freakin' so what?" Cal said. "Live and let live, that's what I say."

Charles looked at Theo and then at Harriet and Connie. "Any reason to think he killed the student other than both of them may—I repeat—may be gay?"

A large beer-delivery truck rounded the corner and drowned out Harriet's words.

The truck moved away and Theo said, "What?"

"He speaks for all of us this time," Charles said. "Harriet, what'd you say?"

"Said that Connie's brother told her that he knew Mel killed him." She turned to Connie. "Didn't you?"

Connie gave Harriet a look that could by no stretch of the imagination be considered positive, and then turned to me. "Yeah, Robbie told me that he knew, but wasn't going to say anything. Said he couldn't prove it and sure didn't want 'Mad Mel,' that's what he called him, to know that he snitched him out. He's called *Mad* for a reason, you know." She turned to Harriet. "I didn't tell you so you'd broadcast it to everyone."

Harriet returned her glare, and yanked her shoulders back. "Up yours, Connie! It's not everyone, only our group, and we were talking about it."

Everyone tried to ignore her but she was so loud that even Theo heard her.

"Okay, okay," Chester said and leaned in the direction we were supposed to be heading. "We've rested long enough. Let's get moving, we're only halfway through our walk."

William had stepped out of the fray. "A superb suggestion."

David, who had started the discussion, said, "I agree with Chester. Besides, it doesn't matter what we think, the police have that man in jail so they must know he did it."

The knot in my stomach continued to tighten as we resumed our hike. David and Cal took the lead, Theo, along with Harriet, who was helping to guide and encourage him, fell to the back of the group, and the rest of us bunched together in the middle.

"Connie," I said. "Did your brother say that he knew that Mel had killed the student?" I had moved up beside Connie and Charles leaned in from the other side to hear what I was saying.

"Big mouth Harriet," she mumbled, but then looked at me.

"That's what he said, but I don't know if it's true."

"I'd like to ask him. Know where he is?"

Charles was on the other side of Connie and gave me a thumbs-up.

"Not really, but I know that he and the other tour-boat guys are meeting tonight at the Surf Bar. They meet once a month, but I think tonight's get-together is something different. They're trying to figure out how they can distance themselves from the murder. Robbie said that it sure will be good to have one less boat captain out there, but the murder will hurt business in the short haul. Let me give you his cell number."

She took her phone out of her fanny pack and showed me his number. I plugged it in my phone and she excused herself saying that she needed to slow down enough for Harriet and Theo to catch us. "Think she's trying to get her hooks into old ET," she said and chuckled. "I think he's sweet on me, but I need to remind him that he is. His memory." She shrugged.

Twenty minutes later, the group gathered on Chester's porch. Harriet griped about how her feet hurt from the walk; Chester went around high-fiving everyone for completing the long walk; David said that he needed to buy more life insurance on himself if Chester "made" him walk more; and Connie brought Theo a glass of lemonade. William had a grin on his face and said that it was a "refreshing experience," and Cal strummed an air guitar and sang, "Six days on the road and I'm gonna make it home tonight."

Charles and I inched away from the group and conspired about how we were going to just happen to be at the Surf Bar tonight, and to be surprised when we saw the captains. Then we were going to invite ourselves to join them. Not a great plan, but the best we could come up with after the exhaustion from .5's longest walk ever.

Chapter Twenty-Three

Our plan to meet at the Surf Bar was thwarted by an early-spring thunderstorm, so I picked Charles up at his apartment and found a parking spot a block from the popular watering hole. We entered, shook water off our hats, and looked around for the captains. They were nowhere to be seen, so we ventured to the patio where they were huddled around a table in the corner. The table closest to them was vacant so we sat with our backs facing the group. They were in animated conversation and wouldn't have noticed if a rhinoceros had parked its ample rear in a chair beside them. There were three captains, three times that many empty beer bottles on the table, and each man had a grip on another bottle. They had arrived long before the rain.

Loud splats of rain hitting the roof and the din of happy diners at four nearby tables made it difficult to hear what they were saying, but Timothy was the loudest and I caught bits of conversation.

He was fuming and didn't try to hide it. I turned to watch the group and caught "Hell yes, he did it," and "Can you believe that macho queer making a pass at a college student forty years younger than him?"

Nemo pounded his hand on the table. "I don't give a rat's posterior who he was hitting on. He's given us a bad name."

Robbie took off his FB cap and rubbed his bald head. "All we have to do is weather the storm, and we'll make more money with him gone. Hope he fries."

Robbie finished his beer, held the bottle in the air to get the waitress's attention, and spotted us. He put his arm down and leaned closer to his two tablemates. Out of the corner of my eye, I caught him put his forefinger to his mouth and say "Shhh," and something about "…friends…Mel."

Charles was closer to their table and heard the rest of what Robbie had said. That was all it took. Charles leaned his chair back and almost touched Nemo's arm. "Oh, hi guys. Didn't see you there until I heard you talking about Mel." He turned his chair toward the captains and scooted it closer to their table. "Mind if we join you?"

It was a moot question since his chair was now closer to their table than to ours.

Nemo had on the same *Hard Rock Café, Toronto* T-shirt that he'd worn the first time we'd met him here and his hair was still pulled in a ponytail. He glanced over at Robbie and then Timothy. Neither of them said yes or no, and Nemo said, "Why not. It's raining old ladies and sticks out there. We're not going anywhere."

Charles pulled his chair closer to their table. "Doing what?"

Nemo scooted his chair to the left so Charles could get closer to the table. "It's a Welsh idiom. It means the same thing as raining cats and dogs."

"Damned PhD talk," Robbie said.

I suspected the other two would have given Nemo several reasons why we shouldn't join them if Charles and I hadn't been listening.

Before Nemo had finished his Welsh idiom lesson and his feeble okay, Charles pointed to their empty bottles. "Next round's on me."

I knew who *round's on me* referred to, but it appeared to mitigate our invasion.

Robbie's hand holding the beer bottle went back in the air and the waitress returned for the additional drink orders.

"Terrible about what happened to Mel, wasn't it?" Charles said like he hadn't heard what they had been saying.

Once again, Nemo glanced at his fellow captains and

turned to Charles. "Never good when something bad happens to someone in your group."

Timothy said to no one in particular, "If Mel killed that kid, he needs to be thrown in jail."

I leaned closer to the table and to Robbie. "Glad we ran into you, Robbie. I was talking to your sister and she said that you knew for certain that Mel did it."

Robbie looked at the beer bottles and then up at me. "I may have said it, but if I had to swear on a stack of Bibles, I'd say I don't know."

"Why'd you tell her that you knew?" Charles asked.

Timothy interrupted. "I'll tell you why, because it's true. It doesn't take a genius to see that if Mel had put the make on that kid while they were at that deserted beach, the kid would have been repulsed. Mel had to shut him up, plain and simple."

Nemo pointed his empty beer bottle at Timothy. "You don't know that for a fact. Just because Mel's gay, doesn't mean he did anything wrong."

"Queer and living with a nig...an African man, you mean," snarled Timothy.

"Timothy, don't be such an ass," Robbie said. He turned to Charles and then to me. "Sorry guys, we're all shook about this. Timothy doesn't mean anything bad about it. Mel's okay."

Didn't mean anything bad, right, I thought.

Nemo glared at Robbie. "You think he did it too? Don't get all apologetic and saccharine because Mel's buddies are here."

Robbie shook his head. "All I said was if Mel wasn't taking so much of our business, we would have enough to survive. To your question Charles, I don't know if Mel killed him."

Nemo pointed to the empty bottles in front of Robbie. "Not what you said two beers back."

Timothy reached toward Nemo and accidently knocked over an empty bottle. "It's such a mess," Timothy said. "My wedding's going down the crapper." He waved his hand around toward Robbie and Nemo. "Our business sucks. This murder has everybody nervous. Crap, it's a mess."

"George W. Bush said, 'It will take time to restore chaos

and order.'"

It was only a matter of time before Charles tried to top Nemo's Welsh idiom.

Robbie took off his FB cap and pointed it at Charles. "You're worse than Nemo with weird talk."

Nemo ignored Robbie. "Chaos is already here."

It didn't take Nemo's PhD to figure that out.

The waitress returned with the drinks and cleared the empties off the table.

Charles took a sip and looked at Nemo. "So you think that Mel killed the student?"

Nemo said, "You bet." The other two nodded.

For the next twenty minutes, the captains shared a lot of bantering, mild arguments, countless reasons why business was down, and somehow how it was all Mel's fault. Their speech began to slur, and I realized that we had learned all we were going to.

Rain, old ladies and sticks, and cats and dogs continued to pound the roof, and I wondered if there was a Welsh idiom for throwing Mad Mel under the bus, or in this case, boat.

Chapter Twenty-Four

Charles and I hadn't had as much to drink as the other three guys, but the next morning my head felt like it had a balloon inflating in it. I had drifted in and out of sleep and was nowhere near rested when I pulled myself out of bed. I kept thinking of Mel on Boneyard Beach with the students and not being able to come up with any scenario for him to harm the student. It also bothered me that a group of his colleagues would have jumped to the conclusion that he was guilty based on his sexual orientation. It seemed more like wishful thinking to eliminate a competitor. They were homophobic, but were they so petty to want him out of the way because of his competition? Or was I that wrong about Mel?

Then there was Abe's murder. I knew Larry better than I knew Mel, but realized that there were dark corners of his past that he'd never shared. He and Cindy had a whirlwind romance and were married after knowing each other a few months. Did she know what he was capable of? And finally, why did I open myself to serious problems by not telling Detective Adair the reason that I was at Abe's? Was friendship worth going to jail over?

I didn't have ready answers, but I knew one thing. I had to mend fences with Cindy. We had been good friends for a long time and I hated how our conversation at Crosby's had ended. Instead of sulking around the house, I called to see if she was available for lunch. At first she hesitated and started making excuses, but then said she could find an hour for me. We agreed to meet at Rita's for an early meal.

I arrived ahead of Cindy and opted for an outdoor table. Last night's heavy rain had cleared out the humidity and it was turning out to be a nice day. I hoped that after my lunch with Cindy I felt the same way.

Since I'd arrived on Folly, Rita's Seaside Grille was the third iteration of a restaurant on one of the island's prime restaurant locations. The outdoor patio faced the Folly Pier, the Tides Hotel, and the Sand Dollar, Folly's iconic bar. Early lunch arrivals wore everything from bathing-suit cover ups, to dress shirts, and one table of diners had already started happy hour. My head throbbed when I saw five beer bottles on their table.

Cindy parked her unmarked car in front of the Pier, saw me, and smiled. A good sign, I hoped.

"So what's with the lunch invitation?" she asked as she sat across from me. Her smile was intact but didn't seem as sincere as it did when she was crossing the street.

No reason to beat around the bush. "I want to apologize."

She nodded. "I admire a man who starts a conversation that way. But since I'm not great at catching nuances, you'll have to explain what you're apologizing for."

The waitress arrived before I told her. I'd noticed over the years that police chiefs get quicker service than us common folks.

Cindy ordered a Pepsi and the "biggest, baddest" burger the chef could "fry up," and I stuck with a burger and told the waitress that it didn't have to be that big or bad.

The waitress headed to the kitchen. "Smartass," Cindy said, and wasn't referring to the waitress.

I didn't deny it. "I apologize for not telling Detective Adair why I was at Abe's." I hesitated but Cindy didn't say anything. "I was afraid that if I told Adair, he'd start looking at Larry for the murder."

Cindy stared at me and then said, "Of course he would, Chris. Any decent cop would, but because Larry had a gripe with Abe, didn't mean he killed him."

Gripe was an understatement. I took a deep breath, and said what I really wanted to tell her. "Cindy, it tears me up to say this, but part of me thinks that Larry may be guilty."

I waited for her to explode.

She continued to glare and then looked toward Center Street before turning back to me. "You've known Larry longer than I have, but I think I know him better than you do. I hope I do. He hadn't even mentioned Abe to me until he moseyed into town to stomp on Larry's happiness. Even now, I feel that there's a lot of their shared past that Larry's not talking about, and that's okay. We all have stuff hidden in caves and crannies that we don't want brought into the light of day." She grinned. "Some of the stuff I did back home when I was a youngin' would've given my parents reason to adopt me out if they found out; my preacher would've had to add extra sermons; and the local cops would've been shopping for more handcuffs. But I digress. To be honest, I've given a lot of thought about what happened. As a cop, I know he doesn't have an alibi and has more reasons to want Abe dead than he did for him to live. And ...."

She broke eye contact and looked down at her water; a tear ran down her cheek. I wanted to walk around the table and comfort her, but I knew that she would break my arm before she'd let me hug her in front of a dozen people.

She looked up, wiped the tears from her cheek with the back of her hand. "Do I think Larry killed him?" she said in a low voice, and moved her thumb and forefinger about an inch apart. "Part of me does, but I want with all my heart to believe that he didn't. I have to believe that, I do."

I resisted reaching across the table for her hand. "I know."

She blinked back another tear and wiped her nose with her napkin, and said, "I won't tell you what to do, and I'll still love you—in a sisterly sort of way, of course." She tried to smile but failed. "I'll love you regardless what you choose to do."

I took a deep breath. "I'm going to tell Adair why I was there. I know it might get you in trouble; I suppose I'll be in trouble too; and worse of all, it will put Larry in Adair's crosshairs."

"Do what you have to."

"Cindy, last year when members of First Light church were getting killed, I underestimated another one of the detectives,

Michael Callahan. Other than Karen, I had little faith in the detectives from the sheriff's office."

"With good reason," she said.

"True. Regardless, Callahan came through, and from what I hear, Adair is as good. I need to trust him. If Larry's innocent, and my gut tells me that he is, Adair will find the killer."

"Do you think he didn't do it?"

"Yes, the more I think about it, it wouldn't have made sense for him to shoot Abe that night."

"Because you were at Abe's house and Larry wouldn't have risked hitting you?"

"That, and because Larry had no idea what Abe and I had discussed and what we may have agreed to. If he'd bought my story about Larry not having any money and your hubby's plan to tell everyone about his past, there wouldn't have been a reason to shoot him."

"True, but—"

Her cell phone interrupted. She looked at the screen, said she had to take the call, and walked to the back of the patio.

Our food arrived while Cindy was on the phone.

I watched as she said a few words, listened for what seemed like an eternity, said a few more words, and listened more. She took the phone from her ear, muttered a profanity, and returned to the table.

"Everything okay?"

She plopped back down in her chair. "You're not going to like it."

I motioned for her to continue.

"That was Detective Cox."

The name wasn't familiar. "Who?"

"He's one of the detectives working with Adair on the Drew Casey case. I met him last year; seems like an okay guy. He used to surf over here so he's familiar with Folly."

"And why won't I like what he said?"

"I called him the other night and he said he'd let me know what they had on Mel. He was vague and said that he wasn't sure he could get into it until Mel's attorney got all the information.

They've got it now." She took a bite of burger.

I still didn't hear an answer in what she had said, but, unlike Charles, I was going to let Cindy tell me when she felt like it.

She looked around the patio and leaned closer. "When they searched Mel's house, they found a bloodstained rag in an old tool box in the garage."

My heart sank. "The kid's blood?"

She nodded.

I looked at a young mother carrying her crying toddler to the side exit and then toward the ocean. "Mel's not stupid," I said. "Why would he keep something as obvious as a rag with the kid's blood in his garage? He's being framed."

"There's more. One of the students who was on the boat swears that he saw Mel near where they found the body."

I tried to remember everything Mel had said about that night. Hadn't Mel said that he stayed with his boat except to go to the bathroom and then he went in the opposite direction of the group and from where Casey was killed?

"How did the witness recognize Mel in the dark? And, from what Mel had said, most everyone was almost drunk when they got to the beach and all were when they left. How credible is the witness?"

"I'm just repeating what Cox said." She tilted her head and lowered her voice even more. "Chris, even if it's almost dark, Mel's easy to recognize. It'd take a mighty high blood-alcohol content for someone to confuse him for a twenty-year-old college student. Cox is confident about their case."

Cindy had a valid point about recognizing Mel, but why would the ex-marine lie about staying with his craft if a dozen people—drunk or not—could have said otherwise?

"I think you're wrong about this one," Cindy said.

I had lost my appetite and pushed the fries around on my plate; the burger remained untouched.

I wondered if I was the only person who believed Mel was telling the truth, and more importantly, wondered how I could prove it. The weather was still beautiful, but my head was filled with storm clouds and fog.

Cindy had to get to the office for a meeting with one of her officers and thanked me for the apology and the food she had barely touched. She left through the side exit and I took a couple of bites of cold burger and realized that I was no longer hungry. There would never be a good time to call Detective Adair, so I called the cell number listed on the card he'd given me. Part of me wanted it to go to voicemail, but instead he answered and I told him that I had some information about the Pottinger shooting and thought he might be interested. He was quite interested and said that he'd be at my house in a half hour.

***

Detective Adair was more rumpled than he had been the last time we'd met. He still wore his like-new blazer, but his tan and blue striped tie had what looked like a mustard stain on it, and his white shirt had lost its starch. I invited him in and offered him my chair. He looked around for options; seeing none, he unbuttoned his blazer and sat. I offered him something to drink, and like during his previous visit, he declined.

He took the small notebook out of his pocket. "So what do you have?"

"I was shook and not thinking straight when we talked in Chief LaMond's car at Pottinger's house. I realized later that I forgot to mention something that you should know."

I gave him a summary of Larry's involvement with Abe and how Abe had attempted to blackmail him. I also shared how Larry had asked me to talk with Abe to see if I could get him to back off his blackmail plot.

Adair listened without interrupting and while he had a pen in his hand, he hadn't written anything. His face didn't give anything away. Maybe it wasn't going to be as bad as I had anticipated.

He started to speak and his facial features turned rigid. "Mr. Landrum, are you aware of what obstruction of justice means?"

"Vaguely."

"I'm certain that if I arrested you this second, your attorney would be glad to give you the legal definition. I can assure you that there's not a court in South Carolina that you wouldn't be convicted based on the cockamamie story you just told me." He sighed. "Do you expect me to believe that you were so shaken that you 'forgot' to tell me the reason you were there, and now several days later, it just popped into your head? How big a fool do you take me for? Wait, don't answer that, it'd just add more charges to the increasing list of crimes you've committed."

"Detective, I—"

He smacked his thigh with the notebook. "Silence. I'm not going to slap cuffs on you—now. But don't think I won't in the next five minutes unless. . ." He paused and glared at me.

If there had been a glass of water between us on the table, it would've turned to ice.

"Unless what?"

He took a deep breath, paused for what seemed like an eternity, and said. "I'm going to ask you to repeat your story, every detail, regardless how miniscule, and once you're finished, I'll decide what to do. Is that clear?"

"Perfectly."

He flipped open his notebook and readied his pen. "Begin."

Detective Adair wasn't kidding when he said every detail. For the next thirty minutes I shared everything from Larry's first comments about Abe Pottinger coming to town to when I looked across the street from Abe's house and saw the shooter walking away. And then throwing my two cents' worth in on why I didn't think it was Larry. Many details I shared multiple times.

"Does Chief LaMond know this?"

I hadn't mentioned while I was telling and retelling the story that Cindy had been present during the discussion about me approaching Abe, so I regressed to telling the truth, simply not the whole truth.

"I don't know how much Larry's told her."

He didn't push me on it and his glare lessened, but ever so slightly. "Mr. Landrum, you know more about the people here than I do. If Larry didn't shoot Pottinger, who did?"

"I wish I knew. Considering what Larry's told me about Abe, it could be anyone from his sordid past."

"Isn't it unlikely someone from out-of-state followed him?"

"Yes."

"So who here?"

I'd already withheld information from Adair that might end up getting me thrown in jail. Should I tell him about my thoughts that Abe was pulling a con on members of the .5? Thinking about the composition of the group, I couldn't imagine anyone being able to handle a rifle well enough to hit Abe from across the street.

"I don't know anyone. Sorry."

He gave me a skeptical look and shook his head.

"Mr. Landrum, you're not off the hook. I don't believe that you forgot to tell me about Larry. I'm not arresting you, and you can thank Karen, Detective Lawson, for that, but you're walking on paper-thin ice. One more thing." He gave a sly grin. "Here's a line I love to throw at suspects. Don't leave town."

I assured him that I wasn't and he stood to leave and I should have walked him to the door, but instead asked, "Learn anything from the bullet?"

He looked back at me. "The things I've heard about your meddling are true."

I shrugged.

"It's no secret. The damned reporters already have it and will be blabbing it to everyone. The bullet was .270 caliber. It's been around for decades; it's popular and easy to get; good for deer and elk hunting. There's nothing to be learned there, unless we have a rifle to test it against." He smiled, slightly more sincere this time. "If you come across one, please don't *forget* to let me know."

I told him I would and asked, if that caliber bullet would have been accurate from the fence across the street from Abe's.

"Why, afraid you were the target and the shooter missed and hit Pottinger?"

"Just wondering."

"Yeah, it's accurate from longer distances than that, but it still took someone who's done a lot of shooting, or the luckiest person on the island."

Chapter Twenty-Five

April showers may bring May flowers, but May showers are prone to bring flooding and areas of standing water to the Lowcountry. Overnight rains left a small lake in the front yard, flooded several streets, and gave early-morning kayakers a couple of new temporary streams, one through the middle of the historic market in Charleston. The storm had moved out and it looked like another nice day for the group's walk.

As was becoming habit, Charles and I met at the foot of the pier before the rest of the group arrived. I shared my conversation with Detective Adair. Charles asked what flavor of cake to bake a saw in. I told him that I failed to see the humor and he said that was because I was looking at it through my obstructing-justice eyes. He also asked if Adair had any leads and I said he didn't mention any, and that since I had become an obstructer of justice, I doubted that he would have been forthcoming with confidential information.

Chester's entourage arrived, followed by Cal's car, and everyone piled out excited about today's hike. More accurately, most of them moaned and groaned as the struggled to get out of the car, and Harriet complained about the cramped quarters and her aching back. After Chester acknowledged Charles and my presence and Cal joined us and said that William had to go to school for a meeting and wouldn't be walking today, Chester assumed his self-anointed leadership role.

He raised his hand in the air. "Okay walkers, here's the

plan. If we're going to achieve our lofty goal, we must push harder, so we're heading up Center Street to the Folly River Park. That's about twice as far as we went the other day and more than half as far as our trek to Boneyard Beach."

I was pleased that Chester didn't open today's route for debate. That cut five minutes off the time we usually wasted arguing.

Harriet shook her head and reminded all of us about her aching back. "Probably'll take us two or three days to make it."

"We can do it," David said.

Cal took two steps toward the street. "Let's head out."

Harriet looped her arm around Theo's and nudged him toward Center Street and the group's longest walk in recorded history.

Cal was already twenty yards in front of David and Connie. Theo, with the aid of Harriet, came next, and Chester, Charles and I lagged behind.

The black ribbons from the previous walk were absent.

I looked at Chester. "No ribbons?"

"Nope, we talked about it and decided the official mourning period's over. We didn't like him that much anyway."

Charles and I had made the walk from the pier to the Folly River Park many times. Unless Charles stopped to talk to everyone on the sidewalk, talk to each canine along the way, and stop for ice cream at Sugar Time, the trip took ten minutes. Today, after the first twenty-five minutes, I was beginning to believe Harriet's prediction that it may take three days. Charles, David, Cal, and I had moved a block ahead of the rest of the group. Fifteen minutes later my group was at the small park and spread out on the picnic table under the gazebo. Cal and David were talking about some of the cities in which Cal had played his distinct form of traditional country music when he toured the south, and Chester leaned against the table and rested.

Charles and I were nearby when Charles's ears perked up when David said, "Did you hear about Abe?"

The others had arrived and looked like that had walked across the Sahara desert. Cal gave his seat to Theo, and Harriet, who had been limping, squeezed in beside him. Chester leaned against the gazebo and Connie brought up the rear.

Chester looked at Harriet who was massaging her ankle. "What happened?"

"Twisted it on the sidewalk over there." She turned, winced, and pointed to the steps into the park.

"What about Abe?" Charles added. He wouldn't let a twisted ankle stand in the way from finding out what David was talking about.

David looked down at Harriet's ankle and then at Charles. "They were talking about his death, and—"

"Who was?" the information-bloodhound asked.

"The radio. Last night on the news. Something about him being suspected in a stock fraud case in Georgia a few years back and running a Ponzi scheme somewhere else."

"What's a Ponzi scheme?" Connie asked.

David looked around to see if anyone was going to answer. Seeing blank stares, he continued, "Where a crook takes your money and says he'll invest it and promises you great returns."

"What's wrong with that?" Connie asked.

Again, David looked around and failed to see any takers. "The crook only pretends to invest the money."

"So how does he pay the investors?" Connie asked.

"He pays the first few who bought in with money he gets from the next suckers. That way he tells others about how great the first group did, even gives them as references."

Chester had been taking in what David had been saying, and then interjected, "Then the crook skips town with all the money leaving everyone but the first people he brought in with an empty bank account and busted dreams?"

David nodded. "Exactly."

"Are you sure it's our Abe?" Connie asked.

David said, "Guess so. The news guy said Abe wasn't convicted but some others involved were in jail."

That was consistent with what Larry had said and I wondered if Detective Adair had known it when I was talking to him.

"What else did they say?" Charles added.

"That's all."

Cal asked, "Could that Ponzi thingee work with reverse mortgages?"

David looked around the group. "Suppose so, but I don't know how he'd get his money. He'd have the title on the houses but how could he convert that to cash if someone still lived in them?"

I wasn't an expert but had owned two rental properties before moving to Folly and had some experience with companies that bought large numbers of rentals. Most were legitimate, but some were sharks with big smiles and little consciences.

"Someone with deep pockets or investment companies could buy the paid-for houses from Abe at rock-bottom prices," I said. "They would have time on their side and wait until the person living in the house either died or moved because the reverse mortgage check would stop coming, and then the investors sell the houses for market value."

Charles said, "So the investors were crooks too?"

I nodded. "They would have had to know what was going on. And, Abe would have his money and skip town before the scheme started tumbling down."

"So wouldn't they get arrested?" Cal asked.

"Not necessarily," I said. "They would have legitimate titles to the houses they bought from Abe and could claim that they didn't know anything about his activities and how he got the houses."

Cal said, "All so danged confusing."

"Yep," Charles agreed. "Harry Truman said, 'If you can't convince them, confuse them.'"

"Wonder if his murder had something to do with all that?" Cal asked, sharing the question that most of the rest of the group probably felt.

"What?" Theo asked.

Harriet leaned to about an inch from his ear, and repeated what David had said about the radio report. Theo's faced dropped. "Oh my. It can't be our Abe."

I knew it was and suspected everyone else did as well.

David stepped forward. "Here's what I think. One of the swindlers from Georgia who isn't in jail shot Abe so he wouldn't testify against him or maybe one of the Ponzi financers wanted him eliminated. I bet Abe moved here to hide."

Harriet kept her arm around Theo's neck and turned to the rest of us. "Doesn't surprise me. I didn't think much of it at the time, but after we walked the other day I was talking to him about the reverse mortgage plan. He was acting skittish so I asked him what was wrong." She paused and looked around the park.

Charles asked, "What'd he say?"

"He hemmed and hawed but finally confided that he was afraid that someone from where he used to live had followed him. He said he was worried."

"Worried about what?" Charles asked.

Harriet looked at each of us and then focused on Charles. "He wouldn't say. I thought it was strange and asked him, but he laughed it off and said that he was just being paranoid. There was more to it than he was saying, but it was like he snapped out of it and continued talking about reverse mortgages."

"Did anybody else hear him mention being worried?" I asked.

David and William shook their heads.

Cal turned to me. "Tell you what pard, I may have. We were talking about stocks, bonds, and money-market stuff. Actually, he was doing all the talking; most of it went in one ear and out the other and the rest of it flew over my head like a jet plane. He said something about Atlanta and a friend who brought him into the business and how well he had done with it."

Charles said, "What's that have to do with someone following him?"

"He didn't say someone was here," Cal said. "But when he was talking about the other guy, he got more nervous."

I leaned close to Theo so he could hear. "Theo, you said that you'd seen Abe's prospectus about the stock he was wanting you to buy." Theo nodded. "You said he took it back." Theo nodded again. I looked at the others. "Anybody have a brochure or other material from the stock or the reverse mortgage company that Abe said he was working for?"

Chester shook his head and looked at Connie and David. Connie shook her head and David shrugged. Harriet said, "He told me that the product was so new that they hadn't had time to print anything about it. I remember he called it a jumbo reverse mortgage, if that means anything."

Other than sounding better than a regular, run-of-the-mill reverse mortgage, I doubted it meant much, and said, "So nobody got marketing materials?"

"He gave me a three-page application," Connie said and turned to Chester. "Hard to believe, but it was longer than your stupid application to get in this group."

Chester smiled.

Connie looked around the group. "You all got applications, didn't you?"

"Sure," David said. "It was a standard application. Looked like the ones I use for insurance."

"Did it have the name of the company on it?"

"Of course, but I don't remember what it was."

"Alexander Lifetime Security Inc." Harriet said. "Knew that because it was the same name that was on the paper that Theo filled out for the stock. Remember Theo?" She put her arm around his shoulder.

"Yes." Theo squeezed her arm and looked at me. "Are you saying that Abe wasn't on the up-and-up?"

The group didn't have benefit of what I had learned from Larry, and I wasn't going to get into it with them. It wouldn't take much of a leap to see that Abe's reverse mortgage, jumbo or otherwise, deal and the yet-to-go-public stock were scams.

"That's how it looks."

"Well, how's that for a kicker," Cal said.

"And I was ready to give him a million dollars," Theo said. "Am I stupid or what?"

"Of course you're not stupid, Theo," Cal said. "Thievin', egg-sucking, con artists are good at what they do. Anybody can be taken by them."

Harriet moved her arm from Theo's shoulder and put it around his waist. "It's lucky someone shot him when they did."

Chester stood and waved his hands. "Enough gruesome stuff. Sounds like we all got off lucky. I didn't give him any money, did any of you?"

No one responded.

"Good," Chester said. "Now I've got an important announcement." We all stopped and stared at our leader. "It came to me after watching some of us huffing-and-puffing, some of us wheezing, some of us limping, and some of us taking about a week to walk from the pier to here. I realized that the river over there will freeze over before we can walk to Boneyard Beach." He stopped and pointed in the general direction of the Lighthouse Inlet and Boneyard Beach.

I wanted to shout, "Duh!" Chester was serious so instead I frowned and nodded.

"Anyway," he continued, "don't fret. We're going to get to Boneyard Beach. After we get done today, I'm going to look for one of those marsh guides who can take us there without charging an arm and a leg. Seeing that our legs aren't working too well nowadays, that's important." He smiled at his weak joke. "Now," he turned serious, "don't try to protest and get all upset, I've made my decision and it's final."

I looked around the group and didn't see a glimmer of protest; thrilled would been how I would have described the reactions. Theo said that he thought it was the best idea he'd heard since, well, he said, "Since I don't know when." And Connie said that she was speaking for everyone else when she told him that he'd made a wise decision, and "probably prevented a heart attack or two."

We stayed at the park for another fifteen minutes until everyone's heart rate lowered to a pre-stroke level, and then we headed back. Along the way, Connie told Chester that if it was okay with him, she'd ask her brother if he'd take us to Boneyard Beach. Chester grinned. "Sure, but he'd better be cheap."

Mel would have been the perfect person to ferry the group, but since he was restricted to a jail cell, he wasn't an option.

Harriet mumbled something about Chester being a tightwad and griped about her sore ankle the entire walk back, and I decided that Chester should win the Noble Peace Prize for calling off the .5 walk to Boneyard Beach.

Chapter Twenty-Six

Morning began with sounds of a delivery-truck driver unloading cartons of produce at Bert's and a call from Cindy asking if I could meet her at her house. I asked when and she said the sooner the better; Larry was at work and she wanted to talk to me without him around. I said to give me fifteen minutes.

Ten minutes later, Cindy poured me a cup of coffee, and we moved to the back patio and she thanked me for coming.

Sun was rippling off the gently-rolling waves on the Folly River and a small fishing boat was beginning its morning quest for a bountiful catch. I sat back in a chair, sipped coffee, and waited for her to get to the reason for calling. She sat, looked around, and started to speak, hesitated, and shook her head. She was the picture of discomfort.

"Last night, Detective Adair and three deputies showed up with scowls and a search warrant for here, Larry's truck, and the store." She paused and I waited. "They were here two hours and then escorted Larry to the store and spent two more hours there. It was after midnight before he dragged his exhausted tush to bed."

I mumbled something about being sorry and asking what they were searching for.

"Adair, of course, wasn't specific; the warrant talked about pertaining to, knowledge of, blah, blah, blah about Abraham Pottinger. It's obvious that Larry and Pottinger had a prior relationship, and anything that would tie him to being at the scene of the crime was fair game."

All I could think was that none of this would have happened if I hadn't told Adair about Larry's conversation about Abe. "I'm sorry. What can I do?"

"You're the only person I can talk to about it. Larry said that he didn't do anything wrong so there wasn't anything to be concerned about. I tried to explain that from the detective's perspective, Larry was the most likely suspect."

"What'd he say?"

"He said he knew that but for me not to worry." She shook her head. "I can't talk to anyone at city hall; crap, I'm the police chief, for God's sake. I don't have any other close friends to yell and scream to about it. The way he's acting, I can't even have a sensible conversation with Larry. Chris. I know I can trust you, and you'll level with me about what you think."

"I appreciate that, but I don't know how I can help."

She looked at the river. "Talking helps."

"Did Adair find anything?"

"They sure as hell didn't find a rifle, but they took our computer, Larry's cell phone, and two pairs of his shoes."

I said, "The soil where the shooter stood is sandy and so is the path beside the tennis court. I suppose they're trying to trace samples from his shoes back to the park."

Cindy shook her head. "You've been in Pewter's side lot, it's covered with sand. Larry's there all the time fiddling with the pipes and lumber. I'm sure there's sand in his shoes. That doesn't prove anything."

I agreed. "Did Abe send Larry e-mails?"

"Don't know. The times I knew about them communicating, it was by phone or in person." She lowered her head. "Chris, I'm scared."

And had good reason to be, I thought, but said, "Larry's right, if he didn't have anything to do with it, they can't find convincing evidence that he did."

"I guess."

"Cindy, don't shoot me for asking this, but—"

"Bad choice of words."

"True, so don't get mad, but is there a chance that he did it?"

We'd covered this ground before, but I needed to keep going back to it. I wanted to push her to be as objective as possible.

I was expecting a blow-up or at least a nasty look. Instead, she whispered, "A powerful case could be put together that he did. But, I don't think so, I really don't." She looked up and shook her head. "Let me ask you something."

I nodded.

"You've known him for eight years, gone through a few tense times together, and spent a bunch of time with him. Has he ever lied to you?"

"Not that I know of."

"Me either," she said, and smiled. "He's the most honest crook I've ever known."

I knew what she'd meant and returned the smile.

"I really don't think he did it, Chris."

"So, if Larry didn't, who did?"

"One whale of a good question."

I remembered yesterday's conversation with members of the .5 group and how Harriet and Cal had hinted that Abe had been worried that someone from Georgia may have followed him. I mentioned it to Cindy.

My distraught friend looked at the river and turned back to me. "Abe was a con artist, a blasted good one according to Larry."

"Did Larry ever mention anyone who might have followed Abe to Folly, someone from his past who may have killed him?"

Cindy looked at the floor and then back at me. "He never mentioned anyone, but someone could have. As they say back home, where's there's a big pile of manure, there's sure to be a large critter nearby and a flock of flies. A con artist leaves a string of unhappy campers in his wake and has a bunch of acquaintances on the wrong side of the law. I suspect some of them would have been pleased to have the opportunity to deposit a bullet in him."

"Why don't you ask a couple of officers you trust to ask around and see if they hear of any strangers in town or any vehicles with Georgia plates from the counties near Atlanta? Other than sand in his shoes, Detective Adair probably doesn't have any evidence. I'm sure he's checking with the police in Georgia and getting what, if anything, they have on Abe. I suspect he'd appreciate anything your officers turn up that may help with his investigation."

"Won't it look like I'm only trying to help Larry?"

"I wouldn't worry about that. Again, if Larry didn't do it, someone did, and Adair could use the extra eyes. Besides, you can say that one of your folks uncovered the evidence, you didn't. Isn't that what the police are supposed to do?"

"Yes, but. . ."

"No but, you're the chief doing your job."

"Even if there is someone, there's no reason to think he's staying on Folly. Could be anywhere and now that the scumbag is dead, whoever shot him could be long gone."

"True," I said. "But it's all you can do.

"I reckon," she said, with little conviction.

***

I pulled out of the drive, and repeated to myself, *if not Larry, who?* I also had the nagging feeling that something that was said on the group's walk yesterday was bothering me, but what?

I stopped at Charles's apartment and caught him as he was heading out the door. He said that he had been cooped up in the apartment all morning and needed fresh air. We walked around the side of his building to the front that had housed the Sandbar Seafood and Steak Restaurant, and sat on a bench overlooking the Folly River and the Mariner's Cay marina and condo complex on the other side of the waterway.

"Why the visit?" Charles said. He removed his Tilley and set it on the bench.

I shared my conversation with Cindy. He asked if I thought it was possible that Larry could have shot Abe. I rehashed what I'd told him before when I said I didn't think so. He said that he wouldn't bet the farm that Larry was innocent, although he'd be surprised if he did it.

I didn't ask him what farm he wouldn't bet, but instead asked, "Why?"

"Larry's past is a sore spot with him. We talked about it several years ago, probably before you arrived. He didn't want everyone here to know about it, but if it had to come out, he'd have mixed feelings. Said he would be relieved and would find a way to weather whatever storm followed."

"He'd also said that to me."

"But it was BC."

"Before Cindy," I said.

Charles nodded and said, "He's protective of her—overly protective."

I agreed.

"Now that she's chief, it'd kill him if something from his past caused her any hurt or threatened her job. The boy may be short, but he's got a spine of steel. I wouldn't want to mess with him if I said anything bad about his woman."

"So you think he may have done it?" I said.

"No," Charles said. "But if I carried a badge and a gun, I'd be on him like spit on a cowlick."

I hoped he was right about the first part.

We sat in silence watching absolutely nothing happening on the river.

Charles looked across the stream at the marina. "I'm glad Chester decided a boat's the best way to get to Boneyard Beach. Think if I had to hear Harriet gripe about one more thing and Theo walk at the speed of the Washington Monument, I'd be searching for a gun to send them chasing after Abe. Those two are made for each other."

"What do you mean?"

"You see the way Harriet's been doting on Theo? If they were younger, she'd be accused of stalking."

I had noticed how she had helped him yesterday and spent most of the time serving as his human hearing aid. "Think she's after his money?"

"According to Chester, she's sweet on him. Don't know if she's after his money or his winning smile and sex appeal." He snapped his fingers. "Oh wait, he doesn't have a smile, winning or otherwise, and if he ever had sex appeal he used it all up around the time Truman was camping out in the White House." He leaned back on the bench and gazed over at me. "It's the money."

My analysis would have been a bit different, but I couldn't argue with his conclusion. It also reminded me what was bothering me about yesterday's walk.

"Remember yesterday when Cal and Harriet were talking about what Abe had said about someone following him?"

"Yeah, so?"

"Cindy and Larry are crystal clear that Abe was a con artist, a good one."

"So?" Charles repeated.

"If he was working a con on Harriet and Cal, why would he tell them anything about someone following him unless it would help him with the con?"

"And telling them about someone following him wouldn't benefit him."

"Not that I can figure."

"I didn't hear everything Cal and Harriet were talking about," Charles said, "but they weren't clear about what Abe had told them. Now with them knowing he was murdered, it might have clouded their recollections and made them read more into it than Abe had meant."

"True, but look at it this way. What if one of them had killed Abe and made up the story about someone following him to deflect attention away and pass the blame on someone else?"

"You're kidding!" Charles picked up his cane from the ground and pointed it toward town. "You think little ole' scrawny, complaining Harriet or our bud Cal shot Abe with a hunting rifle from across the street?"

"Why not? It's just as likely as Larry doing it?"

"Don't think so," Charles said. "Larry had a motive. What motive would Harriet or Cal have?"

"You just told me Harriet's motive."

"I did?"

"Didn't Theo tell us that he was going to hand Abe a million dollars? Didn't you imply that Harriet was after Theo's money?"

"That little gal can't weigh a hundred pounds. How could she handle the size gun used to take out Abe?"

"She grew up on a ranch in Montana," I said. "I'd be surprised if she didn't spend time hunting, and if not, she probably would've been around guns most of her life."

Charles rubbed his chin. "Think she said they took care of each other back there. Bet that included killing any predator that threatened their livestock."

I nodded.

Charles returned his cane to the ground. "If Harriet pulled the trigger, why would Cal have said what he did about Abe seeming afraid?"

"Let's ask him?"

Charles slapped his Tilley back on his head, grabbed his cane again, and stood. "You're sounding more like me every day. There's hope for you yet."

Chapter Twenty-Seven

It was noon but Cal didn't open his bar for lunch unless the mood struck him. The front door was locked so I assumed the aging country crooner wasn't in the mood to entertain diners or early drinkers. Charles and I went to the unlocked side door and were greeted by the smell of stale beer, George Jones belted out "The Race Is On" from an antique Wurlitzer jukebox, and Cal, live and in person, sang harmony as he swept under the tables. He saw us and went to the jukebox, reached behind it, and turned the volume down. "Welcome to the George and Cal show, one performance only, and standing room only."

Chairs were on top of the tables so he could clean the floor, and I smiled at his joke and he tipped his Stetson in my direction. Charles said, "What's for lunch?"

Cal looked toward the tiny kitchen and back at Charles. "Cold hot dogs, frozen french fries, and cold beer. The grille ain't fired up, and I'm not turning it on for you."

"Cold beer sounds good," Charles said. "Got any chardonnay for my wine-snob friend?" He pointed to me although Cal probably knew who Charles was talking about. "He's too good for beer."

"Think I can find some." He walked behind the bar and turned on the neon Corona Extra beer sign that a movie crew left behind last year after they filmed a movie using Cal's as one of the sets. They'd renamed Cal's The Bar and thought the Corona sign looked better than his Bud Light sign. The movie turned out to be a disaster, both during shooting, and in the box office. Removing the Bud Light sign was not the reason.

"You're about nine hours early for my set and from the piss-poor crowds I've attracted lately, I don't think you needed to get here just yet to claim a table." He waved toward the bandstand and the tables. "Reckon there's another reason for the visit."

Charles took a sip of Budweiser and said, "You reckon right. Lay it out, Chris."

Cal lifted three chairs off the nearest table. "Park your butts."

We did and I told him that we had been rehashing the conversation concerning Abe from the other day on the walk, and that we were confused about something Cal had said.

Cal looked at Charles and back at me. "What'd I say?"

Not a good sign, I thought. "Harriet was saying that Abe told her that he was worried about someone following him to Folly, someone from his past that he was afraid of."

Cal removed his Stetson, laid it on the table beside his beer, rubbed his hand through his long, gray hair, and nodded. "I remember. Believe she said Abe was antsy about someone."

"Yes. After that, didn't you say he told you something like that?"

Cal took a long drag on his beer and looked at the water-stained ceiling tiles. "Sort of."

Charles leaned closer to the bar owner. "Sort of said it or you sort of remember what he said?"

"Abe was jabbering about the greatest stock deal since Apple and using all sorts of words that I'd need nine years of college to figure out, so I was only half paying attention. He mentioned being from A-Town. I remembered that because I played a few shows there in the seventies and got stiffed by a scumbag promoter. Atlanta may be high in the alphabet, but it's at the bottom of my list of places to entertain. You see—"

Charles interrupted. "What'd Abe say?"

Cal looked at Charles like he would at a drunk heckling his singing, but returned to the track. "He said he'd sold stock there and his clients did real good."

If there was anything in there about being afraid of someone I missed it.

"And?" Charles asked.

"And all I remember was that he seemed nervous when he was talking about it."

"He didn't say anything about someone following him?" I said.

Cal Smith sang "County Bumpkin" in the background, Cal Ballew stared at the jukebox, and said, "Not that I heard. Why?"

Cal had rented an apartment ever since he'd been here, so I knew he wasn't a mark for Abe's reverse mortgages, excuse me, jumbo reverse mortgages, so I asked, "Did Abe convince you to buy stock he was peddling?"

Cal chuckled. "Even if I wanted to, which I didn't, I would've had to sell my car, bar, and guitar to scrape together seventy-three dollars. Doubt the late Abe would've considered my wealth a big chunk of his retirement nest egg."

If there wasn't a country song in there somewhere, I'll eat Cal's Stetson. I also couldn't think of a reason Cal would have for killing Abe. He didn't have a story about Abe being followed so he wasn't trying to misdirect blame. He hadn't given Abe any money; didn't have any to give. There wasn't a financial reason to kill him. And besides, I had always known Cal to be honest, honest to the point of harming himself on occasion. To be sure, I tried one more question.

"Cal, you were here when Abe was killed, weren't you?" I hoped it didn't sound too much like I was fishing for an alibi.

"Sure was, pard. I was standing right over there when old Roger stormed in and said there'd been a killing. He didn't know who but said there were a slew of cop cars and an ambulance out by the tennis court."

Cal got us another drink and plopped back down in his chair. "Fellas, if I was the suspicious type, I'd think you're looking for Abe's killer and that I was near the top of the chart with a bullet."

So much for subtlety. I looked at Charles, he gave me a slight nod, and I turned back to Cal. "Not really, Cal. The other day it sounded like you thought Abe was saying that he was worried about someone from back home. That didn't make sense. If a con artist was trying to screw you, he'd show confidence in whatever he was selling so you'd fall for it. He'd be good enough not to let his feelings muddle up the conversation."

"Guys," Cal said, "in my fifty-something years travelling the country, I've seen more con artists than the Better Business Bureau. Abraham Pottinger was one of the best." He raised an empty bottle in the air. "I wouldn't let him invest this bottle, much less any of my hard-earned petty cash."

Charles raised his near-full beer bottle and tapped Cal's. "You're a wise man, Cal."

"Tell us what you know about Harriet Grindstone," I said, as the bottle-clinking ended, and Randy Travis sang "On the Other Hand."

"Wow," Cal said. He twisted his head to the left. "That's a whiplash transition. Where'd that come from?"

"We're curious," Charles said.

Cal chuckled. "Yeah, right. Suppose you'll tell me when you get good and ready."

I nodded which seemed to satisfy Cal.

Cal leaned one elbow on the table and put his hand under his chin. "She's a tough old bird."

Interesting choice of words since she and Cal were the same age.

"What do you mean?" I asked.

"She's come in here a few times and threw back more than her share of brews. Told me that she reared three kids and kicked them and her husband out of the house about twenty years back. Said she's now, 'living happily ever after.'"

"What about her and Theo?" Charles asked.

Cal grinned and pointed his bottle at Charles. "Can't slip anything by you. She'd like to be on him like a mosquito on a baby's butt."

"Have they been in together?" I asked.

"Nah, don't think Theo gets out much other than his every-other-day crawl. If cancer spread as quick as Theo walks, we'd all die of boredom at 153."

Charles said, "How do you know she's out to reel him in?"

Cal pointed to the raised bandstand. "I've stood up there and on stages, truck beds, hay bales, and anything else I can stand on and performed for way too many decades and behind that bar for going on three years." He hesitated and pointed to the bar. "Know what I've learned after all those years?"

"What?" Charles asked.

"Learned, a thousand country songs, about as many ways men can look stupid trying to dance, how beer kills brain cells, and a few hundred pick-up lines and flirtin' looks."

"So?" Charles said.

"So, Harriet's used most of those looks on Theo while she's trying to catch him in her web. Heck, when we're on our .5 shuffles, she can't walk down the street with him without him tripping over her flirts."

"Think she shot Abe?" Charles asked.

Cal stared at Charles, started to speak, hesitated, and finally said, "Didn't see that coming. Why would she?"

"Abe was after Theo's money," Charles said. "Harriet was after Theo. She could have been after him for love, you've said how she doted over him; but the biggest reason was for his money."

"I can see that. So you think she shot Abe to keep him from getting the dough."

"Just a thought," I said. "The problem I have with it is why she would shoot him from across the street. She's strong for her size and could have handled the rifle, but it seems like it would have been much easier and less risky to do it from close-up."

Johnny Cash was singing "Ring of Fire" and Cal looked at the jukebox, turned to Charles, and back to me. "I'm from Texas."

I nodded.

"They're more guns per-square-foot there than in Cabela's. You know what state stomps Texas in percentage of gun-owners?"

"Nary a clue," Charles said.

"Montana," I said.

"Really?" my trivia-collecting friend said.

Cal said, "You can bet your Remington on it."

Charles looked at me. "How'd you know?"

"Guessed. That's where Harriet's from, so I figured Cal was making the point that she'd know how to handle a rifle."

"You figured right," Cal said. "And she was raised on a ranch. Shooting would've been as normal to her as teasing her hair. What do the cops think?"

"They're focused on Larry," I said.

Cal shook his head. "You're pulling my spurs."

"He's serious," Charles said.

"I'd heard rumors, but why?"

Cal was one of the few on Folly who knew about Larry's checkered past, so I shared a little about what Larry had told me and the chain of events leading to the murder.

"You don't think he did it, do you?"

"If I did, I wouldn't be trying to figure out why Harriet said what she did."

"Then you've got to talk to that detective and get him straightened out," Cal said.

Easier said than done, I thought. I didn't tell Cal about my last conversation with Detective Adair, but did say that he was right and that I'd tell Adair what I was thinking.

"Good," Cal said. "Larry's my little bud, can't have anything bad happening to him. And speaking of detectives, heard anything else about Mel? I can't believe they think he killed that kid."

I told Cal that I hadn't heard anything new other than Mel was still in jail.

"They must think they've got a heaping-good case against him," Cal said.

I told him about the bloody rag in Mel's garage, Mel being at the gay bar in Charleston that the student frequented, and the other student who claimed to be an eyewitness to Mel being near where the kid was killed while the others were getting drunk at another part of Boneyard Beach.

"That's one saddlebag full of coincidences. Someone's framing my Magical Marsh Machine's man."

"I agree," I said, and thought, *how can I prove it?*

And Ricky Van Shelton was singing "Somebody Lied" as I left Cal's.

Chapter Twenty-Eight

Cal had persuaded Charles to stay and help clean before Cal's opened for the late-afternoon drinkers, so I left him and walked down Center Street looking for reasons to not call Detective Adair and share my suspicions about Harriet. I had come up with five extraordinarily inane excuses for not calling before realizing that I might as well get it over with. I was closer to the gallery than home so I went in, left the front lights off, moved to the back room, and called the detective's cell.

"Yes, Mr. Landrum, what can I do for you," came the steel-cold voice.

I would have preferred hello or good afternoon, but forwent telling him that and said I'd like to talk about Abe's murder. He said that he would be on Folly in an hour and offered to meet me at the gallery. I took a deep breath and lied. "Sounds good."

My five inane excuses had begun to sound better, but it was too late.

As I sat and waited for Adair, the musty smell in the room coupled with the cold air blowing out of the air conditioner, brought back memories from years in this space. Most of the memories were good and the more I thought about them, the more I wondered if I should reconsider closing.

Adair's arrival interrupted whether I should remain open.

"So what's so all-out important?" he asked as I greeted him at the door.

I offered him water or a soft drink, figuring I wouldn't

make a friend by offering him a beer or a glass of wine. He brusquely declined and repeated, "What's so important?"

I pointed him to a chair at the table. He looked around and sat and I took one on the opposite side of the table.

He folded his arms and stared at me. I took a deep breath and shared my observation that Harriet had been paying more than a friendly interest in Theo, a member of the walking group, and that Theo had agreed to give Abe a significant amount of money to invest in a stock that he had been touting. Adair interrupted and asked more about Theo. To the detective's credit, he took notes.

I shared that I believed that Harriet didn't want Abe to get to Theo's money and that she shot him to prevent it from happening.

Adair asked for a physical description of Harriet, and I told him about her age and petite size. He didn't say anything, but from his skeptical look, I figured that hadn't helped my argument. I added that she had lived on a ranch in Montana, and my belief that marksmanship would probably have been a part of her past. I doubted that he was convinced.

The detective shut his notebook, returned it to his coat pocket, sighed, and gave me a police glare. "Mr. Landrum, what evidence do you have that Ms. Grindstone had anything to do with Mr. Pottinger's death?"

I wanted to slap him with his notebook and scream, *Isn't that your job?* Instead, I said that what I had told him was only speculation, but that it made sense. *More sense than accusing my friend Larry*, remained unsaid. To bolster my case, I told him that Charles Fowler and Chester Carr also felt the same way.

He appeared unimpressed and glared at me. "That's it?"

I nodded.

"Let me throw my speculation at you," He leaned both elbows on the table. "Larry LaMond is a friend of yours. I've heard it from several people—"

"Yes, but."

"But nothing. Let me finish."

I closed my mouth.

"He's your friend, I get that, but, he's your friend who had a lengthy criminal past. He's a friend who never hesitated to break in houses and steal valuables from innocent homeowners, often while they were asleep in the same room. He's a friend whose past came back to haunt him when Mr. Pottinger showed up. How am I doing so far?"

I wanted to argue that Larry had been a model citizen for way more years than he had lived outside the law, and how he had established a stellar reputation on Folly Beach. Instead, I said, "Go ahead."

"Not only did Pottinger come to Folly, but I learned, from you, I might add, that he had threatened Mr. LaMond. He threatened to tell everyone about Larry's past which not only could have ruined Larry's reputation and business, but would have made a laughingstock out of his wife, your police chief."

"Larry had already planned to tell everyone about his past," I said, realizing it sounded defensive.

"So you say."

"Didn't Larry tell you the same thing?"

Adair balled his hand into a fist. "What else would he have said?"

I leaned back in the chair, doing my best to not let him intimidate me. "I also said that I had volunteered to tell Abe that Larry was going to tell everyone about his past, and that he had no way to pay the extortion money, even if he wanted to. I told you that I had met with Pottinger with that message."

"Yes." He shook his head. "I believe that's the story you *forgot* to tell me the night of the shooting."

I didn't have a good response, so I continued, "I was leaving Pottinger's house after talking to him about Larry."

"That we agree on."

I held my hand up, palm facing him. "And that was when he was shot." Adair nodded. "Would Larry have murdered Pottinger before hearing the outcome of the meeting? Why would he have shot Pottinger when in your words, Larry's *friend* was only inches from a deadly bullet?" I leaned forward and stared at the detective. "Why?"

He met my stare and upped it. "Let me tell you two things I

do know, Mr. Landrum. I've been a cop for a long time, much of it investigating what seems like countless murders. First, I know that logic, *making sense,* and intelligence seldom prevail when people are killed. And second, I know that your *friend* has no alibi for when Pottinger was gunned down; your *friend* has one heck of a good motive for shutting Pottinger up. Not a thing you've said has convinced me otherwise."

Nothing like an open mind, I thought. "You don't know him, but Larry's one of the most honest, aboveboard, and trustworthy people I've ever known. He may not have an alibi, but I doubt that most people over here who know Pottinger have one, and I've given you a motive for Harriet Grindstone. Why don't you check it out? And now that I think about it, you searched Larry's home, truck, and hardware store, did you find anything to indicate that he was the shooter?"

Since Larry was still free and since I was convinced that he was innocent, I knew what the answer had to be.

"Anything?" I repeated.

I was surprised when he grinned.

"Mr. Landrum, you know I'm not going to answer that. What I can tell you is that I know that Larry LaMond shot Abe Pottinger. It's only a matter of time before I prove it."

Adair didn't storm out of the gallery, but didn't waste any time letting me know that our meeting was over and exited before I could respond.

I was convinced of two things: Larry was in more trouble than I had anticipated, and I hadn't helped him any. And, while I was still convinced that my friend had nothing to do with Pottinger's death, I knew where the detective was coming from. He had far more reason to suspect Larry than I had to accuse Harriet.

It was also clear that Adair wasn't going to be doing anything but focus on Larry. If anyone was going to pursue other possible suspects, it had to be me. Theo had said that he didn't have any paperwork on the stock he was going to fork over a million dollars on so that was a dead end. He wasn't a candidate for a reverse mortgage, but Alexander Lifetime Security Inc. was the company selling the product. I did a Google search and turned up two companies named Alexander Security, but both provided private security services for companies, and there were no listings for Alexander Lifetime Security, Inc. While I was on the computer, I looked for references about Harriet Grindstone and found only four people with that name. Unfortunately, none of them had been arrested for shooting someone, and none had lived in Montana. Wishful thinking was simply that. I knew Harriet had been married and wasn't sure if Grindstone was her maiden name or her husband's name.

What I was certain about was that if Abe was as good a con artist as Larry had portrayed him to be, he wouldn't have let anyone, much less someone he was conning, see that he was afraid of anything. Harriet had been lying. I was certain that she had grown up in Montana, and almost as certain that she'd know her way around rifles. From what Cal had said, she was protective of Theo and probably was out to "hook" him, which would have put Abe in her sights if she felt he was trying to rip him off; in her sights only hours before Theo was going to hand Abe a million dollars.

How was I going to prove it? A simple question, but one with no simple answer.

Chapter Twenty-Nine

The next .5 walk started almost identical to previous outings. Charles and I were at the pier early. Chester pulled his station wagon into the lot at the starting time, followed by Cal in his Caddy with William by his side. Harriet complained about everything else, including, her ankle, the weather, the bugs, and Chester's erratic driving. David Darnell defended Chester saying that it wasn't his fault that the "hippie on the bicycle" pulled in front of Chester so he had no choice but to drive up the sidewalk.

What was different was that there was less debate about the route. Chester made it clear that he was in charge and that the path to be taken was his to choose. Even Harriet, the consummate complainer, seemed to acquiesce to Chester's leadership. Chester began by offering a silent prayer in memory of Abe Pottinger, and then said we were going to "head up Center Street, hang a left at West Erie, and rest our weary legs while we sip Joe at Black Magic Café."

It was only three short blocks to West Erie, and the locally-owned café was fewer than fifty Theo-paces from the corner of Center Street. From what I had heard, and from the walks Charles and I had been on with the group, this would be one of the shortest walks; I doubted that Theo would have objected, even if he'd heard where we were going.

If there had been any question about Harriet's intention about Theo, it was answered before the group hiked a block. She had her arm around his sleeveless T-shirt and kept whispering,

"You can make it, sweetie." Of course, for Theo to hear, Harriet's whisper was heard by everyone.

After what seemed like three months later, but closer to a half hour, we gathered around two round tables on the café's outdoor deck, and William and Cal went inside to get coffee for all of us except William who'd requested hot tea. Harriet still had her arm around Theo and fanned his face with his USS Yorktown ball cap. Chester told David that he had a special announcement to make when Cal and William returned with the drinks. And Charles and I sat at the second table and watched the others acting like they had just completed a mini-marathon, or in Chester's parlance, a 12.1.

"See what we have to look forward to?" Charles said.

I reluctantly agreed.

Cal and William began distributing drinks to the rightful owners. Considering the several thousand coffee and ingredient combinations available, I was impressed that it only took a few minutes to get the drinks sorted out. Charles said it was because Cal ran a bar and had figured out how to get the right drink to the right customer—something that had taken him three years to master.

Chester took a sip and tapped the side of his mug with a spoon. "Listen up."

Everyone quieted except Theo before Harriet nudged him and put her index finger to her lips and then pointed to Chester. Theo smiled and turned to face the leader.

"I have great news," Chester said. "Some of you know Connie's brother, Robbie. He owns a marsh tour business. Well, Connie talked to him and he agreed to take us to Boneyard Beach."

Theo said, "In a bus?"

"No," Chester shouted, "in his boat. It'll hold all of us and he's giving us a real good deal." Chester turned to Connie. "Thank you, Connie."

"When'll we float out there?" Cal asked.

"Day after tomorrow," said Chester.

"How much?" Theo asked, the person who had more money than the rest of us combined.

Chester held up his hands and wiggled his fingers. "Only ten bucks a head. That's a great deal. Thanks again, Connie."

She smiled.

"I hear that the police know that Larry from the hardware store killed Abe," Theo said, like it was the most logical comment to make after Connie was praised for getting a good deal on the trip to Boneyard Beach.

"I don't believe it," Cal said, who turned to me. "Larry's a friend of ours."

Instead of wondering how we had transitioned from the boat ride to Larry, I said, "Yes, he has been for years."

"From my limited contact with the store's proprietor," William added, "he appears to be a fine, upstanding gentleman."

Cal was now fanning his face with his Stetson. "Well I can tell you this, my friend here will find out who the killer is." He sat his hat in front of him and pointed at me.

All eyes turned in my direction.

Before I could say that ten dollars sounded like a good deal, Cal continued, "Yes sir, my friend, with the occasional help from Charles, has solved several murders that stumped the cops. A couple of you know how he saved me from getting killed by that deranged guy who owned the bar before I got it. " He gave a stage nod. "Yes sir, Chris will figure out who killed Abe." Cal picked up his hat and waved it in a semi-circle. "Right, Chris?"

"It's in good hands with the police." I hoped that Cal would let it go.

"I believe my friend, Chris, is correct," William said. "It's a matter for the proper law enforcement authorities. Shall we offer a round of applause for Chester and Connie for collaboratively finding a solution to achieve our goal of reaching Boneyard Beach?"

Thanks, William, I thought and raised my coffee mug to Chester and Connie. Everyone else offered polite applause.

We stayed on the patio for as long as it would take to recuperate from open-heart surgery, before Chester said it was time to head back. David was in deep conversation with William about long-term care insurance as they led the group off the patio. The rest of us followed Chester, the unlikely leader of a band of walkers.

"Chris, Charles," William said after we had turned off Center Street toward Chester's cottage. "Could I perhaps commandeer a few moments of your time in private at the conclusion of our excursion?"

I translated that to mean that he wanted to talk to us without the nosy ears of the others, and said, "Of course."

Charles said, "Okay by me."

We had in Chester's words our "traditional post-walk refreshments" at his house before going different ways. Connie had cornered me to ask what Cal had been talking about when he said that Charles and I had caught some killers. I skimmed over the incidents and she didn't press for details. Theo, with the aid of Harriet, had moved over to my side of the porch and asked me what we were talking about. Fortunately Harriet yelled for him not to worry about it and he dropped the subject. Since we had overloaded our bladders with coffee, little time was spent drinking lemonade and chit-chatting.

Cal asked William if he was ready to leave and the professor told him that it was such a pretty day that he'd walk home. Cal said his adieus, tipped his Stetson at his fellow walkers, and moseyed out.

William looked over at me and tilted his head toward the door. I told the group that I was leaving, Charles said he was as well, and William said that he would walk us out. I felt like I was in the middle of a spy movie and William was going to pass us coded messages in fortune cookies. And I thought how unlikely William would be at espionage; and then again, perhaps that would make him the perfect spy.

We walked back toward town and William asked, "Shall we take a brief walk on the pier; perhaps find a venue with more privacy?"

I said that was fine, and Charles repeated, "Okay by me."

It was noon and the pier was more crowded than usual so we walked to the far end to find a bench that was both in the shade and isolated. Along the way, William never hinted at what he wanted to talk about but talked about the panoramic view of the beach from the pier, and how he planned to try his hand at fishing when he was fortunate enough to retire.

We settled on a wooden bench in the shade overlooking the east end of the island, and William looked around to see if anyone was within earshot. We were alone.

He looked at Charles and then at me. "May I be perfectly candid?"

I said of course, and Charles sounded like a broken record when he said, "Okay by me."

William grinned, looked toward the shore, then at me. "You don't believe that your friend Mel Evans killed Mr. Casey?"

"No," I said, "but to be honest, it's easy to see why the police think he did. They have a rag from Mel's garage with Casey's blood on it; Mel hadn't been forthcoming about how many times he's gone to that bar in Charleston; and most damning, the police have a witness who can place Mel in the area where the body was found, Mel had said that he only left the boat to urinate, and he had gone in the opposite direction from where the body was found."

William said, "Ah, the witness. That's what I wish to confer with you about. For you see, I am aware of who he is. The gentleman's name is Darnell Embley, and like the late Drew Casey, Mr. Embley is one of my students." William paused.

William was hesitant to talk about others, and I hoped that Charles wouldn't push him. The stars must have been aligned because Charles remained silent.

William continued, "As you can imagine, the death, especially by such despicable circumstances, of someone known by many of our students, has become a major topic on campus. Since Mr. Embley was part of the ill-fated party, and has gained extraordinary notoriety from being the individual who saw the killer, he is prone to expound upon the experiences at every opportunity." William hesitated.

I was beginning to wish we were listening to Dude.

"Notwithstanding," William said, "I believe there are a couple of things that Mr. Embley has said that detracts from his credibility; things, I must confess, I overheard at a time I shouldn't have been listening."

I said that it was okay.

William took a deep breath, and slowly exhaled. "Mr. Embley was speaking to two students who were present at the party. They were standing in the corridor outside my classroom, and I couldn't help but overhear." He took another breath.

Once again, I was surprised by Charles's silence.

William continued, "Mr. Embley was laughing and said, and these were his words, 'Were we soused or what?' And one of the others said that he couldn't remember because he was so drunk that he couldn't tell if he was on the beach or in the library. The third student said that everyone was so sick the next day that they never wanted to see another beer." William shook his head. "Mr. Embley said he quickly overcame that aversion."

William hadn't said anything that I hadn't suspected, but was surprised that the only witness admitted to being "soused" and wondered if detectives were aware of it.

Charles couldn't hold his silence. "So that's it?"

William shook his head. "Perhaps another item that one might call a clue. A young lady, someone who hasn't had the privilege of being in one of my classes, so I don't know her name, approached the gathered gentlemen. I didn't hear her salutation, but she laughed and said something to Mr. Embley to the effect that he was the hero who helped the police catch the perpetrator. Mr. Embley laughed and said that he didn't exactly recognize Mel near the scene, but, and again these are his words, 'It was an old bald guy in dark clothes. Who else could it have been?' To my untrained law-enforcement ears, that sounded inadequate as a positive identification of Mr. Evans."

I told him that I agreed. William then said that he knew we would want that information and agreed to tell the same thing to the police if they talked to him. I thanked him for sharing, he said he was uncomfortable listening in on his students' private conversation, but was glad he could tell us what he had heard.

William headed home, and I asked Charles if he was up to a beer on the outdoor deck at the bar at the Tides.

The record was still stuck. "Okay by me."

***

The weather was nice and the bar crowded. We ran into Jay, the omnipresent and personable bellhop, greeter, and all-around nice guy, who told us that an accountants' convention had invaded the hotel, and for some strange reason, the participants appeared more interested in the bar, the view of the ocean, and sunshine than being in a seminar about how to depreciate heavy equipment under the new tax laws. "Go figure," Jay said, with a smile.

We ordered drinks and waited in the shade of the nine-story hotel until two bar-height chairs became available at the long, elevated bar that overlooked the beach and the pier. Finally, two men finished their beers, gazed at the ocean, and headed inside. I said that they probably felt guilty about missing the "highly stimulating" seminar and were returning to the meeting room. Charles said that he could tell from the sweat rolling down their faces that they were hot in their sport coats and ties and were headed to the inside bar to continue "networking." Either scenario, we grabbed their chairs.

"I've still got mixed feelings about Mel," Charles said, as he set his Tilley on the bar. "We don't know him that well; he's got a lot of past that we've never heard about. Besides, the police seem to have a strong case. Got a witness; got a bloody rag; got a motive, sort of; and got Mad Mel locked up."

"Until a day ago, I might have agreed," I placed my hat next to Charles's. "We don't know everything about Mel, but look at what we do know. He's devoted to Caldwell. I can see him frequenting the bar, he's never shied away from throwing back a few beers, but I can't see him there to pick-up college kids."

"I guess," Charles said.

"He's also smart; maybe not book-smart, but I would match his common sense against anyone. Do you think he'd be stupid enough to leave the bloodstained rag in his garage?"

"That bothered me too. But what about the witness?"

"You mean the *soused* one?"

"Yeah, but he was pretty sure the person he saw was old and bald; that wouldn't fit anyone on the trip but Mel."

"Look at the timeline. First, Mel said he asked if everyone was onboard when they were leaving the beach. No one said someone was missing. You had a boatload of drunks; some probably didn't even know they were on a boat. Then no one noticed anyone missing until the next day when the trip's organizer contacted Mel. Finally, my understanding is that the witness didn't come forward until a few days after the trip."

I paused, too long for Charles. "So?"

I looked at the waves rolling in and over to Charles. "Let's say the *soused* witness saw someone. I suspect that after the time he'd learned that Drew Casey was killed there had been many conversations with others from the trip and the witness started thinking all sorts of things. They were trying to figure out what had happened. They probably accused each other of killing him; then talked about him being gay; and then, no telling what else. In other words, days went by before the *soused* student remembered seeing an old bald guy near where the student was killed."

Charles started to interrupt but I stopped him. "I'm not saying he didn't see what he says he saw, all I'm saying is that considering the delay between the killing and him coming forward, it leaves a lot of room for doubt about credibility."

Charles said for me to hold that thought as he jumped up and headed to get more drinks. I spent the time watching a couple with three small children putting their feet in the puddles of water left on the beach as the tide receded, and a teenager walking under the pier. I thought about how many people's worlds were intersecting day in and day out with each being oblivious to the other. Charles returned before I was able to discover the secret of life and our role in it.

Charles set wine in front of me. "So Mel's being framed."

"Yes," I said and took a sip of the cold drink.

"Who and why?"

"Don't know. The first possible *who* would be one or more of the others on the boat, but that seems unlikely. Only the group leader knew who Mel was; and according to Mel, the leader contacted him by phone. Mel only uses his cell and his home address is unlisted, so how would one of them know where he lived to put the bloody rag in his garage?"

"Doesn't rule them out, though. With everything on the Internet—maps, addresses, and stuff I don't have a clue about—someone could find where he lives."

"Possibly."

"But if it wasn't one of the students, the killer had to know that Mel was taking the group out and where they were going; and had to be someone who knew where Mel lived."

"Yes."

Charles looked at the surf and back at me. "If that's true, how likely would it be for that person to know Drew Casey and to want him dead?"

"I don't think he did."

"Huh?"

"I think Drew Casey was killed to frame Mel, not because Casey meant anything to the killer."

"If it wasn't someone from the boat, how would he or she know that Casey was gay?"

"He wouldn't. Mel could still have been framed for killing a student. It turned out that he was gay and that helped the frame, but the gay angle wasn't necessary."

"If that's true, what did someone have against Mel; something that was worth killing over and going to a lot of trouble framing him?"

"That's the real question," I said and looked at a group of accountants competing for bar space, oblivious to what we were talking about.

"So what's the answer?"

The most common reasons for murder, I thought, and said, "Love or money?"

"Unless someone's out to get Mel to break up with Caldwell and put the moves on him, love seems unlikely."

"I'd eliminated that one," I said.

Charles's head bobbed and then tilted. "Money doesn't make any more sense. Mel doesn't have anything more than a pile of debt on his boat and his Camaro. How could money be the motive?"

"Charles, if I knew the answer to that, I'd be talking to the detective instead of to you."

"That's what I thought. Guess we don't know much of anything." He finished his beer and looked at the door to the hotel. "Want to learn how to depreciate heavy equipment under the new tax laws?"

I quickly declined.

"All this talk gave me a headache," Charles said. "I need a nap."

I agreed.

Chapter Thirty

The next morning began with another thunderstorm pounding the metal roof, a parade of work trucks roaring past the house on the way to job sites, and me sitting in the kitchen, drinking scalding coffee from a Lost Dog Café mug, staring at a three-year-old calendar magnet stuck on side of the refrigerator, and thinking about friends. Friendships are strange. They're often forged by things we have in common: children, hobbies, work. The emotional bonds created survive the differences friends have. After the bonds are cemented, and one of the friends does something that the other person doesn't agree with, or that happens to bend the law, the friendship generally prevails. Why? Psychologists and sociologists have pondered this question for decades and are often divided on the answer. Do we recognize and choose to overlook the differences and actions of our friends, or does friendship cloud our perceptions of the actions of others?

The friendships that I have made since arriving on Folly would confound anyone attempting deep analysis. I consider my closest friends to be Charles, Bob Howard, Cal, Amber, Chief Cindy LaMond, William, and word-challenged Dude. I don't have children, so that would be out as a cause for friendships. I could say that Charles and I share photography as a hobby, although before I arrived, he didn't know what end of a camera to look through. And forget work as a common thread.

There are two things my friends and I do have in common. First is a deep love for Folly Beach, its character and characters.

Yes, even Bob falls in that group although it'd take a court order and an orthodontist pulling his teeth with no anesthesia to get him to admit it. And second, we all share a handful of dreadful experiences, often in chase of a murderer, or being on the barrel end of a firearm. One way or another, my friends have saved my life and I theirs. Beyond that, we share dissimilar backgrounds, dissimilar careers, if we even have or had any, dissimilar tastes in clothing, food, housing, and most likely, if we ever got into a discussion about it, politics, religion and the hereafter. With that said, I would give my life for each of them, and I suspected, and I hope never again tested, that they would do the same for me.

I also considered Larry and Mel among my friends. I haven't known them as long as some of the others and both have dark holes in their past. Larry has been more open about his years on the wrong side of the law but they were a long time ago. Since he's been here, he's been a model citizen and unless he chose to share what he'd done, no one would have suspected anything undesirable about him. Mel has never revealed anything other than a bullet-point resume of his life, but I've suspected that there's more than he'd told; more that is best not revealed to the police.

Do I believe that either was capable of murder? Good question. Larry had a powerful motive, no doubt, but I can't see him pulling the trigger, regardless how evil Abe might have been. Then again, has friendship clouded my thinking?

Mel provided me with another dilemma. Yes, I could see him killing someone; and he possibly has during his stint in the military, and maybe as a civilian. But, I can't see him having a motive strong enough to kill the college student. Again, is my belief fogged by friendship?

Friendships have given me more pleasure, more warmth, more comradery, and more depth to my life on Folly, than I had experienced my first six decades. I owed it to myself and my friends Mel and Larry to do everything I could to prove that they were innocent. If they didn't do it, someone else did. Abe's choices in life would have created any number of enemies; enemies from as far away as Georgia and as close as the .5 group. I had no idea who the outsiders might be, but had a strong hunch about Harriet. I would have her much higher on my list if she was twenty years younger, a hundred pounds heavier, and went by Harriet "Annie Oakley" Grindstone. But, she had grown up on a ranch, was probably familiar with firearms, and from how she doted on Theo, would have gone to great lengths to protect him.

Harriet had motive, opportunity, and possibly means; and that brought me to Mel. He had opportunity and means, but to me he had zilch motive. So if that's true, what about the witness? Sure, the student who said he had seen Mel near where the kid was killed, could be discredited in court. He was "soused," didn't come forward until days after the death, and said he was sure the person was Mel because the person he saw was bald and old, so who else could it be? Any defense attorney worth his fee could convince a jury that there were countless *bald and old* potential suspects within fifty miles of the crime scene. Would they have had motive? Of course not, but all the attorney had to do was cast reasonable doubt.

The more I thought about it, the more I was convinced that Mel was set-up. It didn't appear to be for love, so that left money. Who would benefit financially if Mel was convicted? Mel was upside down on his boat and his car. A few years ago, he'd shared that he didn't believe in life insurance; said he came into the world with nothing, planned to go out that way, and was "damned sure" he wasn't going to let anyone benefit from his demise.

And I remembered a comment made in an earlier conversation; a comment that meant little at the time, but that indicated that there was someone who would benefit from Mel's arrest and probable conviction. But how could I prove it? I'd be laughed out of the police station if I shared my theory with the detectives.

If I thought my mental gyrations would give me the answer, I was a colossal failure. The rain continued, the vehicles continued to roll by the house, and I did the most productive things I could think of to do: I poured more coffee, hoped that the weather would clear for tomorrow's boat trip to Boneyard Beach, yanked the outdated calendar off the refrigerator, and dropped it in the trash.

Chapter Thirty-One

With Charles in tow, I showed up at the entrance to Mariner's Cay condos and its marina where Robbie's boat was docked and punched in the gate code that he'd given us. Mariner's Cay Marina was more up-scale than the Folly View Marina where Mel's Magical Marsh Machine spent its free time. Since we were operating on Charles Standard Time, I doubted that Robbie would be at the boat so we waited in the car.

The captain's Nissan pulled in beside us as I started to tell Charles my suspicion about who might have killed the student. Robbie looked around, smiled, and walked over to the car. He looked captainly in navy shorts, a tan safari shirt, and an FB ball cap.

He chuckled. "No worms here."

"Huh?" Charles said as he got out and shook Robbie's hand.

"You're early birds. Catching worms, get it?"

"This is Charles's version of on-time," I said.

We spent the next ten minutes talking about a new gift shop in town, how slow gallery and tour businesses were, and how Connie had conned her brother into taking us on the trip for such a low price. I told him how much the trip meant to Chester and how we appreciated his generosity, although it didn't appear that he had anything else to be doing.

The awkward what-next silence was broken when Chester's Buick and Cal's convertible pulled in beside us. Cal and

William hopped out, while Chester, Harriet, Theo, Connie, and David exited the Buick at the speed of an earthworm. I stifled a laugh when I saw that each of them wore a bright red cap with *.5 OR BUST* on the crown. Even Cal had replaced his Stetson with one. Chester handed Charles and me identical hats and beamed with pride as he said that he had them made for today's "historic" adventure. Crediting myself for wisdom that came with age, I didn't mention that our "historic" adventure was being accomplished by way of boat rather than the walk that was the goal of the group and the reason for .5 on the caps. Instead I replaced my Tilley with Chester's thoughtful, inaccurate gift.

Cal pulled his much-travelled guitar case out of his back seat and announced that Chester had suggested that since we were riding, Cal could share a few travelling, boat-riding, and beach tunes with the group. It didn't take much to encourage the country crooner to break into song, and I was glad that Chester had asked. Cal whispered to me that he had iced his *strummin'* hand all morning to keep his arthritis in check. David lugged a medium-sized cooler and said that all he knew about it was that Chester said it was a surprise. I'd had enough surprises recently and wasn't as enthused as David appeared to be.

Connie hugged Robbie and thanked him for taking the group; Chester echoed her sentiments without the hug, and Robbie led us to the entrance to the marina. Unlike Mel's boat that had numerous battle scars from years on the marsh and heavy partying, Robbie's Carolina Skiff was spotless and looked like it had come straight from the factory. I glanced at the bottom of my shoes to make sure I didn't track dirt aboard. Robbie managed to get everyone seated, a wise move since I suspected that some of the passengers would topple over once we began.

We moved out of the no-wake zone close to the marina and Robbie gunned the powerful Suzuki engine as we moved under the new bridge connecting Folly from the rest of the continental United States. Chester was trying to say something but the roar of the engine drowned him out. Robbie was in a hurry to get the trip over with, but pulled back on the throttle after Chester pantomimed for him to slow down.

The Folly River was sandwiched by marsh and ran behind the island. Larry and Cindy's house was to the right, and I gave a brief thought to the trouble that Larry could be in and how the person I believed killed Abe was ten feet from me.

My thoughts were interrupted when Theo pointed at a large house along the marsh. "That's mine!" he screamed as if he had to talk over the Suzuki. The engine was idling so Theo could probably be heard by his fellow passengers, and also by people miles away walking along the Battery in Charleston. Harriet leaned over and put her arm around his waist and kissed him on the cheek. Robbie must have figured that we'd had enough quiet time and gunned the engine as we continued to where the river narrowed and snaked a path through the increasingly dense marsh grasses. He had slowed to avoid running aground in the pluff mud, oyster beds, and other obstacles lurking beneath the surface. The putrid smell of decaying plants and animals assaulted my nose.

Robbie tried to point out some of the ecological features but only David listened. Connie and William were huddled together talking about how much she hated boat rides and William was countering by how much more enjoyable the ride was than trying to make the trip on foot. Theo, who couldn't have heard anything anyone was saying even if the engine had been turned off, looked off to the left and appeared deep in thought.

Harriet leaned toward Charles and me and put her finger to her lips, and whispered, "Theo and I are getting married."

She said something else that I didn't catch, and I leaned closer and said, "Congratulations. When's the big event?"

Harriet glanced at Theo who continued to stare at the marsh. "We, umm, haven't set a date."

Filtered through my belief that she had killed Abe, I wondered if Theo knew about their marital plans. Either way, it made me even more confident that she was the reason Abe wasn't making the historic trip with us.

It was low tide so Robbie couldn't take the more direct route to Lighthouse Inlet and the four mile trip was taking longer than usual as we weaved through the circuitous stream avoiding the shallower tidal creeks. We were moving at a snail's pace, and

Chester was walking from person to person sharing his excitement about reaching Boneyard Beach.

William moved to my side of the skiff. "Have you learned more about the precarious position Larry finds himself in?"

"Not really," I said. "Don't think the police have talked to him again."

William grinned. "Perhaps the police will not be able to figure it out, but history would indicate that you will find a way to clear his name."

David moved closer to us. "You don't think he killed Abe?"

"No," I said.

"Interesting," David said.

"Chris is positive he didn't," William added. "He'll catch the perpetrator."

I appreciated his confidence, but wasn't as positive and said so.

"I do know that you are looking," he said.

I shrugged. "All I know is that Larry's innocent."

"And you will find a way to extricate Mr. LaMond from his dilemma," William added.

"What's that all about?" Theo asked.

"Nothing," Harriet said. "Enjoy your big day."

A small fishing boat passed us as it headed toward the dock. To its three occupants we looked like a meeting of a redneck chapter of the Red Hat Society with our red caps bathed in sunlight. Connie was standing at the helm beside her brother. I couldn't catch all of their conversation but heard bits and pieces about Timothy's wedding and how he still needed money. Connie said she felt for him, but didn't have any to loan; Robbie said he didn't and was afraid that the wedding may be off.

Cal stood behind Connie and Robbie and started strumming, "Redneck Yacht Club." The song was many years newer than Cal's preferred playlist, but he sang a passable version of Craig Morgan's hit; besides, with the engine revving loudly, few of the travelers could hear him.

The narrow waterway intersected the wider Lighthouse

Inlet and Robbie steered the boat right toward the Morris Island Lighthouse and our destination. Cal was on much more comfortable musical ground as he transitioned into "On the Road Again," and the termination of Chester's dream trip was in sight.

Robbie inched the bow of his craft onto the sand; the opposite of how Mel had when he had nearly thrown me overboard when he rammed the Magical Marsh Machine on the beach. I suspected Robbie was more concerned about his new fiberglass hull than for the aging bones that could have been broken on some of his passengers if he'd hit harder.

Chester was first off. If he had had an American flag, he would have planted it in the sand before announcing, *one small step for .5 kind.* Charles and I were the next on shore and we gave a hand to the others as they exited the craft. Theo remained seated as everyone else got off. Harriet stood in front of him and leaned down and asked if he was okay. He said he was a little queasy and wanted to stay on the boat a few minutes. Robbie said he was going to stay close, and would watch after Theo. Harriet reluctantly agreed and Charles helped her to shore.

Ten minutes later, Cal had moved to the nearby graffiti-covered foundation ruins left from the Coast Guard property, had taken his guitar from its case, and began an impromptu concert. With the lighthouse and Lighthouse Inlet as a backdrop, he waded into his more-familiar songbook with a medley of Hank Williams Sr. heartbreak songs. Connie and William had walked to a small grove of dead, bleached trees, and David, Harriet, and Chester moved closer to Cal as he sang, "Your Cheatin' Heart." I was thrilled that Chester's group had made it to their destination, regardless if by foot or float.

Cal finished strumming and Chester raised his hands and clapped them together over his head. "Group, gather round." He waved for us to move closer. Theo was still on the boat with Robbie but Chester didn't seem to notice. Chester motioned for David to set the cooler on the top of the foundation and Chester pulled out two bottles of cheap champagne and a stack of clear plastic cups. "I propose a toast to the best damn walking group this side of the Folly River."

A safe statement since it was the only walking group on Folly, and Charles yelled "Here, here!" as Chester fiddled with the foil on the top of the first bottle. Charles saw him struggling and grabbed the second bottle and started opening it. And, for reasons that I didn't understand, Cal started singing "Auld Lang Syne." Chester, with a grin as large as a Frisbee, sang along, followed by Connie, David, and William. As I listened to the group fumbling through the words that only seem coherent to a room full of drunks on New Year's Eve, I realized the true meaning of "it's the thought that counts."

I also realized that Theo, the primary reason we had taken a boat to Boneyard Beach, was still on the boat, and Harriet seemed engrossed in singing and drinking champagne. Robbie and Theo were in deep conversation, but since Theo was missing the festivities, I wanted to break him free and help him hobble over to the group.

Robbie's back was to me and Theo faced me as I approached. He assumed that everyone heard as poor as he did, so quiet was not in his vocal range. He said, "How do you know?"

Robbie's response was drowned out by the water lapping against the side of his boat and Cal singing, "How Can I Miss You When You Won't Go Away?"

Theo shook his head and pointed his finger at Robbie. "Okay." He saw me and waved me over to the boat. "Hey, Chris, give me a hand. I need to get to the fun."

Robbie leaned against the throttle and watched as Theo, with a great deal of my aid, managed to get off the skiff. Harriet noticed us and rushed to help her "fiancé." The three of us walked toward the foundation/bandstand/bar and Robbie followed closely behind.

The first bottle of champagne was empty but the second was hardly touched. Cal had returned his guitar to the case and the group began pairing up and walking around the deserted beach. William and Cal walked down one of the handful of paths leading from the beach to the marsh, with Cal pointing to something along the side of the path and laughing. Chester, Connie, and David explored a clump of trees the beach had been named after. Connie laughed when Chester tried to pull himself up on one of the trees. He would have had better luck if he'd been a minnow. Harriet and Theo seemed satisfied to remain at the foundation while Theo made up lost time imbibing. Charles and I stayed with them since we had explored the area several times over the years and I had been here a few days ago with Mel. And Robbie had returned to the boat, spread out on one of the bench seats, and appeared to take a late-morning nap.

I smiled to myself and thought how wonderful and cathartic the trip was for each member of the group. I smiled until I realized that Mel was in jail for killing someone within a couple of hundred yards of where we were, and that Larry was the prime suspect for killing a member of this group.

Chapter Thirty-Two

Like most return trips, the ride to the marina seemed shorter than the trip over. The excitement of reaching their goal, combined with champagne, sunshine, and a combined lifespan approaching the age of coal, had taken its toll. Charles and I were the only members who weren't dozing. I was sitting beside Chester who was snoring louder than the roar of the Suzuki. The others were quieter, but still asleep.

We were near the bridge when we were bounced by the wake of a larger boat heading the other direction, and most of the group were jarred awake. Chester removed the red cap that had been covering his eyes and clapped for everyone to pay attention. All but Theo responded and Harriet had to shake him awake. Chester said that he was proud of everyone for their incredible accomplishment and said that Robbie deserved a hand for taking the group at a reduced rate. I was slow to applaud because I was trying to figure out how the boat ride was such an incredible accomplishment. I didn't waste much brainpower on it and joined the rest of the group as we applauded while Robbie docked his pride and joy.

Chester laughed and patted each member on the back and hugged the two ladies as we stepped on the wooden dock. It was good seeing him this happy. His smile disappeared when Harriet missed the step and fell hard. William, ever the gentleman, rushed to her, asked if she was okay, and tried to help her up. She said she had reinjured her ankle and to give her a minute. David carried the cooler to Chester's car and Cal took his guitar case to his Cadillac while the rest of us gathered around Harriet.

"I'm fine," she said to Chester. "Could you drop me at my house instead of back to yours?"

William helped her up and acted as a human crutch as she gingerly hobbled to the car. They were so slow that Theo beat them to the vehicle and moved to the back seat instead of his customary spot in the passenger's seat so Harriet could have easy access.

Charles and I beat Cal and William to Chester's house and it was another half hour before the group leader pulled up and only he and Connie climbed out.

"Did Theo and David fall out?" Charles asked.

"Theo said he was a wee-bit exhausted from the trip and wanted me to drop him at his house," Chester said. "David said he had an appointment and would get his car later."

"I'm only here to get my car," Connie said. "Sorry, Chester."

Chester's smile faded. "Our biggest adventure, and look who's left to celebrate it."

I had planned to sneak out early, but seeing that his post-adventure party only consisted of Cal, William, Charles, Chester, and me, I knew I was in for at least an hour of lemonade, stale cookies, and reliving our big adventure. I hinted for Cal to get his guitar, but he either didn't catch the hint or was crooned out.

Chester had been rejuvenated from his nap and was ready to party. Charles and I hadn't had the advantage of a nap and I wondered how many more times I could hear Chester say how exciting today had been before I dumped the pitcher of lemonade over his head. Cal saved Chester when he said that he'd had "about as much fun as an inebriated hyena could have," and excused himself. William didn't put it that way but said he'd better call it a day, and Charles and I jumped on the bandwagon, or the mass exodus, and followed Cal and William off the porch.

"Hold up a sec," Chester said, as I reached the car. "I nearly forgot. Theo asked me to give you this." He handed me a folded piece of paper, thanked us for being part of the "really big day," and headed in the house.

I got behind the wheel, turned up the air conditioner, tossed my red cap in the back seat, and opened the folded paper.

I caught myself holding my breath as I read: *Need to talk about the killer.*

I read it a second time and handed it to Charles who had been leaning over trying to make out Theo's words. Charles read the note and looked at me. "What're you waiting for?"

On the way to Theo's, Charles asked if I thought that Harriet had confessed to killing Abe and Theo wanted to tell us. I didn't respond but thought it had to do with something more recent, something that reinforced my hunch about who'd murdered the student.

I pulled in Theo's drive and looked up at the massive two-story elevated structure and was once again impressed by its size and view of the marsh. Theo came out the front door and waved us up the stairs.

He smiled and motioned us in. "Thought that'd get you here."

I had never been in the house, but wasn't surprised by the interior. From the entry, there was a clear view through the kitchen to large windows overlooking the marsh and the river. I envied him and his sunset view. He led us to the great room filled with substantial, light-colored, wood furniture and offered us seats on a latte-colored couch. There were original oil paintings of coastal lowlands on three of the walls and expensive looking knickknacks on the tables. I recognized the name of two of the artists. Either Theo had a sophisticated eye for design or the home was professionally decorated. I told him it was stunning; he said he supposed so, and that it cost him a mint to have someone get it that way.

That answered my first question, so I led into my second. I pulled his note out of my back pocket and said, "Killer?"

"First, thanks for coming. I didn't know who else to go to. I figured the cops would laugh at me and I knew you're a detective."

I started to protest, but Charles jumped in. "Go ahead."

Theo looked at Charles and back to me.

"Let me ask you something," he said.

I nodded.

"Did the police tell anyone where the kid's body was found?"

"Sure," Charles said, again before I could speak. "Boneyard Beach."

Theo sighed, "I know that. That's a big place. I mean exactly where they found him?"

I thought about what I had heard both around town and from Cindy about who knew the exact location. "Don't think so." I glanced at Charles who shook his head. "Why?"

"I'm being rude," Theo said. "Want something to drink?"

I wanted to scream "No! Get on with your story?" Instead, I said "No thanks."

Theo looked at Charles who shook his head, and then he turned to me. "I'm old, ancient according to some; I know my memory's not what it used to be. I'm slow afoot, ask anyone in the group; and, I'm almost deaf." He shook his head. "There's one thing I'm not. I'm not stupid."

"You're definitely not stupid," I said.

"Remember this morning when I stayed on the boat?"

"Sure," Charles said.

"Captain Robbie was with me. I'd talked to him about everything I could think of to pass the time. I'd run out of things to say, so since we were in the vicinity, I asked him if he knew where they found the body."

I thought I knew where he was going but wanted him to get there.

Theo looked at Charles, and at me, and out the large bay window toward the marsh. "Well, the captain stood up and pointed out past the foundation where you all were partying and said, 'About a hundred feet to the left and back a small trail to the marsh.'" He cocked his head, looked out the window, and turned back to us. "Fellas, how would he know that unless he was there?"

"Good question, Theo," I said. "Was that what you were talking about when I came to get you off the boat?"

"Youngsters like the captain, think that because someone's

old that he can't figure things out. Can't wonder about things that seem off. Yeah, I had asked him how he knew where the body was when you showed up."

Charles leaned toward Theo. "What'd he say?"

Theo frowned. "I was getting there. The captain stumbled through his words and mumbled something about hearing it around town. Sounded like a crock. That's when I asked for Chris's help off the boat."

"Is that all he said?" I asked.

"Yes, I know that's not anything that means that he killed the kid, but it sounded wrong, just plain wrong. And I'll tell you one other thing, that fellow sure was antsy after I asked him how he knew. That's why I figured you were the best person." He glanced at Charles. "Best *people* to tell. I know you're good at catching killers."

"You sure that's all he said?" Charles asked.

"Huh?"

Charles repeated the question.

"Did you forget the part about me not being stupid? Yes, that's all. Now you fellows get busy and figure out how you can prove he did it." He yawned, hesitated, and said, "I'm going to call my buddy Chester and thank him again for pulling the trip together, and then take a nap."

We were almost out the door when he added, "Don't tell anyone in the group, but I also know the real reason they call me ET." He then grinned and saluted us.

On the way down the steps, Charles asked, "What do you think?"

"Robbie killed Drew Casey."

"Whoa, you're that sure because Theo said Robbie knew where the body was?"

"Mel didn't kill the kid so someone else did," I said.

"Profound."

"There's more."

"I'm all ears."

"Motive," I said. "Remember when we first met Mel's buddies, the captains?"

Charles nodded.

"One of their big complaints was that there wasn't enough business to go around, and I think one of them even said that there were too many captains doing the same thing. Robbie has a new, expensive boat, and a bunch of kayaks and he told his sister that he didn't have any money to lend his friend Timothy for his wedding. He's probably in financial straits and eliminating competition is one way to get out of the hole."

"What about the gay tie in? That's what the police are pinning their case against Mel on."

"True, but I don't buy it. There's no way Mel would have made a pass at that kid. Because they frequented the same bar doesn't prove anything. I haven't heard that the police have even put them there at the same time. I think both being gay was an unfortunate coincidence. And there are way too many people who want to think the worst about someone because of sexual orientation. Mel's an easy target."

"What about the witness who saw him?"

"The witness admitted to being drunk and didn't come forward for several days. For the sake of argument, let's say the witness did see someone near where the murder took place. The witness admitted that it was dark and he couldn't get a good look. He said it was Mel because Mel was the only *old bald* guy on the boat." I looked out the window and turned back to Charles. "What do Robbie and Mel have in common?"

Charles closed his eyes and nodded left and right. "The same height, same build, and both ... bald. But Robbie's younger."

"To a college student in the dark and through alcohol-infused eyes, he would still be an *old bald* guy."

"So he saw Robbie and thought it was Mel."

"Exactly."

"How would Robbie have known they were going to be at Boneyard Beach? Why kill Drew?"

I grinned, "Remember what Mel told us the captains talked about during their monthly gatherings?"

Charles put his forefinger to his cheek. "Bitched and moaned about cheap vacationers, stupid things that happen on their trips, and fixing prices."

"Yes, I said, "Plus, what trips they had scheduled."

Charles nodded. "So he could have known about the Boneyard Beach excursion and been there when they arrived. Wouldn't Mel have noticed Robbie's boat?"

"No doubt, and that's why I think Robbie walked from the end of Ashley Avenue to Boneyard Beach."

".5 miles," Charles added.

I nodded. "I think he killed the college student to frame Mel. Drew Casey's only crime was being in the wrong place at the wrong time."

"And Robbie put the bloody rag in Mel's garage?"

"Yes."

Charles shook his head. "So what are we going to do about it?"

"I'm going to drop you at your apartment, and call Detective Cox and lay out my thoughts and hope he doesn't laugh his head off. All I have is speculation, and Cox thinks he already has the killer. I hope he is as good a person as Cindy says he is. I hope he listens."

Instead of getting Detective Cox, I got a metallic sounding voice mail message asking me to leave a message. I told the cold machine who I was and requested that Cox call me as soon as possible. I was exhausted but needed to run to the grocery, and hopefully could slip in a nap while waiting for the call.

Chapter Thirty-Three

I was carrying two bags of what I call groceries, or what nutritionists deride as junk food, up my front steps, and wondering if I had the energy to get them put away before falling in bed for a nap. It was an hour since I had called and I wondered why the detective hadn't called back. I stepped through the door and my focus abruptly changed.

"About time," said the strident voice of Harriet Grindstone. She stepped out of the kitchen to meet me.

I'm not the detective some have accused me of being, but it didn't take one to know this wasn't a social call. A black, semiautomatic Beretta pointed at my head gave it away. I also realized that my bag of Oreo cookies may raise her cholesterol, but would be no match for the handgun.

I looked at the groceries, and tilted my head toward the kitchen table. She waved the gun in that direction and I set the bags on the table.

"What do you want Harriet?"

Her cackle reminded me of the Wicked Witch of the West. She motioned for me to sit. I obliged.

She lowered her thin frame in the chair opposite me at the table, and kept the gun pointed at my head. "Let me tell you a story."

I nodded as if I had a choice.

"When I was seven, we lived on a ranch. I went to school like all the other little boys and girls and learned the same kind of things that I bet you learned. English, math, reading, and even some history helped me get to where I am today. But the real learning came from my Pop." She hesitated and looked toward the window, but the Beretta's aim never wavered. "Montana ranch life was tough, but Pop loved every second of it. One day I was playing out behind the barn when a gray wolf peeked its head around the corner. I'd never seen one that close and thought it was as cute as could be and figured it would be a mighty-fine pet. I inched a little closer and it wasn't as skittish as I thought it'd be. I was wondering how to catch it, when all of a sudden, the cute thing's head went and exploded. Boom! I was stunned. I looked around and there stood Pop, his big-ole Winchester in his hand and a wicked frown on his face. I was so mad at him that I ran to the house crying."

I stared at Harriet and waited. She stood and walked to the sink and looked out the window. Her limp had disappeared and I realized that she had faked the injury so she could be here when I got home.

She returned to the chair. "Now the lesson. Pop let me get in a good cry, and then made me sit in front of him. He said that that lovely creature he shot was put on this earth for one purpose, and that was to kill and eat—to kill and eat our livestock, my chickens, and even little girls if enough wolves were in the pack. He said they may be beautiful, but that I shouldn't be deceived. We had to overlook their appeal and kill them every chance we got. They were no good, he said. Know what else he taught me?"

I shook my head.

"Pop didn't have the benefit of a good education, had to cheat to finish high school he said, with a little embarrassment in his voice, but he told me there was one lesson he learned early on. Said that if you set your mind to doing or getting something, you need to use all the wherewithal in your power to do it."

The phone rang.

Great, now the detective calls.

Harriet gave it a dirty look. "Let it ring."

We both stared at it until it stopped and she continued, "Pop said it wouldn't always be easy but if I wanted it, I shouldn't let anything stand in my way."

"Like Abe?"

She grinned but her eyes were cold. "I've had several relationships in my life, some of them were good." She grinned again. "Most of them sucked. Then Theo came along. He's a sweet man, you know."

And a wealthy one, I thought.

"Sure he's got a few problems, but who doesn't. Speed walking's not his thing, his memory's not quite all there, and when it comes to the bedroom … never mind. The point is he likes me, and I think I'm falling for him."

And his money. "Abe stood in your way?"

"Let me put it as delicately as I can." She shook her head. "That sneaky, conniving, conning, son of a bitch, was a damned gray wolf. He was after Theo's money and would've taken him for every penny if I'd have let him. The million that Abe had already talked Theo out of was only the beginning. He had more 'great deals' he was talking to poor Theo about." She glared at me. "You see, I couldn't let that happen."

"So you did what your dad did to the wolf?"

"You bet your ass I did. Another thing Pop taught me was how to shoot a tin can off a fencepost at fifty yards. Sorry you had to be there. If you hadn't fallen out of the way, I would have waited for another time to exterminate the damned wolf. Sooner or later, I would have got him. You know, we do what we have to do to protect our self-interests. I. . ."

The phone's shrill ring interrupted a second time.

I thought she was going to shoot the phone, but instead slid it out of my reach and scowled at it until it stopped. I took the interruption to look around for something I could use as a weapon. All that came close was the Mr. Coffee machine; no competition for a semiautomatic.

"I get why you killed Abe, but why are you here?"

She sighed. "The police are after your buddy, Larry. I wasn't on their radar and never would have been, and then a detective knocks on my door and starts asking questions and fishing for connections to Abe. He finished his questions and I asked why he was talking to me. He said it was routine." She frowned. "I hate it when people think because I'm getting older that I'm stupid."

I thought how similar that was to Theo's comment about Robbie.

She continued. "I knew that was BS and asked him who gave him my name. He gave me a polite smile and said he couldn't say. He didn't have to; I knew it was you and your damned nosiness. Everybody tells me how you butt into murders and keep asking questions until you get the goods on someone. I looked you up on-line and saw they were right. You're a good friend of Larry." She shook her head. "Sorry, but you need to go." She leaned back but still held the gun on me. "We're going to sit here until dark and I'm going to escort you to my car and then we're going to head off-island so I can give you a proper *adios* where you won't be found for a while." She grinned. "If ever. Then I'm going to be back in my house moaning and groaning about my sprained ankle. I couldn't have been out-and-about killing anyone; couldn't even get off the couch."

Dark was an hour away so I had some time to come up with a plan. I didn't have to wait that long. Pounding on the front door startled both of us. Would Detective Cox have come to the house after I didn't answer? No, that wouldn't make sense.

Harriet started to push away from the table, was momentarily distracted. This was my chance. Before she could stand, I rammed the table into her midsection. She tripped over her chair but regained her balance before hitting the floor. The Beretta was still in her hand.

Three things happened almost instantaneously. I shoved the overturned table out of the way and lunged for the gun. I had suspected that Harriet was stronger than she looked. I was right. She scooted back and kicked my shin. I grabbed the pistol's barrel and tried to twist it out of her hand.

The barrel blast was six inches from my head. The sound was deafening and the high pressure muzzle flash blinded me. I barely noticed the sting on my temple.

Then, Charles's size nine shoe kicked in the front door.

I ignored the stream of warm liquid running down my cheek and twisted the weapon away from her. Harriet screamed as her trigger finger yanked backwards. I wrenched the weapon from her grasp and hurled it across the room. I jerked her left arm behind her back. She screamed a second time and fell on her stomach. Blood from my head dripped on the back of her blouse as I grabbed her other arm and twisted it behind her.

Charles moved closer. I yelled for him to get duct tape from the drawer by the sink.

Harriet kicked, let out a bloodcurdling scream, and rolled from side to side. It took both of us to hold her still enough to tape her hands together and then taped her feet together for insurance. Once she was disabled, I sat on the floor and touched my head. Charles grabbed a towel and I pressed it to the wound while he called 911, Cindy's cell phone, and left a message for Detective Adair.

Between the time Charles called the cavalry and when the house filled with police, I must have passed out. The next thing I remembered was lying on the stretcher with an IV in my arm and an EMT smiling and saying "Welcome back."

I knew I was going to be alright when Officer Allen Spencer leaned over the stretcher. "Didn't I say that you needed a better lock?" He was referring to an incident last year when the police had broken into the house to catch someone suspected of murdering members of a film crew. I smiled when I realized that Larry would now be around to install it instead of being behind bars.

I argued that I didn't have to go to the hospital but the EMTs politely, but firmly, disagreed and I finally gave in. I gave Officer Spencer a quick rundown of what had happened as the medics wheeled me out the door. He assured me that Harriet would be leaving with him, and Charles said he would follow the ambulance in my car.

Chapter Thirty-Four

An hour later, I was in an exam room in the ER at Charleston's Roper Hospital. I had spent so much time in the emergency room the last few years either as a patient or visiting friends that I asked the nurse if I could get the employee discount at the cafe. She faked a smile and said something about a shot in the head makes people say weird things. I didn't know about that, but knew that I had a terrible, pulsating headache and the side of my face felt like it had been held over Larry's grille.

I had been X-rayed and the first doctor to check on me had a nurse put salve on the facial burn that had been caused by high pressure gas and unburned gunpowder from Harriet's gun. The bullet had only grazed my skull and the wound was minor, no stitches necessary. Before rushing to more serious emergencies, the doc said he didn't think there was any serious damage, but he wanted to keep me overnight to be safe. I was lucky, he said, and I agreed. Did I ever!

Charles waited with me until they moved me to a room and had the need to say weird things without benefit of being shot in the head. I didn't realize how many stupid jokes could be made about my hard head and how the best way to grab a gun was the grip instead of the barrel. My head hurt too much to appreciate his stand-up comedy routine, so I changed the subject.

"Why were you at the house?"

"You said you were going home and taking a nap, so where else would you be? I called and you ignored the call. I called again and you ignored me a second time, so I thought I'd head over and pound the door until you got your lazybones out of bed."

I didn't think it was necessary to tell him that I didn't answer because I had a deadly weapon pointed at me. Besides, I owed my life to his impatience, something else that I wasn't about to acknowledge.

It kept running through my lucky head what Harriet had said about us having to do whatever necessary to protect our self-interests and despite my aching head, began to focus on Mel. Once I eliminated him as a killer, all signs pointed to Robbie. And Robbie knew that Theo was getting suspicious. Was Theo in danger?

I asked Charles to get my cell out of my slacks.

"If you're calling for a pizza, get pineapple on it," he said.

If my head hadn't hurt, I would have uttered a smart remark, but instead I closed my eyes and held my hand out for the phone. He handed it to me, huffed, and plopped down in the only chair in the room. I saw where I'd missed a call from Chester and that he'd left a voicemail. It could wait, and I called Theo, only to get a recording. I left a message for him to call me as soon as he could.

After I disconnected, Charles said, "Theo doesn't deliver pizzas. What's up?"

I shared my fear that Theo wasn't good at hiding his surprise that Robbie knew where the body had been, and that the captain might go after him. My head hurt but everything else appeared to be working properly so I scooted my legs off the side of the bed and sat. After a minute, the room stopped spinning, and I asked Charles to get my clothes. He shook his head and asked if the bullet in my head made me forget what the doctor had said about me spending the night in Hotel Roper.

"The bullet isn't in my head. I'm leaving."

Charles's response was to hand me the bundle of clothes. I had lied about feeling fine; my head pounded and the side of my face still felt like I'd laid it on an electric stove's red-hot burner. I dressed before anyone in a white coat returned and tried to tie me down.

"Don't suppose you'll let me push you out in a wheelchair?" Charles said.

I smiled even though it made my face sting more, and waved for him to follow me. We managed to avoid anyone who would want to keep me and I conceded to my condition by letting Charles drive.

I closed my eyes as soon as he pulled out of the parking lot. I finally got my nap.

Charles nudged my arm. "Now where?"

I opened my eyes and realized we were on Folly. "Theo's."

Theo's new, black Mercedes was in the drive but no one answered the door. I suggested that we check the back door and Charles and I walked around the house and up the steps. The door to the screened-in porch was unlatched and we could see that the mahogany door into the house was standing open. From our higher vantage point, Charles looked around the back yard and out Theo's private pier that ended at the river. I pushed the door the rest of the way open and called for Theo. Charles said he wasn't outside and no one answered inside.

I had a clear view of the kitchen and nothing looked out of place.

"Think we need to call reinforcements?" Charles asked as we stepped into the kitchen.

"Not time. Theo may be hurt."

Charles whispered, "And Robbie could be here waiting to kill us."

I shrugged and moved to the great room. Things appearing normal ended there. A lamp from an end table was on the floor, its bulb shattered, its shade twisted. A porcelain seahorse that had been on the table was in hundreds of pieces strewn across the floor. And, what looked like drops of blood were in a serpentine pattern leading toward the master bedroom.

Charles whispered, "Now can we call the cops?"

I put my finger to my lips, followed the stream of blood, and inched my way toward the bedroom. The only sounds I heard were my heart beating against my ribcage and a couple of creaks from the floor as Charles and I moved toward the bedroom.

The bed was as neat as it would have been if it had been made by a five-star hotel housekeeper; nothing seemed out of place except the drops of blood leading to the master bath. I moved toward the bath, and I dreaded what I might find. I could picture Theo's frail body, broken, bloody, and stuffed in the tub.

Relief spread over me when there was no one in the room—dead or alive. What was there was a white, blood-soaked, *TS* monogrammed hand towel. The blood was still tacky so I knew whatever happened wasn't too far in the past.

I looked back at Charles. "Now we call the police." Instead of dialing 911, I called Chief LaMond.

She answered on the second ring. "Where the hell are you? I'm at the hospital with a freakin' vase of flowers in my hand and there ain't no Chris to give them to."

I told her where we were and a quick rundown on what we had found. Thankfully, she didn't bombard me with questions and said she was on her way. I told Charles I wanted to check the rest of the house to make sure Theo wasn't bleeding to death in another room. Charles said I must have a death wish, but followed me as I canvassed the rest of the rooms. Again, no body. No killer.

Cindy didn't come alone. Two patrol cars converged, sirens blaring, as the chief pulled her unmarked car in front of the house. I met her at the door.

She shoved the vase of flowers in my stomach and walked past me into the great room. "Why aren't you in the hospital?" Her eyes darted around the room and her hand rested on her firearm's grip.

"I thought…"

"Crap," she interrupted. "Never mind, whatever you say, it means you're too stubborn for your own good. What happened?" She waved her hand around the room.

I told her my suspicions about Robbie and why I was worried about Theo. She nodded when she came to the bedroom and face-to-face with Charles.

"Don't suppose you could've hogtied him and hitched him to the hospital bed?"

Charles shook his head. "What do you think?"

"The boy's good at getting in the middle of trouble, isn't he?" she said and walked around the room taking in everything.

Charles watched Cindy check out the room and then walk into the bathroom and stared at the bloody towel. "Abe Lincoln said, 'Whatever you are, be a good one.' Chris's the best trouble sniffer I've ever known."

Officer Spencer was next to arrive. He said, "We meet again," and asked how I was without making any cutting remarks and asked Cindy what he could do.

The chief looked at me. "Any idea what Robbie drives?"

"Old, silver Nissan Maxima."

She turned to Spencer and told him to have dispatch get the license, put out an APB, and if anyone spotted it, to approach cautiously because he may have a hostage.

"Looks like someone took Mr. Stoll," Cindy said. "Hopefully alive. If it was Robbie, any idea where he may have gone?"

"Off the top of my head, no," I said. "I would guess somewhere far away, although he wouldn't know that we found this as quickly as we did. He could still be on the island."

"Don't suppose you know where he lives?" she said.

Charles stepped close to Cindy. "I heard he has a small apartment somewhere around East Seventh Street, but not sure where."

Cindy turned to Officer Bishop, the second patrol officer in the house, and told her to have someone get her the address and to take another officer with her and check his apartment. Cindy asked Charles and me to sit on the patio so we wouldn't mess up the crime scene any more than we already had, while she called the crime scene techs in Charleston and then Detective Adair and filled him in. My head still throbbed and she didn't get an argument from me.

Chapter Thirty-Five

I sat on Theo's patio with my head resting on my hands while Charles prowled around the patio like a lion trying to figure out which unsuspecting zebra to have for supper. Patience was not in his arsenal.

"The crime scene guys are stuck behind a wreck in Charleston," Cindy said. She had been inside the house and surprised me when she was standing in front of me on the patio. I must have dozed. "It'll be a while before they get here. Why don't you go back to the hospital?" She grinned. "Maybe they won't notice that you skipped out on them."

I looked up at her and frowned.

"Didn't think you'd take my sage advice. So go home. I'll know where you are if we need you."

Charles had stopped pacing and told Cindy that was a great idea and that the Charles Taxi Service would be leaving in five minutes. My head still throbbed but I knew when I was outnumbered, so I walked to the car and once again took the passenger's seat, something that I wasn't accustomed to. Besides, the mid-eighties temperature combined with direct sun, was beginning to add to my discomfort.

We pulled to the stop sign at Center Street. Charles started to turn left toward the house. I said, "Turn right."

"Why?"

"To see if his boat's at Mariner's Cay Marina."

He huffed. "You're going to be the death of me yet."

The dock at Mariner's Cay was visible from the bridge but several larger boats blocked my view and I couldn't tell if Robbie's skiff was there. A minute later, Charles punched in the access code and we weaved around the development to the parking area.

"You okay?" he asked.

I skirted the truth and said that I was fine.

Robbie's boat was where he had docked it after our trip to Boneyard Beach and appeared unoccupied. Charles suggested that since we were this close, we should see if there was anything unusual on the craft. I knew he was trying to delicately say signs of a struggle, blood, or Theo.

The floating dock bobbed up and down, and the fear of finding something gruesome on the boat, intensified my headache. Charles, trying to be inconspicuous, leaned close to me to keep me from staggering off the side of the dock. I appreciated how considerate he was being; perhaps I'll thank him—someday.

I blinked twice and looked over the craft's fiberglass gunwale. My fears and anxieties were unfounded. Nothing seemed amiss and the closest thing to a body was a large fly resting on the pilot's seat. I realized that I had been holding my breath.

"Now what?" Charles asked.

I suggested getting back in the air-conditioned car while I called Cindy to let her know there was no need to send anyone here.

Charles smiled. "I look forward to hearing her tell you that you are a nosy, stubborn cuss. Then she'll ask if you forgot where you lived."

I returned his Cheshire grin. "I'll tell her you were driving."

The air conditioner kicked-in full-blast and the sweat from under my Tilley had begun to dry. I called Cindy and had to yell so she could hear me over the roar of the air conditioner. I said where we were and what we had found. I was the recipient of an East Tennessee rant about the only difference between me and a jackass was the number of legs. To make it worse, I had to endure Charles sitting beside me muttering, "Un huh, un huh," and nodding his head although he couldn't hear everything the chief had been saying.

Cindy finished her comparative anatomy lesson and told me that her officers had found Robbie's apartment but not his car, nor had anyone answered the door. His neighbor told Officer Bishop that she had been working in the yard the last two hours and that she hadn't seen anyone come or go from the apartment. Cindy added that Detective Adair had arrived and would want to talk to me later. And finally, she asked if I needed her to send one of her officers to the marina to give us a police escort to my house, because she knew that I was getting old, senile, and couldn't find my way. I thanked her, but said that I would leave it in the able hands of Charles to get me there. She mumbled something about the "bald leading the bald" and hung up.

I remembered the voicemail that Chester had left when I was trying to get Theo. I clicked on voicemail and the icon putting the phone on speakerphone; no sense in repeating whatever Chester had to say to Charles.

"Chris, Chester here. Theo told me what he told you about thinking Robbie killed that kid. Something about Robbie knowing some detail that only the killer would know. He was talking so fast that I couldn't follow all of it." I heard a chuckle. "The poor man was talking a lot faster than he walks. He was mighty hopped up about it. Do you think it could be true? God, I find it hard to believe; he took us to Boneyard Beach; seemed like a nice man. Have you told the police? Should I call them? Umm, that's enough questions. I was just worried and knew you'd know what to do. Sorry I missed you. Call when you get a chance."

I pinched the bridge of my nose and closed my eyes; the headache continued. I tapped in Chester's number and listened as the phone rang five times before the answering machine kicked in. I hit *End Call*.

"Why didn't you leave a message?" Charles asked.

I glanced at Charles and down at my phone. "Go to Chester's."

Charles kept both hands on the wheel and made no effort to put the car in reverse. "I suppose that I could overlook it since you just got shot in the head, but didn't you figure from Chester's answering machine that he ain't there?"

I started to scream, "Drive!" but I owed Charles an explanation. "Robbie's trying to tie-up loose ends. I think he has Theo. If I was Robbie, the first thing I'd ask Theo was who he told about his suspicions."

"True, and you'd be at the top of that list." He hesitated and looked in the direction of town. "But since you've been doing your rolling-stone-gathers-no-moss imitation the last few hours, he doesn't know where you are."

"How long do you think Theo could go without blurting out that he had talked to Chester?"

"Seconds."

"How many hours ago was it when you called my house twice, got no answer, and still came over?"

"And showed up and saved your butt," Charles added as he rammed the gear shift into reverse an almost hit a mini-van that was parked behind us.

Chester's house was less than a mile from the marina and with little traffic we could have made the trip in three minutes tops. No such luck. A Chevy pick-up had chosen the wrong time to pull out of Indian Avenue and was broadsided by a Jeep Wrangler that had two surfboards perched on top. There didn't appear to be serious injuries but the road leading on-island was blocked by two patrol cars, one fire engine, one badly damaged Jeep Wrangler, and two surfboards that had caught their last wave. I considered having Charles pull off the road and us walking the rest of the way, but my head still throbbed and didn't know if I could make it on foot.

I tried Chester's number twice more while we waited. Still no answer. Both vehicles involved in the wreck were moveable and were pushed out of the roadway quicker than I had anticipated.

Chester's Buick was parked in front of his house but I didn't see Robbie's Nissan. I asked Charles to circle the block and see if Robbie's car was nearby. An alley separated Chester's house from the St. James Gate restaurant and a row of shrubs separated the house from the alley. The lot behind Chester's was reserved for residents of a small apartment building and two large trash dumpsters blocked the view of Chester's back door. What the dumpsters didn't block was Robbie's Nissan backed into the lot and not more than thirty feet from Chester's porch.

Charles looked over at Robbie's vehicle. "Crap."

"Park around the corner," I said, as we rolled passed the lot.

Charles ignored three *No Parking* signs placed along the alley and stopped forty feet from the side of Chester's residence. I was out of the car as soon as he shifted it in park and strode along the shrub row and out of sight of the two windows on the side of the small house. The air conditioner in the living room window closest to the front of the house was working at its peak. It was so loud that I suspected that I could have broken the window and crawled in before anyone would have heard me. Instead, I stood on my tiptoes and when I tilted my head just right, could see part of the room through the half-inch gap between the air conditioner's steel frame and the plywood spacer closing the foot-wide area between the unit and the windowsill. I had to stand at an awkward angle and was having trouble adjusting my line of sight to see anything. The blinds above the air conditioner were open and there was enough sun streaming in for me to see part of the room. Charles had moved to the side of the window closest to the street but didn't have the benefit of a gap. He reached around the air conditioner, tapped me on the arm, pointed at the window, held his hands out, and shrugged. I mouthed, "Patience," and turned my attention back to the window.

Theo was splayed out on one of the recliners. He wasn't moving and had a yellow towel wrapped around his head. One corner of the towel had what appeared to be a large patch of blood on it. Chester startled me when he moved into my line of sight. He waved his hands around like he was trying to make a point; he darted around the room like he was on something stronger than lemonade. He pointed at Theo. Chester was talking, but the roar of the air conditioner obliterated his words. I couldn't see Robbie, but I saw a hand holding a baseball bat in the direction Chester kept glancing. I assumed it was connected to Robbie.

I didn't think anyone in the house could see us, but to err on the side of caution, instead of telling Charles what was going on over the noise from the air conditioner, I waved for him to follow me to the back corner of the yard. I told him what little I knew and he said we needed to call the police.

He was probably right, but I said, "Not yet. We don't need a hostage situation. Theo looks in bad shape and no telling what would happen if a bunch of cops showed up. Chester seems so agitated that he could do something that'd get one or both of them killed."

"But, they—"

I put my hand in front of his face. "I've got an idea. I'm going to call Chester."

"You've already called. He didn't answer. Why think he will now?"

"I hope he doesn't."

Chapter Thirty-Six

I reached for my phone and realized that it was in the car. I looked back at the window and at Charles. "Go see what happens when I call."

He didn't demand a detailed explanation. He moved around the shrub and back to the window. The air conditioner continued to roar and I doubted that Robbie would've heard a helicopter land in the side yard much less Charles sneaking up to the window. I grabbed my phone from the console, thought about what I wanted to say, prayed that I wasn't making a huge—possibly fatal—mistake, and hit redial.

Five rings later, Chester's voice mail message kicked in. I glanced at Charles standing on his toes as he peeked through the slot beside the air conditioner. I took a deep breath and said, "Chester, this is Chris. Listen, I just got off the phone with Detective Adair. He knows Robbie killed the student. I told him that Theo had said the same thing. I figured that Theo told you. The police are at Theo's and it looks like Robbie may have killed him; there's blood all over the place. I told Adair that you figured it was Robbie and Adair said he was afraid that Robbie may come after you next." I paused and wondered what else to say. "I'm rambling, but you're in danger. Get out of the house before Robbie gets there. Go to the police station. The police are pulling together the SWAT team and would be headed to your house and should be there soon. They're worried that Robbie may get there first. Anyway, get out."

I punched *End Call,* closed my eyes, calculated the odds on my spur of the moment plan succeeding, and left the steaming-hot car and headed to Charles who had stepped back from the window and pointed to the back of the house.

My ears still rang from the gunshot and the air conditioner's roar didn't help so we moved toward the back yard and away from the distracting noise. Charles leaned close and said, "Theo's alive. Chester's trying to get him out of the recliner. He looks wobbly, but he's moving, moving at Theo speed. What'd you say to the machine?"

"Later. They'll be going to Robbie's car."

Chester's back door opened to a small, wood deck and two steps leading to the path to the Nissan. There was a large oleander shrub on our side of the deck that blocked the view of the industrial-sized dumpsters, and a four-by-eight foot, lattice privacy panel on the other side of the deck.

I pointed for Charles to hide behind the panel and said that I'd be behind the shrub. With luck, Robbie will be too distracted to notice us in the rush to get out with his hostages before SWAT arrives and also by trying to wrangle Chester and the injured Theo. He had been waving a ball bat, so I figured that he didn't have a gun. A lot rested on me being right.

The screen door squeaked open and Chester backed out while supporting his injured friend. Theo wasn't moving fast enough and Robbie gave him a shove. Chester stumbled backwards but caught himself on the rail and tumbled down the steps. His Coke-bottle glasses flew off his head. Robbie grabbed Theo's belt and stopped him from landing on Chester.

Charles inched toward the front of the lattice and within striking distance and I peeked around the shrub at the six-foot two, muscle-bound killer who looked even taller standing on the elevated porch. I had had more ridiculous ideas over the years, but none came to mind as I watched Robbie effortlessly holding Theo up with one hand while brandishing a baseball bat with the other. My feeble plan to tackle him and hold him down until the cops arrived, seemed more doable when I was in the car. I moved closer to the edge of the shrubs.

Robbie was larger, much younger, and stronger than either Charles or me; but, he was occupied with his elderly captives so we should have the element of surprise on our side. That may even the odds on taking him. I continued to move closer to the edge.

Our advantage evaporated when Charles stumbled on a metal trash can lid that had been propped against the porch.

Robbie jerked toward the noise. "What the—" He saw Charles move around the lattice.

Robbie let go of Theo's belt and shoved him to his right. Theo stumbled into Chester who was fishing around the yard for his glasses. Chester and Theo hit the ground like bags of rocks.

Charles lunged at the captain and Robbie moved the bat behind his back ready to swing at my friend. Charles's cover had been blown, but Robbie hadn't seen me. I took three steps toward him and grabbed the bat's barrel as he started to swing.

Robbie was startled. He twisted around to see who had grabbed the bat, and quickly recovered and tried to yank the weapon out of my hands. I held tight. He pulled again and he jerked the bat from my grip. Charles moved in and grabbed him around the waist. I stepped out of the bat's range and Charles tried to twist Robbie to the ground. He was no match for the killer. Robbie clutched Charles's arm, pried it off his waist, and hurled him to the ground. I put both hands on the bat while Robbie was busy with Charles. Robbie was distracted and I managed enough leverage to jerk the weapon out of his hand.

The outnumbered captain flailed around, not making contact with anything. He took a step toward the car and tripped over Theo who hadn't moved since he'd landed. The killer jumped to his feet, glanced at Charles who was pushing up from the yard, and then looked to me. I grabbed the bat and started after him. He turned and took a step toward his car.

Chester was still on the ground to Robbie's left. Even without his glasses, he saw Robbie trying to escape. Chester stuck his leg in the killer's path and caught him by surprise. Robbie stumbled once and all six-foot-two of him hit the walkway like a giant redwood felled by a lumberjack. Chester flung his body over the prone killer while Charles and I regained our balance and hustled to his aid. The three of us piled on Robbie.

The captain may have been bigger, much bigger, than either Charles or me, but with both of us holding him down, he couldn't get enough leverage to push himself up. I asked Chester, who had rolled off Robbie and was sitting beside us on the walkway, if he had any rope.

"Or duct tape," Charles added, as he gasped for his breath.

Chester, still breathing hard, found his glasses, and staggered into the house. He returned with a roll of duct tape and handed it to me. I told him to take my phone from my side pocket and call 911.

"Aren't the police on the way?" he asked.

"No."

"But your message said—"

Charles shouted, "Call the cops!"

Chester still looked confused, but nodded, stepped back on the porch and dialed 911.

Robbie continued to kick but we stayed out of range of his feet and Charles held him down while I wound the all-purpose silver fabric around his hands.

Charles said, "Didn't we just do this?"

If my head didn't ache, if my face didn't sting, and if my hands didn't hurt from Robbie yanking the bat from them, I would have smiled.

Chapter Thirty-Seven

It had been a week since Detective Adair and a gaggle of sheriff's deputies had relieved Charles and me from our struggle with Robbie. It had been five days since the captain had been charged with a multitude of crimes, the most serious being the murder of Drew Casey, the student whose only crime had been going to Boneyard Beach with a group of fellow students for a night of relaxation, fun, and drinking. He had been in the wrong place at the wrong time.

Theo had spent three nights in the hospital. The wounds inflicted by Robbie to force him to tell who else knew of his suspicions were superficial and the main reason for the hospital stay was so he could regain strength.

The gunshot graze to my head was beginning to heal and the burn on the side of my face only bothered me when I smiled. It burned a lot the next few days. Two killers had been taken off the streets, two of my friends had been cleared, and I was alive to savor it. My main regret was that Karen was still at her training program; I had missed being able to bounce my ideas off her and benefit from her years of experience. My face stung one more time when I smiled knowing she would be home tonight.

I was sitting in my comfortable chair in the living room, enjoying the aroma and flavor of a cup of coffee, reflecting on the activities of the last few days, and since it was only nine in the morning, wondering what I should do with the rest of the day.

I didn't wonder long. The all too familiar sound of

someone pounding on the door told me that whatever I had planned would change.

Mel Evans pushed past me as he headed through the living room to the coffee pot. "Yo Chris, got a question."

I felt like I had stepped into the 1990's movie *Groundhog Day*.

"What's there to eat?" he yelled from the kitchen.

I followed the bellowing voice and was surprised to see a smile on my dour friend's face. "You should know that I—"

"Kidding," he interrupted. "There's not a damn thing here that's not stale or tastes like wet cardboard." He took a gulp of coffee and grinned. He had on the same woodland camo field pants and leather bomber jacket that he wore on his last visit when he interrupted my morning coffee and got me into the mess that had dominated most every waking moment since then.

"What's your question?"

He took a smaller gulp, set the cup on the counter, and led me back into the living room. "I lied. There's no question. Move it. We're leaving."

A normal person would ask the simple question: Where are we going? A normal person would have been surprised by Mel's command.

If I had learned one thing since I'd arrived on Folly, it was that among my fiends normalcy was looked down on, and a trip down Normal Street led nowhere. I grabbed my Tilley, slid my feet into my deck shoes stationed by the front door, and said, "Lead on."

Mel's Camaro was sideways in my front yard, Cal's Cadillac was in the drive, and Chester's Buick inched close behind Cal's car. Now I was surprised.

The windows in all three cars were down and I did a double take when Charles, William, Chester, David, and Theo waved at me.

Mel said, "Don't stand there drooling, get in. I'm throwing a sprung-from-the-hoosegow party. You're holding us up."

Fifteen minutes later, the occupants of the three vehicles, two large coolers, a picnic basket that looked like it had spent a decade in Alaska before being run over by a team of huskies, and Cal's guitar case were all loaded on *Mad Mel's Magical Marsh Machine* and headed to Boneyard Beach. On the ride to the boat, Charles had explained that Mel had called him last evening and asked him to put together "the clump of civvies who helped spring him, and hell, might as well invite that damned .5 group too." Mel wanted to thank everyone for what they had done and the only way he knew to do it was throw a party. He also had told Charles that it had to be early in the day because it would be a group of "old farts" and they couldn't stay awake after suppertime.

An hour later, the coolers were almost empty, we were gathered around the graffiti covered foundation where we had celebrated the walking group's successful trip a few days earlier, and Cal was strumming and singing a medley of the greatest country hits of the 1950s. Theo was still weak, and began the day depressed over the loss of someone whom he thought had loved him. But, he had not become successful in the business world by letting the past drag him down, and by the time he'd finished three beers, he was singing a duet with Cal.

Toasts were offered. Mel was the first when he jumped up on the concrete foundation, held his Budweiser can in the air. "I'm not good at mushy stuff, so bear with me. I'm gay and always have been. Don't know if it's right or wrong. I'm not a big follower of that God guy, but if he's everything folks say he is, then there must not be anything wrong with me being queer or he wouldn't have made me that way. So, I'm thankful that everyone knows that the death of that student wasn't because he was gay or because it was anything that I had done, just the warped mind of that damned Robbie." He shook his head. "He killed an innocent kid just to frame me. All because of money. Now ain't that the shits? Well anyway, thanks for believing in me."

Mel was right, he wasn't good at mushy, but everyone knew he was sincere and was trying to thank them.

Mel hopped off the foundation and Chester waved his hand in the air like he either had a question or had to go to the bathroom.

"Okay fellow .5 members and Mel, when Charles called last night to see if I wanted to come today, I wanted to say 'no way, Jose.' A load a bad stuff has happened to our little group. Abe Pottinger got himself killed, deserved to have it happen, but I suppose it was sad anyway. And misguided Harriet had to go and kill Abe. And Connie's brother not only killed the student, but beat up on our good friend Theo and was going to kill him and me. I think .5 is cursed and we should all throw our hats into the sea." Chester pointed toward the open sea, bowed his head, and then walked back to the coolers.

David, who hadn't said anything, moved to the foundation. "I've not been on Folly as long as all of you. In my brief time on your island, I've experienced firsthand, and seen more friendship, caring, and outright friendliness than anywhere I've ever been. Chester, you starting the .5 group is a perfect example of what's right. Sure, you can be a bit dictatorial at times, and that's okay." He hesitated and chuckled. "We need that occasionally. I think it would be a big mistake to disband the group. You're a great leader, and I plan to be at your house tomorrow morning raring to go wherever you tell us to go."

"Me too," Theo shouted. He'd been fitted with hearing aids the day after he got out of the hospital, and had heard everything that David had said.

"I will be in attendance as well," William said.

Charles nodded and I said so would I, and then I told Chester that he was the true hero. He caught—tripped—a killer and was critical in saving Theo's life, and probably mine.

Chester blushed. "Okay, bright and early tomorrow." He looked at Mel. "Would you like to join us?"

Mel gave one of his patented frowns. "Hell no. You won't catch me dead around you fossils."

Now that's the Mel I'd learned to love.

I looked around and figured that several of the 'fossils' were getting tired and we needed to head back. "One more thing," I said and pointed to the spot where Drew Casey had taken his last breath. "Could we gather over there for a moment?"

No one spoke as the group moved to the path leading to the marsh. I didn't know the exact spot where the body was, so I chose a small clearing for the group to stand. "William, could I impose on you to offer a hymn to the memory of Drew Casey?"

William nodded, and began an a cappella version of "Amazing Grace." It brought goose bumps to my arms and took me back to first hearing him sing the haunting hymn a few years ago at a funeral while we were standing ankle deep in snow in the middle of the Great Smoky Mountains. After the first verse, William gestured toward Cal's guitar; Cal took the hint and played along.

I had no doubt that if Drew Casey was in Heaven, God had called him to his side, and they were listening.

William and Cal finished the last notes and the only sounds heard were a high-pitched squeak of an Oystercatcher sitting on one of the nearby wind-swept trees and the low roar of the water as it lapped against the shore.

Charles did what Charles does best. He lightened the mood when he said, "Last one to the boat is a Theo!"

Everyone glanced at Theo who laughed and slapped Charles on the arm.

Actually, Theo wasn't the last one to the boat. I was. My phone rang as I was heading to the boat. It was Karen.

"Just got home," she said. "Did I miss anything?"

About The Author

Bill Noel is author of the popular Folly Beach Mystery series that includes the titles *Folly*, *The Pier*, *Washout*, *The Edge*, *The Marsh*, *Ghosts*, *Missing*, *Final Cut*, and *First Light*. He is a fine arts photographer and retired university administrator. Bill lives in Louisville, Kentucky, with his wife, Susan.

CPSIA information can be obtained at www.ICGtesting.com
Printed in the USA
BVOW05s0408301115

428845BV00010B/107/P